✳ Praise for ✳
MIDDLE SCHOOL'S A DRAG
YOU BETTER WERK!

"What a fun book! I love the book's message of being yourself and accepting others. You better werk! I definitely recommend this book to all kids and teens, but especially drag kids."
—Desmond Is Amazing

"This fun, funny, and heartfelt novel will leave you feeling hopeful and triumphant!"   —Donna Gephart, award-winning author of *Lily and Dunkin*, *In Your Shoes*, and *The Paris Project*

"A funny, fabulous, and ultimately life-affirming story that will uplift and entertain young readers from many different backgrounds. So, should you check this one out? Mikey says, yas queen!"
—*Booklist*

"Lovely . . . Shows that when people give proper due to each other, they learn and celebrate together, and maybe even heal."
—*Lambda Literary*

"A funny take on early adolescence and discovering who you are, with a warmth that's sure to speak to young readers and the adults in their lives."   —*Knoxville News Sentinel*

"This is a heartwarming story perfect for fans of Tim Federle's *Better Nate Than Ever* . . . [and] while the topic of drag performance has been covered in young adult books, fewer novels have discussed kids who perform drag in a way that is accessible to a younger audience. A solid purchase for most public and school libraries."
—*School Library Journal*

Praise for *The Whispers*

"This taut, moving tale delves beyond loss into issues of sexuality, conformity and self-acceptance . . . A masterful exploration into the power of storytelling but also its dangers, including self-denial and escapism." —*The New York Times Book Review*

"With sensitivity and skill, Howard handles themes of sexual identity, self-worth, loss and friendship." —*The Washington Post*

"Howard's personal story helps create a fictional narrative both realistic and relevant, while also calling on the fantastical magic of the imagination . . . A tale of family, friendship and loss, filled with magic and heart." —*Associated Press*

"A dreamy novel recalling *Bridge to Terabithia*." —*Entertainment Weekly*

"A heartbreaking, beguiling debut . . . This poignant journey through the badlands of grief is crammed with tenderness, wit and warmth." —*The Guardian*

★ "This is a story of a boy coming to grips with heartbreak and trying to understand why he is the way he is, who must learn to discern what is real, and who discovers redemption." —*School Library Connection*, starred review

"A moving, thoughtful examination of trauma, grief, and the power of imagination." —*Teen Librarian Toolbox*

"A beautiful, heart-expanding journey into the wilds of grief and back out again. This gorgeous book will give readers' hearts a hug that's filled with hope and possibility." —Donna Gephart, award-winning author of *Lily and Dunkin, In Your Shoes,* and *The Paris Project*

MIDDLE SCHOOL'S A DRAG

YOU BETTER WERK!

ALSO BY
GREG HOWARD

The Whispers

Social Intercourse

MIDDLE SCHOOL'S A DRAG

YOU BETTER WERK!

GREG HOWARD

PUFFIN BOOKS

PUFFIN BOOKS
An imprint of Penguin Random House LLC, New York

First published in the United States of America by G. P. Putnam's Sons, 2020
Published by Puffin Books, an imprint of Penguin Random House LLC, 2021

Visit us online at penguinrandomhouse.com

THE LIBRARY OF CONGRESS HAS CATALOGED THE G. P. PUTNAM'S SONS EDITION AS FOLLOWS:
Names: Howard, Greg (Gregory Steven), author.
Title: Middle school's a drag: you better werk! / Greg Howard.
Other titles: Middle school is a drag: you better werk!
Description: New York: G. P. Putnam's Sons, 2020. | Summary: In Charleston, South Carolina,
a young business entrepreneur, newly out as gay, starts his own junior talent agency and signs a
thirteen-year-old aspiring drag queen as his first client.
Identifiers: LCCN 2019039242 (print) | LCCN 2019039243 (ebook) |
ISBN 9780525517528 (hardcover) | ISBN 9780525517535 (ebook)
Subjects: CYAC: Entrepreneurship—Fiction. | Business enterprises—Fiction. | Talent scouts—Fiction. |
Female impersonators—Fiction. | Gays—Fiction. | Middle schools—Fiction. | Schools—Fiction.
Classification: LCC PZ7.1.H6877 Mi 2020 (print) | LCC PZ7.1.H6877 (ebook) | DDC [Fic]—dc23
LC record available at https://lccn.loc.gov/2019039242
LC ebook record available at https://lccn.loc.gov/2019039243

Puffin Books ISBN 9780525517542

Printed in the United States of America

Design by Lindsey Andrews
Text set in Dante MT Std

1 3 5 7 9 10 8 6 4 2

For Michelle, Hal, and Tom

BE YOURSELF, ALWAYS.

—DESMOND IS AMAZING

1

THE OFFICE

I sit behind the huge oak desk in my office at the world headquarters of Anything, Incorporated, organizing my homework like I do every Sunday afternoon. I spend a lot of weekends in the office. If I didn't, I'd never get anything done. I think CEOs of big-time companies like mine shouldn't be required to attend middle school. It seriously gets in the way of doing important business stuff.

I've created an Excel spreadsheet on my laptop and sorted my assignments into three columns:

```
Teacher Will Check
Teacher Won't Check
Teacher Will Collect but Won't Check
```

Normally I'd have my assistant handle this kind of thing, but she quit last week. It's okay, though, because she was a climber. More interested in having a fancy title than doing a good job for the company. She started as an intern about a month ago, recommended by one of our board members. She was terrible even back then. I could never find a stapler when I needed one, and my printer was always out of paper. I thought if I gave her a real title and some responsibility by promoting her to assistant to the president, she'd step up her game. But she didn't. All she wanted to do was criticize me. Her boss! That's not how it works in the corporate world.

I open my "Brilliant Business Tips" Excel spreadsheet, scroll down to the next empty cell, and type:

Michael Pruitt Business Tip #347: There's only one way to the top. Keep your head down, apply yourself, and do your time.

It sure would be nice to have someone handle all this busywork now that my assistant bailed on me. I'd much rather be spending my time doing real boss stuff, like planning my next exciting business venture. Retail wasn't the right fit for me. Neither was professional sports instruction. But I have a million other ideas. Those are just two recent ones that didn't work out.

Pap Pruitt always says, *If at first you don't succeed, try, try again.*

I've had my share of failures, but I never give up. I know I'll have a successful business empire one day just like my hero, Pap Pruitt. Technically Pap is my grandfather. He taught me everything I know about business.

My desk first belonged to Pap when he started his real

estate business at seventeen years old. When Pap moved into the nursing home, Dad didn't need it for his landscaping business, so he lets me use it. It's a real boss-looking desk and I always feel real important sitting at it. I also feel close to Pap when I'm at my desk. He's been in the nursing home for a while now, and I don't get to see him as much. Plus he's sick a lot, so Dad doesn't always let me go with him to visit Pap. He didn't let me go today, which I guess is why Pap's been on my mind.

Pap was a super-crazy-successful entrepreneur when he was younger. He started his own general store, a dry cleaning business, two fast-food franchises, a hotel called the Old Pruitt Place, a pet-grooming business, a landscaping business, *three* automatic car washes, a boiled-peanut roadside stand, and a whole lot more. I asked him once how he became so successful. I remember the sparkle in his eye when he grinned a little and said, *All it takes is a dream and a prayer.*

I've got lots of dreams. And even though I'm not the best at prayers, the Almighty is pretty used to hearing from me when it comes to a new business idea. Pap started his business empire in his garage with only a hundred dollars, a dream, and a prayer. Pap's blind now because of the diabetes, but he's still a wicked-cool guy. I really want to make him proud, but he didn't have to build his business empire *and* go to middle school at the same time. I guess Pap was a late bloomer.

It's a little embarrassing, having to do homework at your real job. I'll bet Malcolm Forbes never had to do that and he was, like, one of the most successful business guys ever. Luckily my office is pretty private, but that doesn't always keep the riffraff out. Sometimes it can get so noisy in here, especially when the dryer's on its last cycle like it is now. It sounds like a space shuttle getting ready to launch. And there must be a shoe in there, because something bangs against the side every few seconds, distracting me from my work. I lean back in my executive, fake-leather desk chair and stare at Dad's tools hanging on the wall, waiting for the banging to stop.

The annoyingly long honk of the buzzer sounds and the pounding inside the machine finally fades away. I hit the Talk button on the intercom on my desk.

"Mom," I say, pretty loud so she can hear me from anywhere inside the house. And because I'm annoyed that there's a washer and dryer in my office.

No response.

I hit the button again. "Mom!"

A few seconds later, her voice crackles through the intercom speaker. "Yes, Mikey, what is it?"

I sigh and press the Talk button. "Mom, I asked you not to call me that when I'm at work."

"Oh, sorry, honey. *Michael*, what is it? Is the dryer done?"

We've talked about *honey*, too, but I'm too busy to get into that right now.

"Yes, ma'am," I say.

"Okay," she says. "I'll be right there."

Dad found the old-timey intercom system at a garage sale

and hooked it up for me. It's lime green and nearly the size of a shoe box, but at least it works. Dad thought it'd be a perfect addition to my office and an easy way for Mom to call me in for dinner. Dad gets it.

Mom comes through the carport door—*without knocking*—carrying a laundry basket.

"Mom, the sign's out," I say. "You're supposed to knock when the sign's out."

"It's getting late, honey. I thought you'd be closing up shop by now."

She's wearing light blue mom shorts and one of Dad's old white button-down shirts.

"I'm rebranding," I say. "It takes a lot of thinking time."

Wait a minute. That would be a cool business idea. I could be an expert at helping businesses rebrand. Like I could go down to the Burger King on Palmetto Street and pitch them the idea of updating their brand to make it more modern and hip. The first thing they need to do is change their name to something more welcoming of all people instead of just men. Something like Burger Person or Burger Human Being would be a good choice. I open up my spiral-bound *Amazing Business Ideas* notebook and write that million-dollar idea down before I forget.

Anything Modern and Hip Rebranding
A division of Anything, Inc.
Michael Pruitt—President, Founder, CEO, and Brand Expert

"So how come the putt-putt lessons didn't work out?"

"*Croquet* lessons, Mom," I say. "Not putt-putt."

"Oh, right," she says. "We used to play croquet all the time when I was a kid."

"I know," I say.

Grandma Sharon gave me their old set of clubs and balls and taught me how to play last summer. None of the kids in the neighborhood had ever heard of croquet, which was perfect because it made me the local expert. I might have added a few new rules to the game to make it more interesting, but my students never knew the difference.

Mom rests the basket of towels on her hip. A shoe sits on top. I wonder why she only washed one. It's a perplexing mystery.

I write down another incredible idea in my *Amazing Business Ideas* notebook:

Anything Perplexing Mystery-Solving Detective Agency
A division of Anything, Inc.
Michael Pruitt—President, Founder, CEO, and Head Snoop

I put a star beside that one because that's a super-crazy-good idea.

"Well, how many kids signed up for croquet lessons?" Mom asks.

Before I can answer, my little sister, Lyla, appears in the doorway cradling her fat gray cat in her arms. The cat's name is Pooty. Lyla named him that because he farts a lot. I hate that cat.

"He had four students show up for the first lesson," she says with all the innocence of a demon-possessed doll in a horror movie. "They each paid him a dollar, if you can believe that. But no one showed up for the second lesson. He made four dollars, but he gave them each a whole bottle of water, so he probably lost money."

"I haven't run the final numbers yet," I say, looking back at my spreadsheet, trying to ignore Lyla and her gassy cat.

"And kids around here don't know what croquet is anyway," she adds like she's some kind of marketing expert. She's nine.

"That was the beauty of it," I snap back. "Nobody knew if I was teaching it wrong or not."

"It was a dumb idea, if you ask me," she says.

"You were a dumb idea," I mumble under my breath.

"Mikey! That's enough," Mom says.

"She started it," I say in a pouty voice that makes me sound like a little kid.

Mom shifts the laundry basket to her other hip. "She's only nine. Be a better example."

That's Mom's excuse for everything Lyla does. *She's only seven. She's only eight. She's only nine.* You see where this is heading, right? It's never going to end.

"Sorry," I say, even though secretly I'm not.

Lyla smiles at me like she won or something.

There are no trophies for being possessed by the devil, Lyla!

"I'll give a full report on the Sports Instruction division of the company at the next board meeting," I say to Mom.

She kisses me on top of the head. "Sounds good, honey."

I sigh. I don't think she's ever going to get the *honey* thing. And don't even get me started on the kiss.

Mom leaves, but Lyla still stands in the doorway. Both she and Pooty glare at me. The cat hates me as much as I hate him. He always stares at me like he's planning to murder me. That's why I lock my bedroom door every night before I go to bed. You just never know with cats.

"So what's your next big idea, Mikey?" Lyla says, stroking Pooty's head like an old movie villain who's trying to take over the world. I wouldn't put it past her, even though *she's only nine*.

"It's Michael when I'm in the office," I say. "You know that."

She looks around the cramped, unfinished space with tools hanging on the walls like they're standing guard. "You mean our carport-storage-and-laundry room?"

I turn my back to her, attacking the keys of my laptop like I'm typing a really important email. "You didn't mind it when you worked here."

I hear the door close behind me.

Thank God. She left.

2

THE WALK-IN

"My talent was being wasted."

Or maybe not.

Lyla sits in the metal folding chair beside my desk; it used to be her work area. I asked for a cubicle wall to put between us for privacy, but the board denied the request. They said it wasn't in the budget.

"You were my assistant, but you wanted me to make you junior vice president of the company." I shake my head at her. "Not going to happen. You're too young and you don't have enough business experience."

She swings her legs. "Your loss."

Pooty settles into a ball on her lap, staring at me like he's going to eat me. I shake my head again and look back at the spreadsheet. My sister is three years younger than me, but she acts like we're the same age. Or like she's my *older* sister. She's always been weird that way. Mom calls her precocious. I call her a pain in the butt.

A three-rap knock sounds at the door.

"Come in, Dad," I call. Dad never forgets to knock when the sign is out.

He hurries in and over to his wall of tools. "Sorry to bother you, Michael. Just need to grab the spatula. I'm grilling burgers."

Forbes, my cocker spaniel, follows Dad in, but Pooty hisses at Forbes and he retreats with a whine. Pooty's a bully and Forbes is his favorite target. Poor Forbes. Pooty would fit right in with Tommy Jenrette and his jerk friends at school.

Lyla looks up at Dad and plasters on the big baby smile she's way too old to still be using. "Dad, did you know that Mikey's latest business idea was a humongous flop?"

Dad looks over at me. "Oh no. Is that right, Michael?"

I look away, mumbling back, "You'll get a full report at the next board meeting."

"Oh, okay, then," he says, and I can hear the support in his voice.

Like I said, Dad gets it. He built A to Z Landscaping from nothing to one of the busiest in southeastern North Charleston, in spite of the lame name. *Time to rebrand, Dad!* He even advertises in the *PennySaver* and the online Yellow Pages. Pap Pruitt taught him well.

"How was Pap today?" I ask, my voice tightening around the words.

Dad's face sags. Not a good sign.

"Not great," he says, fake-smiling. "But he's hanging in

there. He asked about you. Maybe he'll be well enough for you to visit him next Sunday."

A lump swells in my throat and I swallow it back. I just nod and fake-smile back at him.

"I want to go see Pap, too, Daddy," Lyla whines.

Dad musses her hair. "Like I said, honey. We'll see."

After the shadow of sadness fades from Dad's face, he grabs the big metal spatula off the wall over my desk. "Dinner in twenty, okay?"

"Okay, Daddy," Lyla says, baby-smile wattage at one hundred.

"And don't worry, son," he says. "I bet your next idea will be the one. Pap is so proud of you. I am, too."

I don't say anything because I'm afraid my voice will fail me now. I know Pap and Dad are already proud of me. But we all know that Pap won't be around too much longer. I just want him to see my first big success.

Pooty yawns very disrespectfully as Dad closes the door behind him. I fake-type some more, hoping Lyla will get the hint and go, too. My eyes are itching and no little sister wants to see her big brother cry. Not even Lyla. But she doesn't get the hint. She just sits there swinging her legs and stroking Pooty's back.

"Don't you have homework?"

"Already finished," she says. "What are you working on?"

"None of your business," I say. "You didn't want to work here anymore, remember?"

She cocks her head. "I never said I didn't want to work here. I just wanted a better job than being your dumb assistant."

Before I can respond, there's another knock on the door. Maybe Mom remembered this time.

"Come in," I call out. I can't get anything done today with all these interruptions. I bet Pap Pruitt never had to put up with this.

The door creaks open behind me, but Lyla doesn't say anything, so I spin around in my chair. Standing in the doorway is a kid I kind of recognize from school, but I don't remember his name. I think he's in the eighth grade and I don't hang out with any eighth graders. I only recognize him at all because he's the *wrong* kind of popular at North Charleston Middle School. And I've got enough problems at school without hanging out with kids who are the wrong kind of popular.

Lyla and I just stare at him, which I know is super-crazy rude and unprofessional, but I can't help it. He's wearing sandals, neatly pressed jeans, and a white tank top with You Better Werk! printed on the front. He's taller than me and thick all over. Especially in the stomach area. After an awkward silence, the boy finally speaks up.

"Is this Anything, Incorporated?" he says, glancing around the room with stank face, like my office is the inside of a garbage dumpster. But I can't even be mad at him for that because—*OMG!*—he knows the name of my company. How wicked cool is that?

He glances over at the washer and dryer and then back to me. "I mean the sign on the door says so, but—"

"Yes!" I say a little too excitedly.

I snap out of my surprise at having someone who was actually looking for my office who's not a member of my family and who didn't think this was a laundromat or a hardware store or anything. I've never had a walk-in before.

I stand, extending my hand to him and clearing my throat. "I'm Michael Pruitt, president, founder, and chief executive officer of Anything, Inc."

The boy steps inside from our carport, closing the door behind him. He takes my hand and shakes it. His grip is loose and kind of clammy but he has a bright smile and sparkly eyes framed with—*is that glitter?*

"Yeah, I know," he says, letting go of my hand, still looking around my office, but without the stank face now. "We go to the same school."

"Mikey doesn't have any friends at school," Lyla says, looking down at Pooty, scratching his head. "They all think he's a weirdo loser and that all his business ideas are lame because none of them have ever worked."

And OMG!

I glare at her, my face heating from the inside out. Why did I ever trust her with sensitive company secrets? The boy looks like he doesn't know how to respond to that. Who would?

I clear my throat, plastering on my fake smile again. "Of

course I have friends, Lyla. You remember Trey and Dinesh. We've been friends since first grade."

Lyla smirks and shakes her head. "Nope. Never heard of them."

I grit my teeth through the fake smile. "Don't you have somewhere to be, Lyla? Somewhere that's not here. Like your room? Or China?"

The boy coughs into his elbow. Pooty poots. I wave the air around with my hand like I'm trying to swat a fly so my walk-in doesn't smell it.

"I bought a candy bar at your general store one time," he says, like he didn't notice Murder Kitty's gas attack. "I thought that store was a pretty cool idea. It was in a good location and had plenty of candy bars and other snacks that kids like. I got the chocolate one with peanut butter and nuts."

Pride curls my whole face into a grin. "That was one of my bestsellers. Could hardly keep them in stock."

"You sold three," Lyla pipes up matter-of-factly. "I was in charge of inventory, remember?" She looks over at the boy and sighs, like being a pain in the butt is so exhausting for her. "The Anything General Store got blown away by a baby tornado three days after the grand opening."

I swear to God.

The boy gives me a sympathetic look. "Oh. Sorry. I wondered why it was gone so fast. I came back the next week for another candy bar."

My face flushes hot again. "My dad built the store out

of big sheets of cardboard, so, you know—lesson learned."

Dad did a great job on the store. He built it in the front yard close to the foot traffic of the sidewalk. He said that's called *location, location, location.* The store had a wooden frame of two-by-fours, a flip-up sales counter/window, and a real door in back. Well, a real cardboard door. But the store was no match for a baby tornado. Lost all my inventory, too. Our next-door neighbor, Mrs. Brown, thought her bunny rabbit, Hedwig, started pooping magic pellets. I didn't have the heart to tell her they were just Skittles.

The boy nods and smiles at me like he understands. I think it's kind of nice of him.

I point at Lyla, trying to be professional. "This is my *former* associate, Lyla Pruitt, and her gassy and very unfriendly cat, Pooty. They were just leaving."

"Hey," the boy says, waving at Lyla with a big, wide smile.

She stands, but doesn't say anything. She doesn't even smile back. Instead, she hefts Pooty up to her chest, giving my walk-in that creepy-kid stare of hers as she takes her sweet time leaving. It's extremely unprofessional.

Michael Pruitt Business Tip #348: Human-demon dolls make terrible receptionists.

I learned that one the hard way.

3
THE GAZILLION-DOLLAR IDEA

I gesture to the metal folding chair by my desk. "Have a seat, Mister . . . Mister . . ."

But the kid doesn't take the what-the-heck-is-your-name hint. He sits, crossing his legs knee over knee like my parents do.

"I'm not a *mister*," he says, resting his hands on his knees. "I'm Coco Caliente, Mistress of Madness and Mayhem."

He tilts his head a little, like he's waiting for a reaction from me. I just stare at him, repeating the words in my head to make sure I heard him right. I ease back into my chair. I can't believe parents would give their kid that kind of name.

"Um, okay," I finally get out. "That's some name."

I'm not sure what I meant to say, but I don't think that was it. I wasn't trying to be rude, though.

"It's my stage name," he says with a pointed look like I might have offended him. "My boy name is Julian."

He raises one eyebrow at me. Why? I don't know. Maybe he's waiting for me to offend him again. I'm not sure how to respond. I've never heard a dude call his own name a *boy name* before. So I grab a pen and a new legal pad from the stack on my desk. Buying myself a few more seconds, I slowly write at the top of the sheet before I forget:

Coco Caliente, Mistress of Madness and Mayhem

I still need another second to get my thoughts together, so under that I write:

Boy name = Julian

And then:

????

Pap Pruitt always says a good businessperson is one who asks questions and listens more than they talk, which takes a lot of pressure off me right now. I relax in my chair and cross my legs knee over knee like Coco-Julian. Resting the legal pad on my lap, I hold the tip of the pen to my chin because that seems like the professional thing to do.

"How can I help you, Co . . . er . . . um . . . Julian?" I say.

"You can call me Coco or Julian. Either works."

We stare at each other in silence. I still can't figure out why he's here. Maybe he's interested in learning how to play croquet. Or maybe he wants to work for me. He couldn't be any worse than Lyla. But she was cheap. Like free-cheap. But Pap always says, *You get what you pay for.* And, boy, was he right about that.

Coco-or-Julian clears his throat. "I want to be a professional drag queen. You know, like on *RuPaul's Drag Race.* And I want you to be my agent."

He says it with an impressive crap-load of confidence. I nod and write on the legal pad:

> drag queen?
>
> Roo Paul?
>
> agent?

"You're, like, the only businessperson I know," Coco-or-Julian says. "And the name of your company is Anything, Incorporated. So I figure that means you do *anything*, right?"

Finally another kid who gets it. I nod some more because that seems like the professional thing to do. "That's the idea," I say with a shrug so it doesn't sound too much like I'm bragging. "I have lots of different business ideas I want to try. I don't like to be locked into just one thing. I thought the name Anything, Inc., would pretty much cover it all."

Coco-or-Julian smiles. "Well, I need an agent to help me get to the next level. You know, someone who will make things happen for me and get me some gigs."

More nodding. Another raised eyebrow. "The next level. I see."

I write on my pad:

next level

And then:

gigs?

"So you want to hire me to be your agent." I make sure it sounds like a statement and not a question. Pap says you have to show confidence in business meetings, even if you don't know what the heck you're talking about.

Coco-or-Julian nods. Good sign.

"To help you become a successful drag queen." Another statement. Not a question. "Like Mr. Paul."

"*Ru*Paul," he says, nodding. He shimmies up in the chair, sitting even straighter now. "My mom says I have a lot of talent."

I touch the end of the pen to my chin again and squint my eyes for a few seconds. Like I'm trying to decide if this is all worth my time or not.

I scribble on the pad:

talent

"I don't have any money to pay you with," Coco-or-Julian adds. "But I think talent agents make money when their client makes money, right?"

I rack my brain for anything I know about talent agents, which is basically nothing. I need to google that.

"Commission," I say in a whisper, and write the word down on my notepad.

It's the only thing that comes to mind. I think agents get part of the money their clients make. Like a piece of the pie. That's called *commission*. I write down:

Michael Pruitt, Talent Agent

I like the sound of it. It would look good on a business card, too. And now that I think about it, it doesn't have to stop with Coco Caliente, Mistress of Madness and Mayhem. I could get other kid clients. More clients, more commissions, more success. And—*OMG*—I just remembered. The North Charleston Middle School end-of-the-year talent show is coming up in a few weeks. They're always trying to get kids to sign up for it because hardly anyone ever does. So this year, the Arts Boosters donated a cash prize of one hundred dollars for the winner. The more clients I have, the better chance I'll have at one of them winning. I'll bet my talent-agent commission would be, like, half of the prize money. Pap Pruitt would be real proud of me if I started a super-crazy-successful talent agency.

Coco-or-Julian shifts in his chair and uncrosses his legs. "I haven't gotten any gigs yet."

I'll have to google *gigs* later, too, but I keep nodding like I know exactly what Coco-or-Julian is talking about.

"But I'm sure I will soon," he says. "Miss Coco Caliente has lots of pizzazz."

He snaps while making a big half-moon motion over his head. The sudden movement startles me. I jump in my seat, nearly tipping over backward. Wow. *Pizzazz* is a powerful thing.

"Pizzazz," I repeat in another whisper, and I write the word down.

Everyone is impressed by people in show business. If I were a successful talent agent, I'll bet every kid at North Charleston Middle School would be falling all over themselves, trying to get discovered—by *me*. Especially if I make Coco Caliente a superstar. This could be my gazillion-dollar idea. How hard can it be anyway? Like Pap Pruitt says, *All you need is a dream and a prayer.*

I rip off the sheet of paper with my notes and write on a new page:

ANYTHING TALENT AND PIZZAZZ AGENCY
A division of Anything, Inc.
OFFICIAL CONTRACT (legally binding)
Details and Terms: TBD
Michael Pruitt—President, Founder, CEO, and Talent Agent

I draw a line under my name. Then I write:

I draw a line under that.

"I'll do it." After signing my name, I hand Coco-or-Julian the pad and pen. I point to the line under his name. "Sign there. It's just your standard agency contract."

Coco-or-Julian stares down at the page and his eyes widen. "A contract? Don't you want to see me perform first?"

Oh, right. Rookie mistake.

Michael Pruitt Business Tip #349: Always audition talent before giving them an official talent-agency contract.

I clear my throat. "I'll make an exception this one time because I can see you have a lot of pizzazz. And that snap . . . that snap is something else. We'll set up a post-contract-signing audition," I say confidently. Like that's a real thing.

Coco-or-Julian twists his face at me. "Are you sure that's how it's done?"

"I like to do things a little differently around here," I say, forcing my voice slightly deeper than usual for some reason. It doesn't work so well. It cracks. "You'll get used to it. It's show business!"

I clap my hands once real loud in front of his face, trying to match the pizzazz of his half-moon snap. He jumps in his seat a little like I scared him, so I guess it worked. Pizzazz must be contagious.

"Sorry," I say. "Just excited to get started."

Coco-or-Julian looks down and points at the contract. "What does *TBD* mean?"

I give him my most professional fake smile. "To be determined." I learned that from Pap Pruitt, too. "You know, like all the details and stuff. How much I get paid and all that. It's not important right now."

He smiles tightly like he wants to trust me. Finally he scribbles his stage name on the line. It's kind of a messy signature, but I guess he's more used to signing autographs than official contracts.

"Michael." Mom's voice blares through the intercom and Coco-or-Julian jumps in his seat again. He eyes the boxy intercom on my desk like it's an alien egg about to hatch. "Dinner. Now."

How embarrassing. And unprofessional. At least she called me Michael. I hit the Talk button. "I'm wrapping up a meeting, Mom. I'll be there in a minute."

I stand, which makes Coco-or-Julian stand as well.

"I think we should shake on it even though we already signed an official legal contract," I say, holding out my hand. He takes it. His grip is a little more firm this time.

"Welcome to the Anything Talent and Pizzazz Agency," I say, trying to keep my excitement from scaring him again. Don't want to act like I'm not a real-live talent agent signing up new clients all the time. Coco-or-Julian grins from ear to ear. I think I sold it.

"Can you meet tomorrow at school during lunch period for our first strategy and planning session?"

He nods. "I have second lunch."

"Good." I usher him to the door before he can change his mind and tear up the contract. "Me too. I'll make some calls right away," I say, but I don't know why. I don't have any idea who to call. I don't even have my own phone. But it just came out, so maybe I'm a natural at this talent-agent thing. I must have good show-business instincts, and sometimes that's way better than real-life experience.

"Oh, okay," he says.

His smile is huge now and his eyes are sparkling. I can't help feeling like I'm part of the reason for that. I'm about to make all his drag-queen dreams come true, after all.

"Well, bye, I guess," he says, opening the door and stepping out into the carport. "See you tomorrow at lunch."

"Lunch. Yes," I say, waving and following him out.

I watch him walk to the end of our driveway before I dart back inside. Suddenly I have so much energy I could bounce off the walls. A talent agency. It's perfect. Why haven't I thought of it before? There're loads of talented kids at school. Pap Pruitt will be so proud when I make Coco Caliente the biggest drag queen in all of North Charleston Middle School. And maybe Tommy Jenrette and his jerk friends will finally stop teasing me about my failed business ventures and show me some respect.

I hurry back over to my desk and open a Web browser on my laptop.

"Now, Mikey," Mom's irritated voice calls over the inter-com.

I don't answer. This will only take a second and she'll think I'm already on my way in. I open Google and type my question into the search bar.

Michael Pruitt Business Tip #350: Fake it till you make it. When in doubt, you can google anything. Even *What is a drag queen?*

4

THE FAMILY INTERROGATION

"Lyla says you had a visitor in your office today." Dad picks up his burger with both hands and takes a big messy bite out of it.

I glare across the table at Lyla. She stole my thunder. Lyla chews a big mouthful of hamburger while smiling at me like she just did me a favor. I can tell she's swinging her legs under the table by the way her body is rocking slightly. She always swings her legs. It's annoying. Especially in the workplace, when your chairs are only two feet apart. She kept kicking mine. I had to write her up a few times about that.

Mom passes me the salad bowl because I didn't put anything green on my hamburger. Mom insists you have to have something green on your plate at every meal. I take the bowl and tong myself some rabbit food that I plan to eat as little as possible of.

"I was going to tell you about it at the board meeting on Wednesday," I say.

Thanks for nothing, Lyla.

Turns out, Google knows *a lot* about drag queens, and even some about drag *kids*. But all I had time to do was look at pictures. I have a ton more research to do before I can take Coco Caliente, Mistress of Madness and Mayhem, to *the next level*.

"I had a walk-in," I say, picking up my fork. "A new client."

"He was weird looking," Lyla says, mustard smeared across her mouth.

"You're weird looking," I mumble under my breath.

"Mikey," Mom says sharply, frowning at me.

Mom teaches American Lit at North Charleston High, so sometimes she slips into her scolding-teacher voice at home.

"Sorry," I mumble, without looking at Lyla, so I could be saying *sorry* to anyone about anything. It makes apologizing to her a lot easier.

Mom wipes her mouth with a paper towel and pushes loose strands of hair out of her face. "And it's not nice to say someone is weird looking, Lyla. Can you find a better way to describe Mikey's new friend?"

"He's not my friend," I say quickly, but I'm not sure why I said it *so* quickly.

Forbes pushes through the doggy door, trotting happily into the room. Pooty jumps down from the top of his cat condo and hisses at him, sending Forbes right back outside. Poor Forbes.

"Okay, then. Let me see," Lyla says to the ceiling as she

licks mustard from the corners of her mouth. "He was . . . *different looking.*"

"That's racist," I say, looking at my burger and not at the devil child of 666 Kudzu Lane.

Unfortunately that's our real street address. But I don't think anyone else has made the connection between our address and Lyla's *peculiar* personality. Or the fact that her birthday is June 6. Thank God she wasn't born in 2006.

Lyla huffs. "I didn't mean his skin color."

I glance up at Dad. He's staring at me, the tanned, sun-creased lines in his forehead raised.

"He's just a kid from school," I say.

"He's Latino," Lyla adds.

"Oh, that's nice," Mom says, adding careful lines of ranch dressing to her salad. "You could use a little diversity in your circle of friends."

I stare at Mom with my mouth hanging open. I literally have two friends—one is black and one is Indian. And she's met them several times.

"Those croquet students aren't his friends," Lyla pipes in.

Oh. *That's* what Mom's talking about.

"And Mikey doesn't have a circle," the devil baby says.

"Your brother has lots of friends, sweetie," Dad says, petting her head like she's a brand-new puppy.

His voice is always a little higher when he talks to Lyla. I swear they act like she's still five. She could get away with murder around here.

"There's Dinesh and Trey and . . . and . . ." Dad's voice trails off like he can't remember anyone else. But in his defense, that's actually all there is.

"See, Dad," Lyla says with a bored sigh. "Not a circle."

"So, what's this boy's name?" Mom asks, saving me. But not really.

I think for a minute. There's a lot to choose from. *Coco-or-Julian. Coco Caliente, Mistress of Madness and Mayhem. Miss Coco, Mr. Caliente.* I decide to keep it simple and use his boy name.

"Julian," I say.

Mom gets the pitcher of tea from the fridge. "And where is Julian from?"

I realize now that during the excitement of having my first walk-in and starting a talent-agency division of Anything, Inc., I didn't get a lot of background information on my new client. I need to step up my game.

Michael Pruitt Business Tip #351: It's a good idea to get the client's last name and current address—or any address, for that matter—on all legally binding contracts.

"I'm not sure where he's from," I say. "Here, I guess."

"Is he cute?" Dad says, leaning over and grinning at me like a goofy kid.

"Ew, Dad," I say. "I'm twelve."

Dad runs a hand through his hair. "Doesn't mean you're

blind. I was about your age when I noticed how cute your mom was."

Mom giggles and playfully punches Dad's arm. I roll my eyes at them. Sometimes parents can be so lame.

"Why would Mikey think a boy is cute?" Lyla asks. "Only girls are cute."

"Not to everyone, sweetie," Dad says. "Anybody can be cute to someone."

Lyla shrugs like she doesn't care one way or another—as long as the whole wide universe thinks *she's* cute.

Sometimes I wish I'd never told my parents that I *thought* I *might* be gay. I said *thought* and *might* to soften the blow, but it wasn't any kind of blow or even a surprise to them. I thought that was kind of weird and it made me wonder if they knew I was gay even before I did. But I don't know how they could have. They were wicked cool about it right from the beginning, though. I guess I should be glad about that. I'm sure some kids who are gay, or bi, or trans probably don't have supportive parents. But sometimes Mom and Dad can be a little *too* enthusiastic about my gayness. Like asking me every day if I *like*-like any boys at school. I mean, *ew times ten*. I'm only twelve and they're ready to sign me up for *Gay Bachelor: North Charleston Middle School Edition*.

"What did Julian want?" Mom asks, absently stabbing her salad to death with her fork. Seriously, her plate is almost a crime scene. I think she secretly doesn't like green food, either, but she's not about to admit it to me and Lyla.

"He wants me to be his agent," I say, like it's no big deal for a twelve-year-old kid to be a professional talent agent. It sure isn't to me. Pap Pruitt would understand. I can't wait to go see him so I can tell him about my new business.

Dad rests his elbows on the table, boring a hole through me with his blue-gray eyes. "Agent? What kind of agent?"

"A *talent* agent," I say casually.

"Oh," Mom says, looking up at me. "Wow."

It wasn't an excited *wow*. More like a that's-a-super-dumb-idea-Mikey *wow*.

"Well," Dad says. "That could be interesting. What's Julian's talent? Does he play an instrument?"

His forehead is all wrinkled like he's not so sure about my latest business idea.

I shake my head.

"Is he a magician?" Lyla asks.

"No," I say to my plate and not to Lyla.

I don't want to tell them what Julian's talent is before I see it for myself. If I say, *He's a drag queen*, it'll just spark a thousand more questions from Lyla. This already feels enough like an interrogation.

"Is he a singer?" she asks.

"No," I say again. Even though I honestly don't know if drag queens sing or not.

"A comedian?" she continues, because she just won't shut up about this. She's trying to break me down.

"I haven't seen him perform yet, okay, Lyla?" The edge

in my voice draws confused looks from Mom and Dad.

"Shouldn't you check out this boy's act before you decide to be his agent?" Dad asks, but not in a mean way.

I let out a big sigh and slump down in my chair. They're not going to let this go until I give them something.

"Well, his stage name is Coco Caliente, Mistress of Madness and Mayhem," I say, bracing myself for a bunch of questions. But they don't come. Because what the heck can you say to that?

Dad opens and closes his mouth a couple of times like he's trying to figure out how it works, but no sounds come out. Mom squints at me with a constipated smile.

"Well," Mom finally says. "That does sound interesting. We'll expect a full report at the next board meeting, okay?"

That's exactly what I said before. But *thank you very much, Lyla, and have a nice day*. How does such a little kid have such a big mouth? I give her my best get-thee-behind-me-Satan glare. She just smiles real big and cheesy. Like seriously, melted cheese is hanging from the corners of her mouth.

"Mikey—"

"May I please be excused?" I say before Lyla can ask another question.

Mom checks out my plate to make sure I ate all my salad and then nods. I can't get out of there fast enough. I have research to do and this *RuPaul's Drag Race* show isn't going to watch itself.

5

THE WORST GAY EVER

It's May—the last month of the school year—so the students are more restless and rowdy than ever. And some of them—*cough-cough, Tommy Jenrette*—more dangerous. When the second lunch-period bell rings, it doesn't take long for the silent, empty cafeteria to fill with the growing roar of Monday chatter, laughter, footsteps, and the smell of deep-fried Tater Tots. The noise ricochets from wall to wall and ceiling to floor like in the prison cafeterias on TV. At least prison cafeterias have armed guards standing around keeping an eye on things. Not here, though. Today we have my homeroom teacher, Mrs. Campbell, and the drama teacher, Mr. Arnold, as lunch monitors. But they're over in the corner gossiping and laughing, so we're basically on our own. Luckily there's only three weeks left before summer break.

Trey, Dinesh, and I keep our heads down as we make our way through the lunch line and out into the maze of long narrow tables. It's like a minefield out here—watch where you step or you could be blown to bits by the wrong people.

33

Although I'll bet they consider themselves the right people and *us* the wrong people. We've learned the hard way where it's okay to hang out, where it's okay to walk, and most important, where it's okay to sit.

The tables closest to the lunch line are in what we call the yellow zone. That's where the outsiders and unpopular people sit. The middle of the cafeteria is the red zone, where the popular, rich, and athletic kids hang out—mostly eighth graders. We make a beeline for the green zone—the tables closest to the safety of the school's front office—where the not-popular, but not-really-unpopular, regular seventh-grade kids like us sit. We like to blend in and not attract attention from the red-zone crowd. They're the worst. The only problem is, you have to weave your way through the red-zone minefield to get to the green zone. Today we just about make it without any problem until a familiar voice calls out as we're passing through.

"Loser, party of three. Loser, party of three."

I glance over to my left and see that it was eighth-grade horrible person Tommy Jenrette, just like I thought. He's sitting with all his dumb basketball buddies, cupping his mouth with his hands to make his voice louder. His friends laugh like it's the most hilarious thing they've ever seen and heard, so he does it again.

"Loser, party of three. Loser, party of three."

"Just keep walking," Dinesh says, eyes glued to the Tater Tots on his tray.

Snickers follow us all the way to the border of the red zone. Finally we make it to our regular table in the green zone, and Trey and Dinesh sit across from me. Next year Tommy Jenrette and his idiot friends will be in high school and we won't have to worry about them for at least a year.

"Those guys are such jerks," Trey says. He pulls the latest Percy Jackson novel out of his backpack.

Trey reads more than any kid I know. Reading is like his superpower. He actually looks forward to getting our summer reading list every year, if you can believe that. And sometimes he'll read an entire book over the weekend instead of watching TV. Like a *whole book* from front to back—with no pictures. And he never goes to see the movies of the books he's read because he says they're never as good. I wonder if reading is a talent. Maybe I should add Trey to my client roster at the Anything Talent and Pizzazz Agency. I'd just have to figure out how to turn his love for reading into gobs of commission for me. I need to do some googling about that later.

Trey covers his naked hot dog with two plastic packets of mustard, two packets of ketchup, and three packets of relish. His spotless white polo shirt doesn't have a chance.

"I've been meaning to ask you," he says to me. "Why haven't you joined the Pride Club yet? We had a meeting last week. I thought you'd be there."

I'm not sure why, but the words *pride* and *club* together give me instant back sweat. I know Trey expects me to join the Pride Club. He's not even gay and *he's* in the Pride Club.

And he's been on me about joining ever since I told him and Dinesh that I *thought* I *might* be gay a couple of months ago. But I honestly didn't *think* that I *might* be gay. I knew. I've always known. I'm just not ready for all of North Charleston Middle School to know.

There are four people in the whole wide world who know—my parents and my two best friends—and that's been *plenty* of people knowing as far as I'm concerned. I get enough crap from Tommy Jenrette and his jerk friends already. Why give them more ammo? Besides, I'll have all summer to get comfortable with the idea of being an *out* gay. Next year I'll be an eighth grader. Untouchable. At least for a year. In the meantime, I just want to end this school year without the whole world knowing all my business and without Tommy Jenrette having a fresh batch of names to call me. Names with the word *gay* in them.

I squirm a little in my seat. "I . . . um . . . just figured since it was so close to the end of the year, I would just wait and join next year."

Trey gives me a disappointed sigh and shakes his head. "Dude, you're the worst gay ever."

He maneuvers his hot dog to his mouth with both hands. Still, a thick drop of mustard lands right on his shirt.

Dinesh points to the mustard stain and hands Trey an extra napkin. "Nice, dude."

"Crap," Trey says. "Moms are going to kill me."

Trey always calls his parents *Moms* because he has two

36

moms. Makes a lot of sense to me. Trey is easily the best looking of the three of us with his perfectly rounded face, his soft brown eyes, and shoulders almost as wide as Tommy Jenrette's. And his moms always send him to school looking like he stepped right off the pages of a JCPenney catalog, but he never leaves that way. He takes the napkin from Dinesh, dips it into his water, and blots away. He knows the drill.

Dinesh leans in and nods at me. "It's true. Trey is a better gay than you and he's not even gay."

Feeling a little defensive, I pick up a Tater Tot and hold it in the palm of my hand, like a rock I might throw at them. "Is joining the Pride Club mandatory? Are there gay rules that I don't know about yet? I mean, I've only been gay like . . . five minutes."

Not exactly true.

Trey picks up his book. "Whatever, dude."

I don't want Trey to be disappointed in me or to think I'm *the worst gay ever*, even though he's probably right about that. I didn't know there was a right way and a wrong way to be gay, but I guess I'll have to ask Google about that, too.

"I'll think about it," I say, hoping that gets me off the hook for now.

Trey looks over at Dinesh. "What about you? The club is for friends of gay people, too."

"I don't think my parents are going to let me join," Dinesh says, popping a Tater Tot in his mouth. "They said I need to focus on my grades, not *all that*."

Dinesh's traditional Indian parents are super nice, but they think everything is a distraction for Dinesh that doesn't involve passing the bar exam or getting into medical school.

"'All that'?" Trey points to me. "Mikey's gay and you're around him, like, every day."

The words punch me right in the gut. Maybe because he said it kind of loud. I glance around to see if anyone heard him say the words *Mikey* and *gay* together. Thank God Tommy Jenrette is too far away to hear. It's not that I'm ashamed of being gay or anything. It's just easier being the right kind of popular than the wrong kind of popular at North Charleston Middle School. Even though I'm not really *any* kind of popular. I guess sometimes that's the safest kind to be.

"Yeah," Dinesh replies with a goofy grin. "But like you said, he's, like, the worst gay ever, so I don't think it even counts."

They both crack up. And yes, these are my best friends. The ones laughing at me right now. We kind of bonded on the playground in first grade when nobody else wanted to hang out with any of us, so we just started playing together and never stopped. I think that's how some of the best friendships are made.

"You guys suck," I say. I toss a Tater Tot at Dinesh. He catches it and pops it in his mouth. Dinesh's talent is eating Tater Tots for sure, but I don't think there's anything I could do with that, unless . . . I pull a pen and my yellow notepad out of my backpack and write it down before I forget:

Google local Tater Tot—eating contests.

Dinesh clears his throat. I look up. His eyes are wide and he's using them to point over my shoulder, which makes him look way crazy. But I turn around anyway and *OMG!*

"Hey," Julian says. He stands there holding his lunch tray. At our table. In real life.

He's wearing sharply creased jeans and sandals like he was when he came to the world headquarters of Anything, Inc., yesterday—minus the YOU BETTER WERK! tank top. The T-shirt he's wearing today reads, *YAAAS!*

Before this weekend I wouldn't have known what *yaaas* meant. But after my extensive research watching three episodes of *RuPaul's Drag Race*—very informative show, by the way—I know now that *yaaas* is something drag queens say when they're super-crazy excited. Like they might say:

Yaaas, queen! That look is fierce!

Fierce means "good" in drag language, as best as I can tell, but I don't speak it fluently yet.

I look back at my friends. Trey has his nose buried in his book, but he peers over the top, his eyes wide and locked on Julian. Dinesh's mouth hangs open, two half-chewed Tater Tots balancing on his tongue.

I turn to face my new client, heat flooding my cheeks and beads of sweat exploding across my forehead. I'm not sure why, though. I mean it's not like he's standing here in a dress like the contestants on *RuPaul's Drag Race*. Still, I glance over my shoulder to make sure Tommy Jenrette isn't looking this way. Luckily he isn't.

"Hey," I finally say.

But I say it a little sharp and more like a question. Like *Hey* actually means "What the heck are you doing here? At our table? In real life?"

I don't know what else to say, though. So I spit out the stupidest thing in the entire world.

"Can I help you?"

Can I help you? What the heck is this? A drive-through window? I even say it with a little huff. Like I have no idea who Julian is or what he's doing at our table saying *hey* to me. I feel like a total jerk, but that doesn't stop me from looking at him like I don't recognize him either.

Julian glances over at Dinesh and Trey, then back at me. His eyes darken a little and his smile fades. "You said we should meet up at lunch for our first strategy and planning session."

I hadn't forgotten about that, but I figured I would go find him *after* I ate lunch with Trey and Dinesh. I try to round up what's left of my professional manners.

"Oh, right," I say, like I'd forgotten all about our meeting, because *I'm so busy* and stuff like that. "Um . . . um . . ." Because that's a professional response, right? "Where're you sitting? I'll come find you after I eat."

I don't dare look back at my *friends*. I'm sure they're just loving this.

Julian looks around at all the empty chairs at our table

40

and—*OMG!*—for a second I think he's about to just sit down with us. And then everyone in the cafeteria would see me with him—that popular-for-all-the-wrong-reasons kid. And they might think we're friends. But Julian doesn't sit down. And he doesn't ask to. And I don't invite him to. Because I guess I'm a terrible person. Or maybe Pooty somehow got into my room last night and sucked all my nice-person breath out through my nostrils and replaced it with his own evil-spirit breath. I've heard cats can do that.

Julian tries to smile again, but it doesn't take. He actually looks a little sad, or hurt. I feel about two inches tall.

Michael Pruitt Business Tip #352 (learned the hard way): Always set a clear time and location for all business meetings.

He nods over his right shoulder to the yellow zone. "Okay. Um . . . Well, I'll be over there whenever you're ready."

He turns and walks away—straight through the red zone with his head down, ignoring the taunts from the basketball team. I think Tommy yells something about the size of his butt or the way he walks, but I can't quite make it out. Or maybe I just don't want to make it out. Julian sits at a table in the far corner of the yellow zone. By himself. I sigh. *Worst gay ever.*

6

THE WICKED-COOL SMILE

When I turn back to face Trey and Dinesh, they're staring at me all intense and bug-eyed.

"So," I say, casually picking up a Tater Tot and popping it into my mouth like what just happened never happened. "Want to hang out after school?"

"'Want to hang out after school?'" Dinesh says, resting elbows on the table. "Dude. What the heck was that?"

"What was what?" I say, chewing and avoiding their eyes because that seems like the smart thing to do.

Trey closes his book. "Julian Vasquez? Strategy and planning session?"

The last name sounds vaguely familiar, but it takes my brain a few seconds to connect the dots.

Ah. Julian/Coco Caliente, Mistress of Madness and Mayhem, equals North Charleston Middle School popular-for-all-the-wrong-reasons eighth grader Julian Vasquez.

"Oh, that," I say with a wave of my hand, buying a little time to figure out how much I should tell them.

Trey and Dinesh are usually pretty cool about all my business ideas. They've never teased me about them like some of the red-zone kids do. They even help out sometimes. On the opening day of Anything General Store, they stood on the sidewalk and handed out free samples of our green apple Jolly Ranchers to lure people over to the store. They always work on a strictly volunteer basis, though. I would never pay my best friends. It's not in the budget.

And we don't have any secrets either. When I told them I *thought* I *might* be gay, Dinesh seemed the most surprised. But then he shrugged and said, *That's cool.* Trey gave me an eye roll and a drawn-out *duuuh*—whatever that meant. But the way they're acting about Julian right now puts me on guard a little.

"It's just a new business venture I'm working on," I say. "He's my new client. No big deal."

Trey and Dinesh look at each other like I just told them *I'm* a drag queen or something.

"No big deal?" Dinesh says, pushing his tray to the side and leaning in to whisper. "Dude. Julian is gay. Like *way* gay."

This isn't news to me. I guess I just assumed Julian was gay because of the whole Coco Caliente thing. But I guess non-gays can be drag queens, too. It's a free country.

"He is?" I ask. "How do you know?"

Trey looks at me like I have four heads. "His locker is right across the hall from mine. Trust me, everyone knows."

"You made us *swear* not to tell anyone about you," Dinesh

says. "You said you weren't ready for the whole school to know. Especially not Tommy Jenrette."

I nod like making them swear not to tell anyone I'm gay is a perfectly normal thing to do. It is, right? Dinesh looks at Trey for backup.

Trey pushes his lunch to the side and leans in. "Look. It sucks, but he's right. If you start hanging out with Julian Vasquez, trust me, everyone will know your secret. Are you ready for Tommy and his idiot muscle-head friends to find out?"

This feels like a trick question. On the one hand, *absolutely not, Trey, no, thank you very much and have a nice day,* and on the other hand, *why do I care what a jerk like Tommy Jenrette and his idiot friends think of me?* But let's face it, for some reason I do. It's that whole attracting-the-*wrong*-kind-of-attention thing when I've worked really hard all these years to attract the *right* kind of attention. Not that it's worked, though. Still, I'd prefer pats on the back to more teasing and rude notes taped to it. And in three weeks I won't have to worry about those guys for a long time.

Dinesh shakes his head slowly. "He's right, dude."

Dinesh keeps talking, but I stop listening because Colton Sanford just walked out of the front office. He's the new kid who transferred from Columbia to North Charleston a few weeks ago to finish out the school year. Some kind of *family emergency* from what I heard a couple nosy kids say. Miss Troxel, the guidance counselor, has her hand on Colton's shoulder and she's talking to him real serious-like. Colton nods with his head down.

I haven't told Trey and Dinesh that whenever I see Colton in homeroom or pass him in the hall and he smiles at me, it makes my stomach feel like someone put it in a blender and turned it on High. I thought I would give them some time to get used to just the basic me-being-gay thing before I tell them I actually *like*-like someone who is also a dude. I don't think Trey and Dinesh have even met him yet. I haven't actually *met him* met him yet, either.

When Mrs. Campbell introduced him in homeroom, I remember that was the first time I ever saw any kid at North Charleston Middle School wearing suspenders. They were bright blue and they made Colton look real fancy. And there just aren't that many students at school with shiny reddish-brown hair and lots of dark freckles. I have only a few freckles and that's plenty for me. They look perfect on Colton's face, though. But it was his wicked-cool smile full of, like, a hundred sparkling white teeth that I remember the most. He looked at me and smiled after Mrs. Campbell introduced him, but I guess maybe he could have been smiling at Heather Hobbs, who sits behind me in homeroom. All the guys thinks she's super-crazy pretty, so I can't be sure Colton was looking at me and not her. And I'm not even sure if Colton likes girls or boys. Mom says you shouldn't just assume these things.

Colton's not smiling now as he talks to Miss Troxel, though.

I wonder what he was doing in the front office. I wonder if anything is wrong. Or if he's in trouble. Miss Troxel wipes something from Colton's cheek with her thumb the same way Mom wipes Lyla's tears away. But why would Colton be crying? Just the thought of Colton Sanford maybe-possibly crying makes me want to hurl. What the heck is that about? Miss Troxel gives him the teacher side-hug and sends him off in our direction. He glances up and our eyes meet and— *OMG!*—he saw me staring at him.

"Dude? Are you listening to us?" Dinesh asks, waving his hand in front of my face.

"Um . . . um . . ." is all I can get out because Colton is just steps away and he's looking straight at me. Probably because he thinks I'm a creep for staring at him like a stalker. He's definitely not smiling, but he's not scowling either, so that's something, right? His eyes are glassy and he's kind of staring at me the way I looked at Julian when I was acting like I didn't know him earlier. *Ouch.* Pap always says, *What goes around comes around.* And I guess he was right about that.

Colton is close, so I open my mouth to try to say something—*Hi* or *Are you okay?* or *I promise I'm not a creepy stalker* or *You have a wicked-cool smile, so why are you sad?* But right as he passes, the words stumble out of my mouth not as words, but as an involuntary burp. And—*OMG!*—what is wrong with me?

Colton scrunches up his nose probably because my mouth just burped at him. *Loud.* And just like that, he's gone.

I turn back to Trey and Dinesh. They're staring at me like I'm the most disgusting person alive. Or an alien from a gaseous planet. Like Planet Pooty.

"Nice, dude," Trey says. "Burping in a guy's face. Wow. Is that one of your smooth new gay moves?"

Dinesh shakes his head. "That was the saddest thing I've ever seen."

Sometimes I don't like my best friends very much. Maybe now that I'm a professional talent agent I should audition some new ones. I look over my shoulder and spot Colton entering the yellow zone and sitting down at a table, *with Julian*. And they fist-bump and everything. Huh. Julian Vasquez and Colton Sanford are friends? This has to be the weirdest day ever.

I turn back around. "Hey," I say to change the subject before they start asking more questions about Colton. "Trey, you said Julian's locker is across the hall from yours, right?"

Trey looks confused, but nods. I tear off a sheet of paper from my legal pad, scribble a message on it, and fold it, like, a hundred times. Okay, maybe five times.

I hold the note out to him. "Can you slip this through the vents into his locker?"

Trey raises his hands and shakes his head. "If somebody sees me doing that, they'll think it's a love letter or something. *From me.* No way."

I shoot him a glare and lean forward. "I didn't know you were such a homophobe."

Trey holds my stare for a while. It's like we're playing

chicken. But I know Trey's not a homophobe, you know, because of the having-two-moms thing.

"Aw, man," Trey whines, shaking his head and grabbing the note from my hand. "This blows."

I smile and lean back in my chair.

Michael Pruitt Business Tip #353: Using inside information on someone to get what you want is not nice. But it's not illegal, either.

7

THE PROBLEM EMPLOYEE

Trey didn't chicken out like I thought he might, because there was a folded-up scrap of paper in my locker from Julian by the end of the day. I'd apologized in my note for being too busy to meet during lunch but asked if I could see his act after school. His note gave his home address. He said to be there at four thirty and to come on in through the garage door. It was signed *xoxo, Julian.* I'm not sure what's up with all the *x*'s and *o*'s, and I don't think I want to know. But as soon as I got home from school, I did my homework in my office before hopping on my bike with my backpack full of my business essentials—a few pens, a pencil, my notebook, a calculator, a stapler, and some paper clips. I've never held an audition before, so I want to be prepared for anything.

I ride my bike down Julian's street checking the mailboxes, looking for number 239. Sprawling magnolias line both sides of the road, their sagging limbs dotted with fat white blooms like giant popcorn growing in the trees. I guess that's why this is called Magnolia Way. We don't have any magnolia trees in our subdivision, and the houses over here are bigger. The grass is also way greener and the cars in the driveways are nicer, too. It's weird that Julian lives in the subdivision next to ours and I never even knew it. I thought I knew just about every kid from school who lives around here, but I guess not.

I finally spot number 239, between numbers 237 and 241. I've never understood why there have to be all even-numbered houses on one side of the street and odd-numbered houses on the other side. It seems like a very confusing system. Maybe I should go down to city hall and sell my services as a professional re-addresser and get North Charleston all straightened out once and for all. I need to remember to write that down in my *Amazing Business Ideas* notebook when I get home:

Anything Non-Confusing Re-Addresser Service

A division of Anything, Inc.

Michael Pruitt—President, Founder, CEO,

and Address Specialist

So many ideas, so little time. That's what Pap Pruitt always says, and man, is he right about that. Thinking about Pap causes a weird little pang in my stomach. I wonder if he's feeling any better today. I hope I'll be able to visit him this Sunday. I can't wait to tell him about my new company. Pap might even have some super-crazy-good business advice for me. But he's been getting sicker and weaker lately. I really want him to see one of my ideas take off before it's too late, and I think the Anything Talent and Pizzazz Agency is what Pap calls a home-run idea.

I pedal into the driveway of 239 Magnolia Way and stop beside a shiny, dark blue BMW that looks brand-new, parked just outside two closed garage doors. The license plate frame reads, VASQUEZ FINE AUTO—NORTH CHARLESTON.

I'm a little surprised by the size of Julian's house. I don't know what I was expecting, but it's, like, twice the size of ours. A lot fancier looking, too, with real white columns on the front porch and a bright red double front door framed by lots of tiny windows at the top and sides. Dad keeps our yard in tip-top shape, but this lawn is like plush dark green carpet. You could definitely say that Julian's house is *fierce*, at least on the outside. A muffled but steady bass beat drifts out from the garage—it could be Beyoncé or Lady Gaga, I'm not sure. I guess I should learn the difference if I'm going to be the talent agent for a drag queen. And, you know, gay.

A familiar but irritating bicycle bell dings twice behind me and *OMG!*

"Who lives here?"

Lyla pulls up beside me. Hopping off her pink-and-white Hello Kitty bicycle like she's supposed to be here, she gives me the creepy-kid smile as she knocks the kickstand down.

I roll my eyes at her. "What are you doing here, Lyla?"

"I followed you," she says. Like secretly following people without their permission is a perfectly normal thing for nine-year-olds to do.

She's wearing a purple Disney Princess dress over jeans, and her devil horns are hidden by flimsy pigtails tied up in yellow ribbons.

"Who said you could follow me?" I say.

"Dad," she replies with a smirk.

Thanks a lot, Dad.

"So, who lives here?" she says, crossing her arms over her chest, staring up at the house.

"None of your business," I say, still straddling my bike. "Go home."

She turns and then heads for the front door of the house. "Okay. I'll just find out for myself."

"Wait!" I say, hopping off my bike and chasing her down. I grab her shoulder and spin her around. "You can't do that. This is an important business meeting. You're going to blow it for me."

She crosses her arms and squints up at me. "Does the boy who came to the office the other day live here?"

I look around to make sure no one has seen us yet. "Yes. But you still have to go home." Mom says I sometimes have *a tone*, so I try to talk all sugary and sweet to her, hoping that will work. "I mean, how would it look if I brought my little sister to a business meeting? Very unprofessional, that's how, right?"

She gives me the creepy-kid smile again. "Then you better make me more than just your little sister before we go in. And more than your dumb assistant, too."

OMG! She's blackmailing me. And it's working. I take a second to think this through.

Option A—Lyla crashes the audition and embarrasses the heck out of me, causing me to lose my first and only talent-agency client.

Option B—Rehire her and cross all my fingers and toes that she keeps her mouth shut during this audition.

She hasn't lost her smirky stare. She knows she's got me. Pap Pruitt always says, *When life serves you lemons, make lemonade.* And boy, is he right about that.

"Okay," I say, even though I hate lemonade. "Fine. You are officially the junior talent coordinator for Anything Talent and Pizzazz Agency."

"That's a dumb name for a business," she says.

I ignore her. "But you're on probation for thirty days."

Lyla's face sours instantly. "What does that mean?"

I turn, heading toward the garage. "It means for thirty days I can fire you for any reason I want to, so you better not screw up. And don't even ask for a raise. Same deal as last time."

"But you didn't pay me last time," she whines behind me.

"Exactly," I say.

There's a side door to the garage and I guess that's where Julian meant for me to go in. But I feel kind of weird just walking into someone's house without ringing the doorbell or anything. It seems rude and kind of illegal, but that's what his note said to do.

"Mikey," Lyla says behind me.

I look over my shoulder. "*Michael*. What?"

"What does a *coordinator* do?"

"Everything the boss says to do," I say, turning the door-knob. "And coordinators don't speak unless spoken to."

I open the door and Lyla follows me inside.

"Yeah," she says. "That's not going to work for me."

8

THE AUDITION

The garage is huge, at least twice the size of our carport. It's brightly lit with no cars inside and super-crazy neat. A single row of metal chairs faces a small stage with a black curtain for a back wall. Two women sit watching a girl about Lyla's age dance around onstage in black tights. One of the women looks like an older version of Julian and the other one looks like a super-older version of him. We stand quietly in the back, watching the girl. She's pretty good, I guess, but I don't know much about dancing, so I can't be sure. The thumping song ends and the girl twirls, throwing her hands way up in the air when she stops. The older of the two women stands, clapping excitedly. The other woman pops up out of her chair and walks over to the stage.

"You have to point your toes, mija," she says to the girl, who's already stepping down off the stage.

Dancing Girl nods at the woman and then spots us in the back of the garage. She waves us over. Before I can open my mouth to say hello and introduce myself to the three of them, Lyla pipes up.

"That was really good," she says to the girl. "You have loads of talent and pizzazz."

The girl grins so hard I think her face is going to crack open. I glare at Lyla, but she ignores me. What is she up to now?

"You must be Julian's new friend," the woman says to me, while smiling at Lyla the way all adults do. *Ugh.*

I don't know why she called me Julian's *friend*. He's my client and I'm his agent. We have a professional relationship, that's all. I don't know why that seems important to me to clear up, but I manage to ignore it.

"Michael Pruitt, ma'am." I hold out my hand to her. "President, founder, and CEO of Anything Talent and Pizzazz Agency, at your service."

I don't know why I said *at your service.* I think I heard it on a TV show once and thought it sounded professional. But it doesn't seem to bother the woman, because she shakes my hand and winks at me.

"I'm Julian's mother," she says, the dancing girl leaning in to her side. "This is Gabriela and Abuela."

"Hey, Gabriela," I say to the girl. Then I hold my hand out to the older woman standing beside Mrs. Vasquez. "Nice to meet you, Mrs. Abuela."

She shakes my hand with a little giggle. "It's just Abuela, dear."

"*Abuela* means 'grandma' in Spanish," Gabriela says, chuckling into her hand.

Lyla looks up at me with a giant smirk on her face. "You just called her *Mrs. Grandma.*"

Now they're all laughing and my cheeks are on fire. But I have to admit it's pretty funny, so I relax a little and chuckle right along with them.

"Are you going to make Julian a star?" Gabriela asks, saving me from all the giggling.

I clear my throat and lower my voice a little. I don't know why. "That's the plan, Gabriela."

"You can call me Gabby," she says.

Mrs. Vasquez wraps her arm around the girl. "Gabby just won her third dance competition in a row."

Oh. Now I get it. They were hoping I would catch Gabby rehearsing so maybe I would want to represent her, too. I can't blame them. When you get a chance to perform in front of a big-time talent agent, you take it. I stand up a little straighter and nod at the girl like I'm thinking about if I want to offer her a contract or not.

"That's great," I say to her. "You have a lot of potential."

That sounded good. I think.

Michael Pruitt Business Tip #354: If you're not sure about an idea, say it has potential and put it on the back burner in your brain so you can think about it later. Or you might just want to leave it there forever. But don't forget to turn the burner off so the idea doesn't boil over.

"Well, it's very nice to meet you, Michael," Mrs. Vasquez says.

She has a pretty face and sparkly eyes like Julian's, with a tiny nose and wavy brown hair.

Mrs. Vasquez pushes her hair over her shoulder. "Julian tells us you have big plans for his career."

That catches me off guard, so I clear my throat and try to sound as professional as possible.

"Yes, ma'am," I say. "Sorry, but that's all top secret right now." It's not, but I don't have anything to tell them yet. "You understand. I can't wait to see his audition, though."

Julian's tiny abuela covers my hand with both of hers and leans in. "You are so young. Do you think you can handle Miss Coco Caliente?"

The name rolls off her tongue with a lot of pizzazz. It must run in the family.

"I'm going to do my best, ma'am," I say.

"And who is this?" Julian's grandma says, beaming at Lyla like she's the baby Jesus. Lyla gets that a lot. She even played the baby Jesus in a Christmas pageant once. She was terribly miscast in that role.

"This is my associate, Lyla," I say, trying hard to sound professional and not bothered that Lyla is here.

Stepping in front of me, Lyla shakes their hands. "Lyla Pruitt, senior talent coordinator."

"Junior," I spit out. "*Junior* talent coordinator."

Lyla glares at me over her shoulder. I don't care.

A boy's voice is amplified through the garage. "Please, everyone, take your seats."

I glance up at the stage and down into the blender goes my stomach again. Standing there holding a microphone is—*OMG!*—Colton Sanford. And he's smiling at me. Heat rises to my cheeks. He gives me a little wave even though my mouth burped in his face the last time I saw him. Hopefully he's already forgotten about that. And that's the second time he's smiled at me when he's standing in front of people. And Heather Hobbs isn't sitting behind me this time, so I'm pretty sure the smile is meant for me. I only kind of half wave back because everyone is watching me wave at another dude and this doesn't feel the same as when I wave at Trey and Dinesh in the cafeteria or in the hall on the way to class.

Mrs. Vasquez hurries us to the chairs in front of the stage and we sit—me in the middle with Mrs. Vasquez and Julian's grandma on one side and Lyla and Gabby on the other. Those two are already whispering to each other like they're best friends. But I can't stop staring at Colton up on the stage mainly because I'm so surprised that he's here. I saw him sitting with Julian at lunch today, but I didn't know they were the hanging-out-at-Julian's-house kind of friends.

Once we're settled and quiet, Colton nods to someone behind the black curtain and then out comes—*OMG!*—Julian. No, I mean Coco Caliente. Yeah, this is *definitely* Coco Caliente, Mistress of Madness and Mayhem. North

Charleston Middle School eighth grader Julian Vasquez is nowhere in sight. Coco looks like a giant Christmas tree in red high heels, a long red wig, and a sparkly green dress. Like *a real dress*. It's so glittery that it's almost hard to focus my eyes on him.

Julian twirls like he thinks he looks really good as a giant twirling Christmas tree or something. And he kind of does actually, especially with all that makeup on. He almost looks like a real girl. I had a pretty good idea of what to expect from watching *RuPaul's Drag Race*, but seeing it live and up close, well, it's a lot to take in. I look over at Lyla. She just stares up at the stage with her mouth hanging open. For once, she's speechless.

I can't get over how tall Julian is in those high-heeled shoes, and the poufy wig makes him look even taller. I don't know how he doesn't just topple over, but somehow he doesn't. Julian stands front and center on the stage. Colton hands Julian the cordless microphone, which is much fancier than my antique lime-green intercom.

"Well?" Julian says to me, his voice booming through the speakers.

"Well?" I say back, my voice sounding way smaller than his because I don't have a microphone. And, like—*no fair*.

Julian looks a little confused. He plants a hand on his curvy hip. "Aren't you supposed to tell me what to do? This is an audition, right?"

"Oh," I say, sitting up a little straighter in my chair and raising my voice so everyone can hear me. "Right."

I wish there was another microphone for me, and there really should be, but I won't count that against Julian. My mind races. How do you run an audition? I wish I had my laptop and Google, but I guess I'll just have to wing it. Pap always says, *Fake it till you make it.* And I guess this is the perfect time to do that. Then I remember all the reality talent-competition shows I've seen on television.

I lean forward like those judges do, like I'm talking into an invisible microphone on the invisible table in front of us, because that seems like the professional thing to do.

"Please tell us your name and where you're from," I say.

Yeah—I'm pretty sure that sounded wicked cool and professional.

Julian still looks a little confused, but he smiles anyway, standing up real straight and speaking into the microphone. "My name is Coco Caliente, Mistress of Madness and Mayhem, and I'm from"—Coco glances around the garage—"this house."

Mrs. Vasquez and Abuela look over at me, like they want to know if that was the right answer or not. I just smile, nodding at them as if to say, *Don't worry, he's doing just great!*

I look back at the stage. "And how old are you?"

"Thirteen going on fourteen," Julian replies, all smiles. Like he's proud of being thirteen going on fourteen. And like I don't know that fourteen comes after thirteen. I do, by the way.

"Great, Coco," I say. "And what will you be doing for us today?"

I look down at my lap like I'm not all that interested in what Coco has to say. That's the way Simon Cowell does it on those TV talent shows.

Julian clears his throat. "I will be performing a Beyoncé classic." He pauses, I guess for dramatic effect. "'Run the World.'"

Mrs. Vasquez and Abuela burst into applause. I jump a little in my seat because I wasn't expecting it. I can see now where Julian gets all his pizzazz from.

I lean forward again. "Okay then, Juli—um . . . I mean, Miss Coco. Good luck, and whenever you're ready."

Mrs. Vasquez beams at me. She's probably super impressed by the way I'm handling this audition. I have to admit that I just sounded super-crazy professional and like I judge auditions all the time. *Fake it till you make it!*

Lyla leans over and whispers, "Are you sure that's the boy who came to our office? Maybe Julian has *two* sisters."

I put a finger to my lips to shush her, ignoring the fact that she called *my* office *our* office.

Colton looks down and presses something on an iPad, and music fills the garage. I mean, it's *loud*. But it doesn't seem to bother Mrs. Vasquez or even Abuela. They move their heads to the beat, clapping their hands and grinning from ear to ear.

That's when all the fireworks begin, and *OMG!*

9

THE *IT* FACTOR

Julian dances around the stage, moving his lips like he's singing the song, but he's actually not. That's called *lip-synching* in drag language. It's, like, the main thing drag queens do. They do that a lot on *RuPaul's Drag Race* when they're *lip-synching for their lives*. And that's how I have to think of Julian right now—as Miss Coco Caliente, Mistress of Madness and Mayhem, lip-synching for her life. Because Julian is like a whole different person up there.

The next couple of minutes are a blur of jerky dance moves, twirling, strutting back and forth from one side of the stage to the other, and lots of finger pointing—at us, at Colton standing on the side of the stage holding his iPad, at the ceiling, at the riding lawn mower in the corner, at a bicycle, and everything in between. I may not be an expert yet, but it sure seems like Julian has this drag queen thing down pat—the moves, the look, *and* the attitude. He definitely has the *it* factor. That's, like, the most important thing ever when you're judging a professional audition. You gotta look for someone with the *it* factor. And I should know, because I'm doing that right now.

Lyla and Gabby are really into it. I've never seen Lyla with her mouth open so long without a lot of annoying words coming out. Mrs. Vasquez has this little grin on her face as she watches Julian, like this is nothing new to her. Julian's abuela kind of bounces in her seat and sways to the beat of the song.

As the song winds down, Julian circles the center of the stage a couple of times. Then all of sudden, on the last beat of the music, he drops into a full-on split, throwing his hands up in the air. I can't believe my eyes. I've never seen a big dude do a split before. Especially in a sparkly green dress and red high heels.

For a couple of seconds the garage is completely silent. Then we're all on our feet clapping and yelling our heads off. I even try the two-finger whistle, but nothing comes out. It never does. Julian's face lights up at our reaction. Somehow he wrangles his body out of that split and up off the floor. After taking a dramatic bow, he steps down off the stage like he's worn high heels since he was a baby drag queen. Walking over to him, I extend my hand because I think that's the professional thing to do.

"Hello, Miss Coco," I say. "I'm Michael Pruitt, your talent agent."

Julian shakes his head with a healthy dose of stank face. "Michael, it's me. Julian. You know that, right?"

"Oh. Um. Yeah, I know," I say. "It just feels like I'm meeting

Coco Caliente, Mistress of Madness and Mayhem, for the first time."

Julian laughs at that, but it wasn't a joke. At least he shakes my hand and doesn't leave me hanging. Lyla stares up at him with wonder lighting her eyes. Like he's a drag Santa Claus.

"That was amazing," Lyla says kind of quietly, like she's in church.

"Thanks," Julian says, smiling with his whole face.

Colton comes over to us holding a white hand towel, which he uses to dab the sweat from Julian's forehead like he's a professional boxer and Colton is his trainer. And then everyone is quiet. And they're all staring at me. It's super-crazy awkward. I guess they're all waiting to hear what I thought about Julian's performance. I look at each of their faces—Julian, Mrs. Vasquez, Abuela, Gabby, Lyla, *Colton, Colton, Colton*—trying to remember what the judges on *RuPaul's Drag Race* usually say to the contestants because that seems like the smart thing to do.

"Wow," I say to Julian. "You better werk!"

I wag my finger through the air in front of him, from his wig down to his high heels. I think my head might have moved from side to side a little, too, even though I didn't plan on that. It must happen automatically with whole-body finger wagging.

Lyla looks at me like I have four heads. I guess that's fair. I've never said some of those words before and I've definitely never wagged my finger at anyone. A huge grin explodes across Julian's face. Mrs. Vasquez and Colton seem happy with my response, too.

"You seriously liked it?" Julian asks, straightening his wig a little. "You promise?"

I try to remember some more *Drag Race* judge responses.

"Yaaas, honey!"

I feel kind of silly saying it and it came out a lot louder than I'd planned. It's also the first time that I've ever called another dude *honey* or said *yaaas* in my life, but it makes everyone laugh and not in a Tommy Jenrette–jerk kind of way. Even Lyla chuckles a little.

I clear my throat because I need to get into professional-talent-agent mode. "I mean, of course I see some room for improvement, and I have some ideas for your act. You know, to take it to the next level like you said you wanted."

I really don't have any ideas for Julian's act and I'm not even sure what the *next level* for a drag kid is. But my mouth is on autopilot now and I am helpless to stop it. Sometimes I feel like my mouth is my business partner. And definitely not the silent kind.

"You know, fine-tuning and all that stuff," I add, nodding like they should all understand what I mean.

Julian nods back like he knows exactly what I'm talking about even though *I* don't even know what I'm talking about.

"What did you think about the ending, Mikey?" Colton asks shyly, stepping in beside me.

It's the first time he's ever said my name, or talked to me

directly, which seems weird given how much I think about him.

"Colton thinks I need a bigger ending," Julian says. "Something that leaves the audience gagging. What do you think, Michael?"

"Why would you want the audience to gag?" Lyla asks the question before I can.

"He means *gagging* like losing their minds and going wild," Gabby says to Lyla, real serious, like she's translating a foreign language—which she kind of is.

"Gagging is a good thing these days," Mrs. Vasquez says. "*This* means *that*. *That* means *this*. I can't keep up."

Abuela nods real hard like what Mrs. Vasquez said is the God's honest truth and then some.

"Oh yeah, sure," I say to the group. "Colton's a hundred percent correct."

I don't know if he is or not, but that makes Colton smile with his whole face including all of his freckles and shiny white teeth, and there goes my stomach down into that blender again. On High.

"You have to leave the audience gagging to death—in a good way. But we can work on the ending. It needs to be something amazing. Something . . . *fierce*. Don't worry, Julian, I have some ideas about that."

No, I don't, but my non-silent-business-partner mouth won't shut up. Julian nods his whole red wig real fast at me, like what I just said is the smartest thing ever. It feels good to be taken so seriously for once. Maybe I'm a natural at the whole talent-agent thing. In fact, Julian's so excited, I can't help but share the one idea I actually do have with him.

"But we only have about three weeks to work on it before your first gig," I say, crossing my arms, because I think that makes me look super-crazy important.

Julian and Colton exchange puzzled looks.

"You already booked me a gig?" Julian asks, his face changing from confused to excited on a dime.

"What is gig?" Abuela asks.

"It's a job, ma'am," I say. "A chance for Julian to perform in front of gobs of people."

I don't know how many people will be at the North Charleston Middle School end-of-year talent show, but gobs seems like a safe estimate. Everyone stares at me, waiting for me to tell them more.

Julian punches my shoulder. He's a big dude, so it kind of hurts.

"Well, Michael?" he says. "What's the gig?"

I suddenly remember that I haven't actually signed Coco up for the talent show yet. But everyone's looking at me and they're so excited. I hate to disappoint them.

"The school talent show," I say. "There's a hundred-dollar grand prize this year."

Before I can explain about the contest, Julian shrieks so loud I touch a finger to my ear to see if it's bleeding.

"They're going to pay me a hundred dollars?" Julian screeches. "And they'll let me do drag at the school talent show?"

Mrs. Vasquez explains to Abuela in lightning-fast Spanish. Gabby and Lyla look at each other in wide-eyed disbelief.

"Well," I say. "They'll pay you a hundred dollars if you win. And I don't see why they would stop you from doing drag. It's your talent, after all. I'm sure it will be fine."

Now that I start thinking about it, I'm not sure it will be fine at all. I don't *think* there are any rules about what you can and can't do as your talent in the show, but I don't actually *know*.

Julian is speechlessly fanning himself like he might pass out any minute, so I don't want to worry him with details. According to Google, it's my job as his agent to take care of all those details so my client can focus on his performance. I can't stop grinning, though. Making dreams come true is definitely better than crushing them. Someone should tell Simon Cowell that. Maybe I will myself when they ask me to be a guest judge on one of those TV talent competitions. I mean, it's probably only a matter of time before that happens, the way everything is going.

A loud clacking sound fills the garage, and just like that, Julian's big proud smile deflates like a leaky balloon. Mrs. Vasquez's eyes darken a little as her smile is replaced with a tight, thin line. Gabby and Colton quiet down, too. Lyla and I are left wondering what just sucked all the joy out of the room.

One of the garage doors rises with the grumpy grind of a motor. Gabby runs over to it. "Daddy's home!"

Mrs. Vasquez and Abuela exchange a look. I don't know what it means, but it's definitely not a happy look. They don't seem to be as excited as Gabby is that *Daddy's home*.

When the garage door finally rises, a tall, wide man stands there staring at all of us. Gabby wraps her arms around his legs and he leans down to hug her. But the look he's throwing our way doesn't feel very huggy. Julian pulls his wig off.

"You and Lyla should probably go home now," he says, sounding small and not Miss Coco sassy at all anymore. He glances at Colton. "You too."

Colton nods, guiding me and Lyla to the side door where we came in. Lyla waves to Gabby and I look over my shoulder. Julian's mom and dad meet in the middle of the garage, immediately exchanging sharp-sounding words in Spanish.

Mr. Vasquez pauses and looks over at Julian. "Go change now. And wash your face."

"Is everything okay?" I ask Colton, even though it's kind of obvious that everything is definitely *not* okay.

We slip out, but I can still hear Mr. and Mrs. Vasquez arguing through the open garage door. I glance back inside. Gabby, Julian, and Abuela are gone—I guess inside the house somewhere.

Colton walks us over to our bikes, his head hanging a little. "Julian's dad doesn't understand the whole drag thing."

"Then why did he build Julian a stage in the garage?" Lyla asks.

Colton pushes his silky reddish-brown hair out of his eyes, but it falls politely back into place. "He built the stage for Gabby. She does a lot of dance competitions, I guess."

Lyla hops on her Hello Kitty bike, nodding over to the house. "Is Julian in trouble?"

Colton shakes his head a little. "I don't know. I hope not."

Mr. and Mrs. Vasquez's voices have died down now, so I hope everything is okay. I especially hope Julian is okay and that he won't get into trouble. He was so good up there on-stage. I can't understand why his dad wouldn't be proud of him.

There isn't another bike anywhere in sight. "Did you walk here?"

Colton points to the house next door. "That's my grandma's house. Julian was the first friend I made when I came to stay with her."

"Oh," I say. "That's cool." But secretly I wish that Colton's grandma lived next door to us and that I would have been his first friend when he moved in with her.

"You're from upstate, right?" I ask, even though I know he is.

Colton nods. "Columbia. But I had to come stay with my

grandma when my mom . . . well . . . she had to go away for a while."

Go away? I want to ask him where his mom went, but he stares at the ground and shoves his hands down deep in his pockets, so I don't.

"What about your dad?" I say. "Why didn't you stay with him in Columbia?"

I know I shouldn't have asked the second Colton looks up at me and his usually sparkly eyes have gone dark and flat.

"My dad left us when I was little," he says. "I don't even know where he is now."

I don't know what to say. I can't imagine how Colton feels. So I don't say anything to that. Because the way he looks over at his grandma's house tells me that he really doesn't want to talk about this. I get it.

"Come on, Lyla," I say, grabbing the handlebars of my bike. "We better get home." I look up at Colton one last time. "I'm sorry."

It's all I know to say. And I'm not even sure which thing I'm saying I'm sorry about—his mom *going away* or his dad leaving him altogether. Both things suck. But his eyes glint back to life a little, so maybe just saying *I'm sorry* was enough. I guess it usually is.

"Thanks," he says. And it sounds like he means it.

I mount the bike and walk it backward down the driveway. Colton watches me the whole way.

"See you tomorrow in homeroom," he calls out.

My cheeks feel like someone just struck a match on them. It's a strange feeling and suddenly I'm super aware of Lyla at my side, staring up at me. I wonder if my cheeks are as red as they feel. But if they are, Lyla doesn't say anything, thank God. She gives me a real curious look before pushing off and pedaling down the street. Colton is still watching me. He smiles and waves.

I pedal away as fast as I can before my whole face explodes into flames.

10

THE BOARD MEETING

"I hereby call this official board meeting of Anything, Incorporated, to order," I say loud and clear. I wish I had a gavel, but Mom said that might be a little much.

"Hey, y'all. Happy Wednesday and welcome to Rosepepper's. I'm Caitlyn and I'll be your server tonight. What can I get ya to drink? We've got sweet tea, unsweet tea, peach tea, raspberry tea, fruit tea, mango tea, Pepsi products, and homemade grape soda."

I look up at the rude server, who just appeared out of nowhere, and who doesn't understand that she's interrupting important corporate business without an *excuse me* or anything. Just walks up and plows right into our conversation. *Millennials.* Generation Z has manners. We have goals. Plans. Business ideas. Like the:

Anything Millennial Life Coaching Company
A division of Anything, Inc.
Michael Pruitt—President, Founder, CEO, and Life Expert

One thing I could teach them is how to have a whole conversation without looking at their phones. It's easy for me, because I don't have a phone. That's on the agenda for this board meeting.

"Oh yes, please," Mom says enthusiastically to Caitlyn. A little too enthusiastically if you ask me. Like she doesn't even want to be having our monthly board meeting right now. "I'll have a glass of unsweet tea."

Dad and I each get a fruit tea and Lyla orders the homemade grape soda. That's right, she's crashing our board meeting. I got overruled by Mom, who said it would be unfair not to include Lyla because we're having dinner at the meeting and *she's only nine*. See what I mean?

At least she brought a small spiral-bound notebook and a Hello Kitty pen with purple ink to keep her occupied and hopefully quiet. She's drawing cats in the notebook. None of them look like Pooty. Unless Pooty only had three legs, a lopsided head, one ear, and was, you know, purple.

"First order of business," I say after the rude server leaves. "The minutes from our last meeting. Mom?"

Mom is the official board secretary, so she's in charge of taking notes.

"Oh, shoot," Mom says, digging around in her purse. "I forgot my notepad, Mikey—"

"Mom," I say with a huff.

"Oh, right. Sorry. Mr. Chairman." She tucks loose strands of hair behind her ear. "But I remember we talked about your Sports Instruction division idea. It was approved by the board."

"Unanimously," Dad says.

Mom nods. "Right. And your dad—I mean Mr. Treasurer—gave us the balance of the Anything, Inc., operating account. Oh, how much was it, honey?"

"Seven dollars and eighty-three cents," Dad says with a grin, like he's proud that he can remember stuff.

"Y'all ready to order?" Rude Server Girl blurts out as she drops off the drinks. She just appeared out of nowhere again. Like a ghost. Or pimples. Or Pooty.

"The Tex-Max burger is my personal favorite," she says, and winks at me.

I guess she doesn't have very good gaydar. Trey told me that gaydar is like radar for detecting who's gay and who's not. Sort of like an internal metal detector, but one for detecting gay people and not metal. Trey said I should have a pretty good one, you know, because of me being gay and all. But honestly, mine's just as bad as Caitlyn's. Like, it doesn't work on Colton at all. I'm still trying to figure him out. Maybe gaydar is something kid gays have to grow into. Like when Mom buys me shoes that are a half size too big and says I'll grow into them.

"Oh." Lyla suddenly forgets about her Murder Kitty portrait and sits up straight. "I want a burger, Mom."

Mom peers down at the menu with the tip of her index finger pressed to her lips. "That does sound good, sweetie, but we just had burgers on Sunday. Let me see what else they have."

"Do fries come with sandwiches?" Dad asks, peering over the top of the massive menu at Rude Server Girl.

"Sure do," Caitlyn says. "Bottomless, too. You can get crinkle-cut, steak-cut, waffle, curly, shoestring, garlic, sweet potato, nacho-style, or loaded-and-smothered. But those last ones aren't bottomless. They're just a little heaven in your mouth."

I sigh. Loudly.

Michael Pruitt Business Tip #355: Always hold official corporate board meetings in a professional conference room with glass walls, leather chairs, a whiteboard, a drop-down projection screen, and all-you-can-drink mini bottles of water. Or at the kitchen table, if a professional conference room isn't available. But never at Rosepepper's Tex-Mex Cantina on River Road in North Charleston, South Carolina, when Rude Server Girl Caitlyn is working.

We order. Lyla gets her burger, but Mom tells Caitlyn to put extra lettuce and tomato on it. I order the Rosepepper's Jalapeño Southern Fried Chicken Sandwich with the *little heaven in your mouth* loaded-and-smothered fries. Caitlyn said the sandwich is a new item on the menu. Mom asks me if I've ever had jalapeños before. I haven't. But once I thought about starting a food-tasting business for restaurants, where I'd try out their new dishes and leave a review on Yelp. I thought that was a pretty good idea, so why not test out this new sandwich for Rosepepper's. I can bill them later for my review.

When I get Mom and Dad back on track, we move on to my report about the Sports Instruction division.

"It was a huge flop," Lyla says, looking up from her purple cat portrait.

I glare at her.

"Oh, don't worry about it, son," Dad says. "At least you tried something. Most people never even do that. We're proud of you."

Mom leans in. "Tell us about this new talent-agent thing, honey. That sounds fun."

It's not a thing, Mom, and it's not fun. It's a gazillion-dollar business opportunity, and I need an immediate infusion of capital and an iPhone to get it off the ground. That's what I want to say, but I don't.

Michael Pruitt Business Tip #356: Dazzle them first, then go in for the kill.

"Well," I say, clasping my hands together and resting them on the table. "I saw Julian's act Monday afternoon and I think the kid really has something . . . unique. He's going to be a superstar one day and make the company *a lot* of money. I just need to work with him some to fine-tune his act. Our first official rehearsal is Friday after school."

Dad props his elbows on the table. "What's his talent?"

Lyla looks up from her drawing. "Wearing girl clothes, a wig, and high heels. And pretending to sing Beyoncé songs."

There she goes again. That's not how I was planning to describe it, and now Mom and Dad have confused looks on their faces.

"It's called *drag*," I say.

"I know what *drag* is," Mom says. "I just didn't know kids did it. How old is Julian?"

"Thirteen," I say. "There're a lot of drag kids out there, Mom." And by *out there*, I mean on Google. I count them off on my fingers. "Lactatia, Desmond is Amazing, Katastrophe Jest, E! The Dragnificent . . ."

"Wow," Dad says. "I had no idea. I guess that explains the stage name. What was it again?"

I clear my throat so I can get it all out without choking. "It's Coco Caliente, Mistress of Madness and Mayhem."

"Julian's sister, Gabby, does dance competitions and she's good, too," Lyla says. "I want to take dance classes with her. She's my new best friend."

"I didn't know you had an *old* best friend," I mumble.

"Michael," Dad scolds. "She's only nine."

Ugh.

"And Julian's parents," Dad says. "They're supportive of him doing this Coco thing?"

Lyla pipes up again before I can answer. "Coco *Caliente*, Dad. His mom and abuela are, but not his dad."

I'm losing control of my meeting, so I jump in quick.

"Julian told me at school yesterday that his mom calmed his dad down about it. He just doesn't understand it. But I need to book Julian some gigs before I can make my commission."

Mom and Dad nod. Lyla draws big, sharp teeth on Purple Pooty. Is that purple blood dripping from those fangs?

"And I can't book him gigs without my own phone," I add casually like it's no big deal. "The latest iPhone probably makes the most sense for the president of a big-time talent agency."

"But you're not thirteen yet," Mom says, like I don't know how old I am. "That was the rule. For both of you. No phone until you're thirteen."

"I already have a phone," Lyla says, without looking up from her *art*.

I sigh. "How many times do I have to tell you, Lyla? Your Hello Kitty phone is not a real phone."

"Sure it is," Lyla says. "Pooty calls me on it all the time."

We all just kind of stare at her. I don't know what Mom and Dad are thinking, but I wouldn't put anything past Lyla and Murder Kitty. They probably communicate in all kinds of crazy, Voldemort-like ways, plotting my downfall and ways to terrorize poor Forbes.

I ignore her and focus on Mom and Dad. "And I could use an infusion of capital."

Capital is just money, but it sounds way more professional in a business meeting.

Dad's brow wrinkles. "Well, how much are we talking, bud?"

I haven't really thought about the *how much* yet, but I know I need at least twenty-five dollars for some new business cards. There must be a lot of other expenses involved in starting an international talent agency, too, but I guess business cards would be a good start.

"I think a hundred thousand dollars would do it," I say confidently.

Lyla looks up with wide eyes. "Then you could pay me, right? And I could hire an assistant. Oh, I could hire Gabby to be my assistant. That would be so awesome."

Mom and Dad share a look. I don't know what it means, but Mom's lips are curling up, so maybe she agrees with me.

"One hundred thousand is kind of steep, bud," Dad says, also kind of smiling. "How about forty dollars. And you pay it back from the first forty you make in commission. Sound fair?"

I activate my pouty face. "I guess."

Michael Pruitt Business Tip #357: Always ask for way, way more capital than you need. You might get more than you expected in the first place. But still act disappointed.

I only thought I'd get, like, twenty bucks, so I made out big with forty even though it's just a loan. Lyla slumps down in the booth, I guess realizing that Anything, Inc., won't be hiring an assistant to the junior talent coordinator anytime soon. You know, like, *ever*.

"So what about the phone?" I know I'm pushing my luck, but I might as well go in for the kill while the board is still wounded from my amazing negotiating tactics.

Mom and Dad exchange another look. He whispers something in her ear, and she nods.

"I think I can help you with that, son. We'll work it out when we get home. So what's next on your action plan?"

Pap Pruitt taught me that every good businessperson needs an *action plan*, so of course I have one for the Anything Talent and Pizzazz Agency.

"Well, first I need to have business cards made," I say, sitting up straighter.

Mom and Dad nod. Lyla draws super-long claws on Purple Pooty.

Is he holding an ax?

"And then . . ." I make them wait for it.

"Hope y'all are hungry!"

And—*OMG!*—Rude Server Girl Caitlyn appears out of thin air again, holding a large tray of food and ruining my big announcement. It smells really good, though, as she sets the plates down in front of us.

"I'll be right back with some ketchup," she says, resting the tray on her hip. "Do y'all want regular ketchup, chipotle ketchup, tomatillo ketchup, bacon ketchup, taco ketchup, sweet-and-spicy ketchup, or barbecue ketchup?"

I tune her out because I'd forgotten how hungry I am. Before I go on with the meeting, I pick up my Rosepepper's Jalapeño Southern Fried Chicken Sandwich, take a huge bite, and—*OMG!* Rude Server Girl Caitlyn will have to wait to hear what kind of ketchup I want. And the board will have to wait to hear about the open-call audition I'm planning for this Saturday. Because right now I'm running to the bathroom.

There really should be a warning label on all jalapeño-pepper-related menu items, because I can't feel my face.

11
THE DIVA TAMER

Friday afternoon I stand in front of the stage in Julian's garage with Dad's old flip phone open and pressed to my ear like I'm on an important business call. It's not an iPhone, not by a long shot, but it's better than nothing, I guess. And no one has to know that Dad hasn't taken it to the cell phone store to have it activated yet. After a few nods, *rights*, and *okay sounds goods*, and one *let's do lunch*, I say goodbye to no one, snap the phone closed, and slide it into the front pocket of my shorts.

"All right, people," I say, loud and clear. I clap one time because I guess that's the person-in-charge thing to do. "Sorry about the delay. We have exactly two weeks until the talent show, so let's take it from the top. And . . . five, six, seven, eight . . ."

I clap each number out, but nothing happens on *eight*. No music. No dancing. Nothing. Julian stands on the garage stage dressed in gray sweatpants and a white Lady Gaga T-shirt that barely covers his belly.

"Um, Michael. What are you doing?" he says, looking up

from his starting pose with a hint of snippiness in his voice.

It's only been four days since Julian's audition, so this is our first official rehearsal together. He has to get used to my methods. He'll learn eventually that I'm only hard on him to make him the best that he can be. That's what Miss RuPaul sometimes says to the contestants on *Drag Race* and I think that's a pretty smart thing to say when you're judging someone.

"I was just counting you off," I say.

Colton stands on the side of the stage holding his iPad like a clipboard, looking back and forth from me to Julian. I guess he's wondering who the boss is around here. So am I. I *thought* it was me.

"Just say *cue music*, and Colton will start it," Julian says, still holding his standing prayer pose. He looks like a statue in a church. Julian's family is Catholic, so I guess that's what he's going for.

"We have to stay on schedule," Lyla says to me. "His dad will be home from work in two hours and Mrs. Vasquez said to be sure we are all cleared out by then."

Lyla stands beside me holding a real clipboard with some ruled notebook paper. Well, it's a Hello Kitty clipboard. She keeps writing little notes and tearing them off. Gabby stands beside Lyla and giggles every time Lyla hands her one of them. It's annoying. Distracting. Unprofessional. And I'm about ready to snatch one and read it out loud like Mom says she does when her high school students text each other in class. High schoolers must be the worst.

I brought my laptop so Lyla could work on my new business cards on QuickPrint, but she said she had already finished that at home last night. She didn't even let me see them before she placed the order using Mom's credit card, which I got onto her about. I told her that was strike one.

"What happens when you get to strike three?" she'd asked. I didn't have a good answer ready, so I told her I'd get back to her on that. That seemed like the professional thing to say.

Michael Pruitt Business Tip #358: Never make hasty decisions when it comes to punishing an employee. You could get in trouble with the board. Or the employee might have a murderous cat. Plus, you never know what dark magic the employee has at their disposal. Especially when they've seen every Harry Potter movie five times, say they are House Slytherin, and always root for Voldemort.

Document everything. That's what Pap Pruitt says. I remind myself to write Lyla up for placing the business cards order without my final and official approval on the wording and design.

"Hey, my dude." Dinesh's voice sounds behind me.

I turn and find Trey and Dinesh standing there, looking around the garage.

"Wow," Trey says, checking out the stage. "This looks big-time."

"Nothing but the best for the clients of Anything Talent

and Pizzazz Agency," I say with a shrug. Like I built the stage myself and it's no big deal. *Fake it till you make it!*

I asked the guys to come by this afternoon to see me in action. Plus, I wanted to get their opinion on Julian's act because they're my best friends and they'd never steer me wrong. I point them to the metal folding chairs lined up in front of the stage, where they sit.

"Excuse me," Julian says, the snippiness in his voice a little sharper. "What are *they* doing here?"

He's acting a little bit like a *diva*, just like some of the queens on *RuPaul's Drag Race*. That's not always a good thing in the drag world. There's the good kind of diva and the bad kind. And Julian seems like he could turn into the bad kind superfast.

"Don't worry," I say in a calming voice, like I'm a lion tamer. More like a diva tamer, I guess. "I just wanted to get some feedback on your act from regular people."

Colton's eyes widen. I don't know why. I guess because he knows Julian way better than I do and maybe I just said something not cool.

Julian breaks his starting pose and props a hand on his hip. "*Regular* people? What am I? *Irregular* people? And what do *they* know about drag? Who are *they* to judge Miss Coco Caliente, Mistress of Madness and Mayhem?"

Okay. Wow. I did not see the bad kind of diva coming *that* fast. I don't say anything at first because Julian looks kind of scary right now.

Trey stands like he's in class and has been called upon. "Um, my mom's best friend, Manny, is a drag queen. He's good, too. I've seen him perform at Charleston Pride a few times. This one time he asked me to hold his wig for him."

Trey nods and sits down, like he's proud of his drag qualifications. I look over at Dinesh and give him the it's-your-turn eyes.

He fidgets in his seat but finally stands. "Um, uh, I watched that *Priscilla, Queen of the Desert* movie with my sister one time when our parents were out. It was pretty funny, I guess. My sister laughed a lot. I didn't get most of the jokes, though. I was probably too young to be watching a movie like that."

"A movie like *that*, huh?" Julian says. "Ugh. Whatever."

Julian waves us all away with a flick of his hand like he's swatting at an annoying fly. He takes a deep breath and does one of his around-the-world snaps. He says it centers him before he performs. Then he resumes his starting pose.

"Let's do this," he says. "The clock is ticking."

Lyla leans over and whispers, "He means his dad will be home in two hours, like I said."

"I know what he means, Lyla," I say. I don't whisper like she did, though, because I'm her boss and I don't have to.

Lyla scribbles something on her tattered sheet of paper, rips it off, and hands it to Gabby. They look at each other and giggle like whatever Lyla wrote is the funniest thing ever written. I sigh. Why wasn't I enough for Mom and Dad?

I clear my throat real loud, trying to regain control of the rehearsal. "Is everyone ready?"

Nobody answers. So I look back at my two best friends. Trey gives me a thumbs-up and shoots me one of his JCPenney catalog–ready smiles. Dinesh nods real fast and his thick mop of dark hair nods right along with him.

"Okay, then," I say. "Places, everyone."

Julian looks up again with a frustrated shake of his head.

"I mean, cue music," I say loud enough to fill the whole garage. I wish I had a wireless microphone—a headset one like Miss Beyoncé has.

Colton taps the iPad with his finger and music blares through the speakers. For the next few minutes we all watch in silence as Julian channels Coco Caliente, pretend singing and non-pretend dancing a routine he planned for the song "Like a Prayer" by Madonna. When I told him during lunch period today that I'd never heard of the song or the singer, he gasped so loud half the cafeteria turned to look at us. Google taught me later that it's called a *gay gasp*. I guess I still have a lot to learn about being gay. I just thought it meant that I think about Colton Sanford a lot and I like looking at him. Like, more than anyone else at North Charleston Middle School. And that I wish Colton and I were best friends. But I guess there's a lot more to being gay with all the special words, songs, and the snapping and such. I really hope the around-the-world snapping is optional. I'm not very good at it. I tried it while looking in the bathroom mirror this morning and knocked everything off the counter.

Julian twirls, shakes, points at us a lot, and walks from one side of the stage to the other and back while lip-synching the words to "Like a Prayer." Julian's pretty good today, but it's not the same without the wig, the heels, and the makeup. He just looks like a big dude in sweatpants dancing around the stage. I don't dare look at Trey and Dinesh, though. I'll wait until the end to do that. Trey said he's seen his mom's friend Manny perform, but Dinesh's parents won't even let him watch the evening news because they say it's too racy.

At the end of the song, Julian does the same split he did in his audition. Gabby and Lyla go crazy clapping beside me. I clap, too, because that seems like the polite thing to do. Finally I turn and look at Trey and Dinesh. They're not clapping. Not until I give them the stink eye do they spark to life. Dinesh's mouth hangs open, though, so I guess that's something. After their applause dies down, I say to Trey and Dinesh, "So, what did you guys think?"

"I don't think I'm supposed to be listening to songs like that," Dinesh says, his cheeks a little red.

"Your client has some pretty good dance moves," Trey says. "But it didn't look like he was mouthing all the words right."

"Oh yeah," Dinesh says. "I noticed that, too. Was he saying

peas and carrots over and over? And I guess he could smile more. That would probably make it better."

I glance over at Lyla. "Write that down. *Peas and carrots* and *more smiling.*"

Lyla scribbles something down on the clipboard, tears it off, and hands it to Gabby. When Gabby reads it, they giggle again. *Ugh.*

"So?" Julian says behind me.

I turn and find him and Colton there waiting for my notes.

"Do you think I should do it again in heels?" he says, shifting his weight from side to side. "Yeah, I should probably do it again in heels."

Julian doesn't look as sassy now as he did onstage. He actually looks nervous. His face is tight and he's fidgeting with his hands. I guess super-crazy-talented people sometimes aren't always as sure of themselves as you think.

"Yeah, so," I say. "Just a few notes."

But I know Lyla didn't write down any of my notes, so I have to remember them off the top of my head.

"Nothing much," I say in my soothing diva-tamer voice. "Let's talk over by the stage."

Julian nods and crosses his arms as we walk away from the group. Colton stays behind, talking with Trey and Dinesh.

"Was it that bad?" he says, leaning his butt against the edge of the stage.

I look at him, trying to choose my words carefully. His

short dark hair and his skin glisten with sweat, and his eyes beg me not to say anything too critical.

"No, no," I say reassuringly. "Just a few little things to work on."

Julian hangs his head. "I wanted our first rehearsal to go well. I've been so worried about it. I guess I should have practiced more for today. I forgot the words to the song and everything. I'm sorry I let you down, Michael."

It seems like something more than that is bothering him, but heck if I know what to say. But I guess as his agent, this is part of the job. So I just dive right in.

"Um, are you okay? I'm sorry I invited Trey and Dinesh without asking you first. That was super-crazy dumb of me."

Julian looks up. "I guess that might be part of it. I mean, those guys never even talk to me at school, but here they are judging me in my own house."

Crap. That's a good point. I really screwed that one up.

Michael Pruitt Business Tip #359: Don't surprise your drag-kid client with straight-boy judges from school during the first rehearsal. Especially if those straight boys don't ever talk to your client at school.

I have to be careful with my coaching techniques. Sure, I have to be firm, and be the bad guy sometimes, as his agent, but I don't want to hurt Julian's feelings. Like, at all. Like, ever.

"I can ask them to leave right now if you want." And I honestly do mean it.

Julian's voice tightens as his eyes dart over to the garage door. "No, it's fine. I guess I'm just worried about my dad finding out."

I lean against the stage beside him. "Did you get into trouble after the audition on Monday?"

Julian's shoulders sag. "He said he'd better not ever catch me in girl clothes again."

"But you said your mom talked to him and everything was okay." I cross my arms, because that's what my dad does when I'm telling him something hard.

Julian's eyes are moist and shiny. "My mom tried to talk to him, but my dad's set in his ways. We used to be close and spend a lot of time together. But then he got busy with his car dealership and I got busy figuring out that I liked doing drag."

He laughs a little.

"When did you start?" I ask.

Julian's lips curl up on one side and his dark eyes instantly brighten as he thinks about that. "The first time I tried on my mom's high heels a couple years ago—you know, just playing around with Gabby—it was just so fun. And then when I found *RuPaul's Drag Race*, I was hooked. I studied what the queens did in every episode and tried to copy them. But Dad just doesn't understand how it makes me feel."

I nudge him with my elbow the way Dad does to me sometimes. "How does it make you feel?"

"I don't know." Julian kind of half-smiles at me. "Like I matter. Does that even make any sense?"

I think about all my business ventures and how they make me feel important. And like I matter. And wanting to matter doesn't seem like too much to ask.

I nod. "Yeah, dude. It makes all kinds of sense."

"I just wish my dad could be proud of me," Julian says, his shoulders sagging. "Like he used to be—before Coco Caliente."

We're quiet for a moment, watching Trey and Dinesh talking to Colton, and our sisters giggle-whispering to each other.

"Has your dad ever seen you perform?" I ask cautiously.

Julian shakes his head. "No. But he's caught me in drag a few times. I think he believes there's something wrong with me, but I know there's not. He's afraid it means that I'm gay or trans or something."

I'm not sure what to say because I'm kind of confused myself. "So, are you? Gay or trans?"

Julian grins. "Um, *hello*." He waves a hand up and down his body. "Duh. Of course I'm gay." He narrows his eyes at me. "You are, too, right?"

My face heats up from the inside out like it's about to explode. Nobody's ever just asked me like that before. And my first thought is to say no. Weird.

"Um," I say instead. "I guess so."

Why the heck did I say *I guess so* when *I know so*? Why didn't I just say, *Yes, Julian, I'm the gayest gay in the history of gays*? It was scary when I told Trey and Dinesh, but I didn't say, I *guess* I'm gay. I said I *thought* I *might* be gay. Crap. Trey's right, I'm the worst gay ever. But Julian doesn't call me the worst gay ever for saying *I guess so*. He just smiles at me and nods. I think he gets it.

"How did you know?" I say.

He shrugs. "I see the way you look at Colton."

The heat burning my cheeks spreads around to the back of my neck. Is it that obvious?

"I've only told Trey, Dinesh, and my parents," I say. "I don't think I'm ready for anyone else to know just yet."

I want to add, *Hint, hint,* meaning, *OMG, please, Julian, don't tell anyone. Thank you very much and have a nice day.* But the way Julian nods, I think he understands that I don't want him telling everyone at school about me.

"Not that I'm ashamed of it, or anything like that," I add quickly. But I'm not so sure that's the truth. Why else would I not want everyone to know? Weird. "Plus I'm not very good at it."

Julian kind of chuckles under his breath. "Not good at what?"

I push my hair out of my eyes. "You know. Being gay."

That makes Julian laugh out loud. But I wasn't trying to be funny—like, at all.

"Michael," he says, a wide grin stretching out his cheeks, "there's no right way or wrong way to be gay."

I narrow an eye at him. "Are you sure?"

"Of course I'm sure," he says. "Just be yourself."

It's not like I haven't heard that advice before. But I don't believe him, and I don't want to argue with him.

"You know," I say, trying to get the attention off me and all my gayness, "maybe if your dad saw you perform, like, for real, in a show, with an audience, he would understand."

Julian looks down and shakes his head.

"No, seriously," I say. "If he saw you perform at the talent show with gobs and gobs of people cheering for you, maybe he would be impressed. And proud of you."

Julian pushes off the edge of the stage, still shaking his head. "You might be a good agent, Michael Pruitt, but you don't anything about my dad."

I guess he's got me there.

"So, what are your notes about my performance?" he says. He crosses his arms and gives me a neck-roll warning.

I ease back into talent-agent mode and use my diva-tamer voice. "More smiling, and less *peas and carrots*."

Julian's lips tighten into a thin line before he says anything. "Okay, boss." He lets the tiniest of grins slip through as he climbs the stairs to the stage. "You got it."

I guess I'm getting pretty good at this diva-taming thing after all.

I turn back to the others, clearing my throat to get their attention. "Okay, people, from the top." My own grin wriggles itself free. "Colton, cue music."

12
THE OPEN CALL

Michael Pruitt Business Tip #360: Never let your nine-year-old sister design your business cards. Just trust me on this one.

Before I can stop her, Lyla passes the cards out to all the kids who showed up in our carport for the Anything Talent and Pizzazz Agency's first annual open-call auditions. And by *all the kids*, I mean Colton, Trey, and Dinesh, who aren't even auditioning; Julian, who's already on my roster; Gabby, who's only nine, which is below the minimum age limit that I set at ten—I don't want to break any child labor laws, after all—and four other kids who *are* here looking to get discovered by me.

Maybe I shouldn't have sent Mom and Dad next door to visit with Mrs. Brown during the auditions so they wouldn't embarrass me. At least that would have been two more heads in the crowd. I guess I should be happy with the turnout. Four kids auditioning is more than zero, which is how many Lyla said would come. I just thought that since it was a Saturday, tons of neighborhood kids would show up. Mrs. Campbell let me announce the open call in homeroom yesterday and I put a flyer on the bulletin board in the cafeteria. Maybe I should have done more. Or maybe my junior talent coordinator should have done more. I can't do everything.

Stuart Baxter races up to me in his tricked-out electric wheelchair like he's driving the Batmobile. He's wearing a Spider-Man costume without the mask, but I'm not sure what his talent is yet.

"Hey, Mikey," Stuart says, holding my business card up to his face and squinting at it. "So I don't get it. Are we auditioning for a talent agency or to work at a pizza joint?"

I take the card from him and stare at it for, like, the thousandth time since they came in via overnight express. Lyla paid extra for that and she didn't even ask for approval. The card reads:

Anything Talent and Pizza Agency
A division of Anything, Inc.
Michael Pruitt—President, Founder, CEO, and Pizza Expert

And my company logo is one of Lyla's Murder Kitty drawings. In purple. I'm sure we paid extra for that, too. *Dang it, Lyla.*

"Um, yeah," I say to Stuart. "That's, um . . . a misprint. Don't worry, you're in the right place. Hey, I'll see you a little later, okay?"

I wave Lyla over like an impatient crossing guard. Stuart speeds away looking super-crazy confused.

"What?" she says with a huff, holding her Hello Kitty clipboard close to her chest like it has top-secret information on it. "I'm busy networking."

She didn't even know what *networking* meant until this morning when I gave her her assignment for today.

I hold the card in front of her face. "Why are you passing these out? I told you they have to be redone."

"That's part of networking, Mikey," she says. "You talk to people and trade business cards and tell them you want to go to lunch. But nobody here has their own business card except for you."

She takes the card from me and looks it over like she's never even seen the thing before. "I think it looks very professional like you said you wanted. I did a good job with Pooty's face on this one. I think I deserve a raise for this."

My blood is boiling and I think my head is going to explode right here in front of everyone. And Colton.

"You know what I mean, Lyla," I say, fuming. "You put *pizza* instead of *pizzazz*. My business card says I'm a *pizza* expert. You didn't even let me see it before you placed the order. I think you did it on purpose."

Her lips jut out in a pout. "I already said I was sorry, Mikey. I don't know how it happened. *Pizzazz* is a really long word. Maybe my fingers got tired of typing all those letters."

"It's seriously like two letters more than *pizza*," I say, gritting my teeth.

Lyla's pouty lip quivers. "But . . . but . . . I'm only nine."

Forbes gazes up at me from the floor, whining a little and—*OMG!*—she even has my dog fooled. If I thought she was actually about to cry, I would ease up on her, but I've seen this act, like, a thousand times. It always works on Mom and Dad, but not me. I know Lyla's up to something. She's always up to something. She's probably planning a hostile corporate takeover. I wouldn't put it past her. Or past Pooty for that matter.

"You can stop with the lip thing you're doing," I say, crossing my arms. "I know you're trying to sabotage me."

The pouty lip disappears instantly. *See what I mean?*

"How can I *sabotage* you when I don't even know what that word means?" she says, all sweet and innocent. But a little smirk tugs at the corner of her human-demon-doll mouth.

I hold out my hand. "I don't have time for this. Just give me the sign-up sheet. We need to get started."

She pulls a wadded-up piece of notebook paper out of her front pocket and hands it to me. *Ugh.* Pap Pruitt says that when employees talk back and stuff, that's called *insubordination* and you can fire your employees for acting that way. I'll have to write Lyla up for being insubordinate. *Document, document, document.* I go and stand in front of the two rows of chairs. I wish we had a stage like Julian has in his garage. But I just pretend like I'm standing on one. Dinesh comes over with a girl with long dark hair.

"Hey," Dinesh says, giving me a fist bump. "This is my

cousin Charvi. She's in seventh grade but she goes to Xavier Academy. She's auditioning for you today." He glances at Charvi. "This is one of my best friends, Mikey Pruitt, the super-cool talent agent I told you about."

Charvi smiles at me real big. Her eyes are bright with a hint of blue, holding my attention. Like Dinesh, Charvi is taller than me and she has the same thin nose, high cheek-bones, and long eyelashes. I'm not, like, an expert on girls or anything, but even as a gay dude, I can tell that Charvi is super-crazy pretty—almost like a girl version of Dinesh. Wait, does that mean I think Dinesh is pretty? *Ew.*

"Hi," Charvi says.

She leans down and pets Forbes, who sits obediently at my feet. Forbes isn't a diva like Pooty, who has to be carried around everywhere. And he's not very gassy, either. I banned Murder Kitty from the auditions today. I wanted Forbes around as the official greeter and Pooty always scares him off. Poor Forbes.

When Charvi's done giving Forbes a scratch behind the ear, she stands, extending her hand like a grown-up would when meeting someone for the first time.

"Hey, Charvi." I shake her hand because I know that's the polite thing to do. "So what's your talent?"

Charvi pockets her hands. "I don't know. I didn't think I had a talent. Dinesh made me come."

I give her a big, reassuring smile that kind of hurts my cheeks. "Everyone has *some* kind of talent."

Yeah, that sounded super cool, like something a real professional talent agent would say—which is what I am.

"Charvi's a mystic," Dinesh says excitedly. "She interprets dreams. This one time I was having the same dream over and over about a unicorn that pooped on my bedroom floor. And the unicorn's poop looked and tasted like cotton candy. And I ate, like, all of it every time I had the dream. So I told Charvi about it and she said that the unicorn represented my math teacher, Mrs. Jackson. She was seriously, like, the *only* teacher who didn't give me an A last semester. And the unicorn's cotton-candy poop represented my good grades in my other classes. And the reason Mrs. Jackson was pooping out all my As was because she was rubbing the B she gave me in my face. And that Mrs. Jackson probably had some spicy food for lunch. Isn't that so cool?"

Charvi smiles like she's super proud of her interpretation of Dinesh's dream, but honestly none of it makes any sense. I have a ton of questions, but I settle on the most important one.

"Dude," I say. "Why would you eat unicorn poop?"

A confused look twists Dinesh's face. "Because it looked and tasted like cotton candy."

I don't say anything else about Dinesh's unicorn-poop-eating dream. I guess it was my fault for asking in the first place.

I smile at his cousin. "Thanks for coming and good luck, Charvi."

Dinesh and Charvi go sit by Trey, who's looking at my business card, doubled over laughing. *Thanks a lot, Lyla.*

When I turn around, I find Colton kneeling down, petting Forbes. And it's not just some polite can-I-pet-your-dog kind of thing. He's scratching Forbes behind his floppy ears, rubbing his belly, and giving him kisses on the side of the head. Forbes wags the whole rear end of his body, including his dirty blond nubbin, which means he *really* likes Colton, too. My dog has great taste in people.

"Wow, this is so cool," Colton says, standing.

He flashes me one of his wicked-cool smiles as he scans the crowd. I can't help but smile back, because when Colton Sanford smiles at me with all those freckles and white teeth and shiny reddish-brown hairs, my stomach goes right back into that blender. On High.

It's funny, I knew I liked boys instead of girls way before Colton ever came to North Charleston Middle School, but there wasn't ever a boy that I actually *like*-liked. I mean, I'm only twelve and I don't think a lot of dudes my age are thinking about *like*-liking someone yet. Except Trey does get all tongue-tied when Heather Hobbs speaks to him. And Dinesh has a super-serious crush on Lara Croft. *Tomb Raider* is his favorite video game. I think he feels like he and Lara are on a date every time he plays it. But I'm sure his parents would forbid him from dating a video-game avatar, so I hope Dinesh realizes there's no future there.

"You're going to be the most popular kid at school,"

Colton says, grinning. Like he's proud of me or something.

I know he's going a little overboard to make me feel good, so I don't let it go to my head. Well, not too much anyway. It would be way cool to be the most popular kid in school. The *right* kind of popular, that is.

"I just wish more people would have come out to audition," I say, looking around the carport.

Colton pushes his hands into his pockets and rocks back and forth on his heels. "I thought about signing up, but I chickened out."

"Really?" I say, my voice jumping up an octave in surprise. I dial it back down a notch. "What's your talent?"

His pale cheeks go red. "I can sing. My mom always wants me to sing for her and she says I'm good, too, but she has to say that. I haven't been able to sing for her in a long time, though." He looks down at Forbes.

I'm about to ask him why not, but then I remember what he said about his mom going away for a while. And he kind of acts like talking about it is off-limits. Forbes licks my hand like an official greeter dog would. Not like a murderous cat.

"Well," I say. I hold up the crumpled sign-up sheet. "If you change your mind about auditioning, I could probably fit you in."

Colton nods and flashes me a partial Colton Sanford wicked-cool smile, which is way better than no Colton Sanford wicked-cool smile at all.

I reach into my front pocket, take out my dad's old aviator sunglasses, and slip them on like it's something I do every day. I practiced wearing them in the mirror last night and thought I looked pretty cool in them.

"Okay, people," I say, kind of loud to quiet everyone down. "Thank you all for coming. Please, take a seat. We're about to get started."

I think that sounded super-crazy professional. I have a card table set up in front, where I'll sit and judge everyone. It's standard in the industry, I think. Dad helped me bring out all our dining room chairs plus a couple from the kitchen table, so almost everyone has a place to sit behind me.

Michael Pruitt Business Tip #361: It's always good to have a few people standing because it makes your event look super-crazy important. Like everyone wants to be there even though there aren't enough chairs to go around. But some people don't mind standing because your event is *the* place to be.

Once everyone is settled, I take control of the room—I mean the carport—by clearing my throat super loud.

"Okay, then. My name is Michael Pruitt and I'm the president, founder, CEO, and *pizzazz* expert"—I pause and glare at Lyla, or as much as I can glare at her through Dad's sunglasses—"of Anything Talent and *Pizzazz* Agency. I know you're probably all super nervous, and you should be, because this is probably the most important day of your lives."

There's a little murmuring in the crowd. They're probably totally agreeing with me and telling one another how good I am at this.

"I'm looking to add three clients to the roster of the Anything Talent and Pizzazz Agency today." I just now decided that the number would be three.

I pull out my used flip phone and hold it up. "And I even turned my phone off so we won't be interrupted by all my important business calls." I slip the phone back into my pocket and notice a few people nodding like they're super impressed that I have a phone and that I get a bunch of important business calls on it.

I still have to talk to Dad about getting the phone activated, but no one needs to know that it's not working yet. I pull out the sign-up list, smoothing out the wrinkles so I can read the first name.

"Stuart Baxter," I say. "You're up."

Stuart's face lights up like I'm about to make all his dreams come true. And if he has enough talent and enough *pizzazz*, not *pizza*, I just might be able to. He pushes a lever on the armrest of his wheelchair and it lunges for the spot where I'm standing. I jump out of the way just in time. So does Forbes. I go over to the card table where the eight-by-ten framed portrait of me from last year's school pictures holds my spot between Colton and Julian. They're my official guest judges, but only I can make the final decision—just like Miss RuPaul. I hand my picture to Lyla and sit. She walks over to the recycling bin in the corner and drops the frame in like it's nothing more than a used soda bottle and *I swear to God!* But I try to not let her rattle me. I need to be professional. I sit, give Julian and Colton a professional nod, and then look up at Stuart.

"Okay, please tell us your name, where you're from, and what your talent is," I say, speaking loud enough for everyone to hear me. I'll definitely be asking the board for a wireless-headset microphone in next year's budget.

Wiping his brow with his Spider-Man mask, Stuart clears his throat. "Um, my name is Stuart Baxter, like you just said . . . and I'm from . . . um, um. Sorry. I'm really nervous."

I cross my legs and lean back in my chair. "That's perfectly normal, Stuart. Take your time." I think that sounded super grown-up and professional.

Stuart smiles and relaxes his shoulders a bit. "Okay. I'm from Marion Drive a couple of streets over. And my talent is superhero impersonations."

A few whispers trickle around behind me. I know what some of the kids are thinking, and I have to admit, even I'm a little bit surprised by Stuart's talent, with him being in a wheelchair and all.

"Silence," I say, loud enough to quiet everyone down while clapping twice. It totally works just the way it does for Miss RuPaul. "Okay, Stuart. Let's see what you've got."

Stuart nods once. He pulls the Spider-Man mask over his head and fiddles with something in the seat of his chair. Then, sitting up straight and puffing out his bony chest, he launches into action.

"Stop right there, Green Goblin!"

Stuart yells it pretty loud, making some people jump a little in their seats. Forbes lifts his head and growls, but Stuart just keeps on going. I guess Spider-Man isn't afraid of overweight cocker spaniels. Poor Forbes.

Stuart leans forward, pointing at me. "You can't kidnap my girlfriend, Gwen Stacy, blow up New York City, *and* kick that little dog and get away with it. Not while I'm around. I'm Spider-Man. And your reign of terror is over!"

Everyone is on the edge of their seats waiting to see what will happen next, and that's probably just what Stuart wanted. Because all of a sudden, he throws out both arms and web-zaps us all with cans of Silly String in each hand. Julian screams and I mean he *scream*-screams when the Silly String gets in his hair. Colton yelps in surprise, while Trey and Dinesh laugh hysterically behind me. The Silly String is everywhere, all over Lyla and her Hello Kitty clipboard, all over Forbes, and it completely covers me, Colton, and Julian at the table in a giant web-cocoon.

After the initial shock of the attack, everyone goes still and quiet. I'm sure they're waiting to see how I'll react to Stuart's stunt before they do. After a good, long dramatic pause, I shoot up out of my seat. Burst through the ceiling of the web-cocoon clapping and yelling like crazy.

Now *that's* what I call pizzazz.

13
THE NEW CLIENTS

The last act to audition is Sadie Cooper and her blind, high-jumping, three-legged pit bull, Fifi. And let me tell you, if you're blind *and* a three-legged pit bull that can jump back and forth over Sadie Cooper while she's down on her hands and knees, consider me impressed and yourself a new client of Anything Talent and Pizzazz Agency. The audience goes crazy when Sadie *and* Fifi bow at the end of the act, which for Fifi means bending the one front leg that she still has.

"Wow," I say over the applause. "That was amazing, Fifi. And you, too, Sadie."

Sadie guides Fifi over to the wall to wait beside Lyla for my decision. This is going to be super-crazy tough. It's safe to say that Stuart Baxter is in, the way he brought the house down with his Spider-Man impersonation and his surprise special effects. I mean, I still have bits of Silly String in my hair and I had to take off Dad's sunglasses because the lenses were caked with the stuff. And Julian seemed super impressed with Charvi's interpretation of his dream about his dad having long blond hair. She told him it meant that one day his dad would come around and accept Julian doing drag. It seems kind of unlikely, but it made Julian happy—which gave me a great idea of how to use Charvi's talent. And Brady Hill's jokes were super-crazy funny. I could probably get him booked on *Later Tonight with Billy Shannon* in no time flat.

"Okay," I say, clapping my hands once because that seems like the perfect thing to do at such an important moment in the history of Anything, Inc.

I look out into the audience and ponder my choices. Everyone is staring back at me like I'm about to read the winning lottery numbers for a gazillion-dollar jackpot. I guess this is sort of like that.

"I want to thank you for coming out and auditioning today," I say. "You all did an incredible job. So give yourselves a hand."

"Yaaas!" Julian calls out with his signature around-the-world snap.

Colton laughs and everyone else claps real loud. Trey and Dinesh even add a couple of *whoop-whoop* fist pumps.

I clasp my hands together in front of me because I think that makes me look super-crazy serious and important. "Like I said, I'm looking to fill three open spots on my client roster."

The carport goes silent. Sadie kneels, closes her eyes, and hugs Fifi. Brady and Charvi hold hands real tight. Stuart sits in his wheelchair, pointing two cans of Silly String at me, whatever that means. But that's when I realize something. They *all* want this. Like, bad. And who can blame them? It's the opportunity of a lifetime. Their entire futures are in my hands.

This must be how Simon Cowell feels right before he crushes dreams. But the idea of crushing someone's dreams actually feels a lot worse than I thought it would. And the idea of making someone feel like a loser, the way some people at school make me feel sometimes, well, it just sucks. But Pap Pruitt says when you run a successful business, you have to make tough decisions. Unfortunately I can't, like, go to a commercial and reveal the results when we return to the show. You know, because of this being real life and all.

I clear my throat. "The newest clients of the Anything Talent and Pizzazz Agency are . . ."

It feels right to pause before I announce my final decision. That's called a *dramatic pause*. Miss RuPaul does it all the time on *Drag Race*. When I glance up, I see three bicycles turn into our driveway. No one in the audience notices the intruders because they're sitting with their backs to the street. But *I* see them. And when I do, my heart drops down to my stomach. Tommy Jenrette, Colby Brown, and Trace Williams race up the driveway to the carport going like ninety miles per hour and skid to a stop right behind the audience like they're in some kind of *Fast and Furious* movie for bicycles. Everyone turns in their seats to see what all the ruckus is about.

Tommy Jenrette looks around the carport with a sneer.

Then he looks straight at me. My face goes hot and suddenly I have to pee real bad.

"Oh," I say. "What's up, Tommy? Hey, Trace. Hey, Colby."

My voice is shakier than usual. And I wonder if Tommy knows that a single stream of sweat just ran down my back. Or that I'm about to pee myself. I feel like everyone knows, but I guess that's impossible. Tommy just ignores me, like I didn't say anything at all. He reaches into the front pocket of his jeans and pulls out a blue sheet of paper. I recognize it as soon as he starts unfolding it. It's the flyer that I put up in the cafeteria.

"We came for the auditions," Tommy says. I can tell by the look on his face that they didn't. "But we must be in the wrong place, because this looks more like a freak convention."

Laughing, Trace and Colby high-five each other like a couple of idiots.

Colby points over at Sadie and Fifi. "Oh, man, look at that messed-up dog. That's the ugliest thing I've ever seen."

The three of them laugh hysterically at Fifi and I hope that Fifi can't understand what they're saying about her. It would probably hurt her feelings.

"Maybe that's Mikey's big new business idea," Trace adds. "Freak Conventions R Us."

I let out a nervous chuckle, like that was super funny even though it wasn't. Actually it was pretty mean. And who ever heard of a freak convention? It's a terrible business idea. I clear my throat.

"No, um. We're having auditions," I say. "For my new talent agency. Like the flyer says."

Tommy, Colby, and Trace look at one another and then crack up.

"Talent agency?" Tommy says. "Oh, man. He's serious. Wow. That's the saddest thing I've ever heard."

"The auditions are over," Julian says sharply, without looking at them. "So if you just came to make fun of us, you can leave now."

Lyla takes a small but defiant step toward the boys, pointing right at Tommy. "Yeah. Y'all better get out of here before my big brother kicks your butts."

She points at me and *OMG, Lyla!* We've had our differences since the day she could walk and talk, but I don't think Lyla's trying to get me killed on purpose. The hard, determined look in her eye tells me that she actually believes I could kick Tommy Jenrette's butt. And I guess it's pretty cool that my little sister has that kind of faith in me, even though she's dead wrong.

Tommy and his friends bust out laughing. Like what Lyla just said is the funniest joke they've ever heard. And I'm the punch line. I hope that doesn't mean Tommy is going to punch me.

"Who?" Tommy says with a snort. "Gay Mikey Pruitt? *He's* going to kick our butts?"

I think I stop breathing for a few seconds. Did he just say *gay* Mikey Pruitt? How the heck does Tommy know about me and the whole gay thing? Trey and Dinesh promised not to say anything and the only other people I told are Mom and Dad. Oh, and Julian, I guess. The last thing I wanted was for people like Tommy Jenrette to find out. I *want* to say something. Something like, *Why the heck would you think I'm gay and why would you even say something so dumb, Tommy Jenrette?* But my lips are glued shut.

Colby looks around the carport. "Oh, man. Gay Mikey Pruitt is having a freaks *and* gays convention."

He points at Julian and laughs like a hyena. Trey and Dinesh slouch down in their chairs like they're trying to become invisible. Colton and Julian are sitting in the front row with their eyes glued on the floor. The rest of the kids look completely terrified, all wide eyes and fidgety hands. Even Fifi sniffs the air in Tommy's direction and then cowers behind Sadie's legs. I keep hoping my voice will return any second now and that I'll give Tommy, Colby, and Trace the telling-off they deserve. But it never does. I just stand there like an idiot while they laugh at all of us. It's official—I'm definitely the worst gay ever. I should probably get a trophy or something.

"My mom and dad are right next door and they'll be home soon," Lyla says, planting her hands on her hips. "And then you're going to be in big trouble."

OMG, Lyla, just stop talking! I guess she's given up on the me-kicking-Tommy's-butt thing. And I kind of hate that I've disappointed her.

"Ooh," all three boys say with their hands in the air like Lyla is arresting them.

"We're *sooo* scared of your mommy and daddy," Tommy says with a smirk. "Are they gay, too? Are you gay, little girl? Is your whole family gay?"

More hysterical laughter, and I don't know why Tommy keeps saying that word over and over. I wish he would stop. Now Lyla will want to know what he's talking about. She probably doesn't even know what *gay* means. And if Tommy Jenrette is saying that about me here, then he's probably saying it about me at school.

Tommy, Colby, and Trace eventually stop laughing. I don't know what's about to happen. I pray that Stuart doesn't shoot them with his Silly String webs. Or that Lyla doesn't say anything else—like telling Tommy, Colby, and Trace again that I'm going to kick their butts. I've never kicked anyone's butt in my life and wouldn't know how even if I wanted to. Dad always says it's best not to give bullies any reaction at all. That way they just get bored and move on. I guess it's worth a try. So by silent agreement that's what we do. We all just stay quiet and still.

Finally, Tommy shakes his head and turns his bike around. "Come on, guys. This is lame. Let's go."

Colby and Trace follow Tommy down the driveway. Trace hocks a loogie on the concrete, which seems unnecessary and rude, but what do I know about being a bully?

Everyone stares up at me. They all seem a lot less happy

than they did before Tommy and his friends interrupted the big announcement. Julian isn't smiling or snapping anymore. His face is like stone. Colton's eyes are kind of blank and sad. And the kids who auditioned aren't ready to hang on my every word. They just look like they want to go home. I get it. I'm already home and I want to go home.

I swallow the lump in my throat and find my voice again. "Lyla, please write down the names of the newest clients of the Anything Talent and Pizzazz Agency."

Lyla doesn't hold up her Hello Kitty clipboard like she's going to write anything down, though.

"Stuart Baxter," I say.

Stuart looks up at me like he's super surprised. A smile stretches out his face, and he gives me two thumbs-up. No Silly String.

"Sadie Cooper and Fifi," I say.

Fifi sits up at attention at the mention of her name and Sadie hugs her tight. I figured it was best to take them as a team, even though Fifi's the one with all the talent and pizzazz.

"Brady Hill."

Brady claps for himself and a chuckle rolls around the carport. That kid is super funny.

I pause. Charvi sinks down into her chair, crossing her arms with a super-crazy-sad look on her face. But she doesn't know that I've already decided that nobody's dreams are getting crushed today.

"And Charvi Lahiri," I announce.

Everyone gasps. At least that's what I hear in my head. One big, old, entire-crowd gay gasp. Like they're all amazed by my generosity. And they should be.

They all erupt with applause. Julian and Colton are on their feet clapping, Colton shooting me that stomach-in-the-blender wicked-cool smile of his. Trey and Dinesh are *whoop whooping* and punching the air. Lyla even grins—just a little. Fifi and Forbes bark like crazy at all the noise, between sniffing each other's butt. Stuart chases Brady around in circles with his wheelchair, spraying a can of Silly String, both of them cheering and laughing.

It's nice seeing everyone so happy. I feel warm all over, and have a super-crazy-hard time imagining why Simon Cowell would ever want to crush anyone's dreams.

14
THE VERY IMPORTANT CALL

As soon as I get home from school on Monday, I go straight to my office and make the very important call I've been thinking about making since the auditions on Saturday. I sit in my executive chair with my feet propped up on the desk, staring at Dad's Weed Eater hanging on the wall, as the phone rings a third time in my ear. Dad got it activated for me this morning. Mom only agreed to break the no-phone-until-you're-thirteen rule because it's Dad's old flip phone and you can't use any apps on it or anything like that. And it takes, like, an hour to text three words. But it's okay. The phone part works well enough to connect me to the real-life NBC Studios in New York City. I've already been put on hold three times, which I think is kind of unprofessional, and I'm starting to lose my patience.

This is the kind of thing my junior talent coordinator should be doing, but I have her working on something else right now. She's sitting in the metal folding chair beside me—Pooty the Murder Kitty in her lap, of course—correcting all 250 business cards, turning *pizza* into *pizzazz*. I don't have enough money in my operating budget to have them reprinted, so correcting them by hand will have to do. Lyla agreed to do it only if she could use her Hello Kitty pen with purple ink, though. *Whatever.*

"*Later Tonight with Billy Shannon,* how may I direct your call?" a man's voice finally says.

I clear my throat and lower my voice because that seems like the professional thing to do. "Yes, hello. My name is Michael Pruitt, president, founder, and CEO of Anything Talent and Pizzazz Agency, and I'd like to speak to Mr. Billy Shannon, please. It's urgent."

There's a pause on the line before the man responds. "I'm sorry, what is this regarding? And how did you get this number?"

"Google," I answer.

Lyla looks up at me and I point to the phone.

"I think I got an intern," I say to her in a whisper.

She nods once like she understands my pain and would never want to deal with just an intern, either.

"I need to speak to Mr. Shannon right away. Did I mention it's urgent? I represent the hottest new comedic talent in all of show business. Maybe you've heard of him. Brady Hill?"

Another pause on the line. "Um, no. I can safely say that I've never heard of your client. Are you with CTA, sir?"

I write on my yellow legal pad:

CTA

I'm not 100 percent sure what CTA is, but it sounds like it could be one of my competitors because when I first googled *talent agencies* I saw that a lot of them use initials as their agency name. I google it really fast and find out that CTA stands for Creative Talent Agency. That's a super-crazy-boring name.

"No," I say, turning the name of my agency into an acronym in my head, which I should have thought of sooner. "Like I said before, I'm with . . . um . . . ATAPA."

That actually sounds pretty cool. I write that down, too.

"And I'd like to speak to Mr. Shannon about my client Brady Hill making his television debut on *Later Tonight*. I'm sure it'll boost your ratings. This kid has tons of pizzazz. And I should know, since I have my own talent agency and I'm a pizzazz expert."

Lyla nods without looking up from her work. I guess she approves of how I'm handling this call. Like *she's* in charge and I work for *her*. There's another pause and what sounds like a muffled chuckle on the line.

Lyla taps my shoulder. "What are they saying now?"

I press my index finger to my lips. She shrugs and goes back to adding two z's to the word *pizza* on one of my cards. It's a little messy, but you know, *she's only nine*.

"Mr. Shannon is unavailable," the man says. "But I can transfer you to our booking desk."

I sigh loudly into the phone so the guy knows how unhappy

I am about not being able to speak to Billy Shannon directly.

"Okay," I say. "I guess that will be okay. Thank you, sir."

Dang. I shouldn't have called him sir. It makes me sound like some kind of little kid.

"Hold, please," the man says.

Some cheesy music plays while I'm on hold. I don't think it's anything Coco Caliente could dance and lip-synch to, so I tune it out. I glance over at Lyla. She scratches Pooty's back and his eyes droop like he just ate a whole catnip cake.

"Mikey?" Lyla says. She waves the business card she just corrected back and forth so it can dry, I guess. This is going to take forever.

"What?" I ask, annoyed.

I'm not sure if I'm annoyed at Lyla or at the intern on the phone or at my jacked-up business cards. It's just kind of a natural response whenever Lyla speaks. It's like how Dad says Grandma Sharon's voice sounds on the phone: *like nails on a chalkboard.* Whatever that means. We don't have any chalkboards at North Charleston Middle School, just whiteboards. So I wouldn't know.

"Are you gay?" Lyla says. Right out in the open. In real life. To her boss.

Well, *that* didn't take long.

"It's none of your business if I'm gay or not," I say.

She glances up, all angelic eyes and rosy cheeks. "Lots of people are gay. It's nothing to be ashamed of."

"I'm not ashamed of being gay," I snap.

I don't know why I snapped at her. What she said was actually pretty nice.

"Um . . . hello?" a female voice on the phone says. "This is Allie Rosen in booking. And I'm glad you're not ashamed of being gay."

My whole face heats up like there's a bonfire on top of my head.

"Oh, hi," I say into the phone. "This is Michael Pruitt, president, founder, and CEO of Anything Talent and Pizzazz Agency in Charleston, South Carolina. And I'm calling to let Mr. Billy Shannon know that I'm willing to give him an exclusive on the television debut of the hottest new comedic sensation in the country, thirteen-year-old Brady Hill."

I give Allie Rosen my best pitch about Brady before she can respond. I tell her how funny Brady is, how good he is in front of a crowd, how he's the president of the entire seventh grade of North Charleston Middle School, which he won in a landslide because no one ran against him. I think it's going pretty well. Allie even asks some questions about Brady and a couple about me, too. I only tell one small lie, when she asks how old I am and the first thing that flies out of my mouth is fifty-one. I don't know why I lied, but it seemed like the smart thing to do at the time. I don't think Allie would have taken me so seriously if she knew I was only twelve. Fifty-one just felt right. I'll be thirteen next month so, you know, close enough.

"Can you send me a link to your client's sizzle reel?" Allie asks.

"Of course," I say confidently.

I scribble on my legal pad:

Google sizzle reel.

"What's your email address, Miss Rosen?" I say.

She gives it to me and I write it down carefully. It's an actual NBC email address with the letters *N-B-C* in it and everything. I give her my phone number because I know she'll be needing it soon to book Brady on *Later Tonight*.

Lyla's swinging leg kicks me and she doesn't even look up or apologize or anything. *Ugh.*

"Well, thank you for letting us know about Brady, Mr. Pruitt. We'll check out the sizzle reel as soon as you send the link and we'll contact you if we're interested. No need to follow up."

She called me Mr. Pruitt and it sounded super-crazy professional. Maybe I should make all my clients call me Mr. Pruitt. And Lyla, too. Maybe even my board members.

"Okay, thanks, Miss Rosen," I say. "Next time I'm in New York, lunch is on me."

She giggles. I don't know why I said it and I don't know why she thought it was funny. Who knows if Allie Rosen will even still be working at *Later Tonight* when I make my first trip to New York. Or I guess she might be running the show by then. Like executive producer or something. I don't even know if I'll have enough money left in my operating budget to take anyone out to lunch. I'll bet restaurants in New York are super-crazy expensive.

I give Allie Rosen my phone number, say goodbye, and snap the phone closed, feeling pretty proud of myself and like a real professional talent agent. Forbes trots happily in through the partly open door, wagging his tail. Pooty hisses at him. Forbes turns right around and leaves. Poor Forbes.

"Do Mom and Dad know you're gay?" Lyla says, like that's the most important thing in the world right now.

"Yes, they know," I say with a sigh. She's not going to let this go.

"So it's true," she says, adding one too many purple z's on a card. "You *are* gay."

I take the business card from her and drop it in the waste-basket.

"If you tell anyone, I'll fire you again," I say.

"You can't," she says. "My job is board-approved. You can't fire me without a vote, and Mom and Dad won't vote to fire me because I'm only nine."

Ugh.

I open my laptop to add Allie Rosen to my contact list. "Now you're just making up company policies. None of that is true."

"Besides," she says, "I already knew and I haven't told anyone yet."

I shoot her a glare. "Yet? And how the heck did you already know?"

Lyla looks up at me. "Sisters just know these things, Mikey."

I don't actually know what she means, because, you know, *she's only nine*.

"Plus Dad asked you if Julian was cute the other night at dinner." She turns her attention back to one of the business cards. "Don't worry. I would never tell anyone if you don't want me to."

"I don't want you to," I say. "Just so we're clear. Thanks, Lyla."

She gives me a little smile and nod and then goes back to her work. And for some crazy reason I have the urge to hug her tight like I used to when she was younger. Sometimes little sisters can surprise you.

Lyla hangs her head, going all quiet on a dime, which isn't like her at all.

"What's wrong, Lyla?" I say.

She looks up at me, her eyes heavy and sad. "I missed seeing Pap Pruitt yesterday."

I take a deep breath, trying to keep my older brother cool in check. "Me too. But Dad said Pap was too sick for our regular Sunday visit."

"I know," Lyla says, pushing her hair out of her eyes. I

think she might have done it so she could brush a couple tears away, too.

We're both quiet for a moment. It's awkward. I don't want to talk about this, and I hope Lyla will just drop it and go back to being a pain in the butt. That I can deal with.

"Is Pap going to die, Mikey?" she asks.

Well, I guess we're talking about it.

I swallow hard and take her hand because that seems like the good older brother thing to do. "I don't know."

Mom's voice crackles through on the intercom. "Michael?"

I push the Talk button. "Yes, Mom?"

"Um . . . your friends are here," she says.

My friends? I don't remember inviting Trey and Dinesh over today.

Lyla reaches over and pushes the Talk button. "That's impossible, Mom. Mikey doesn't have any friends."

And we're back.

"Oh my God," I say, about to lose it. "Why do you keep saying that?"

And then I remember. It's not Trey and Dinesh. I flip open my phone and check the time. "They're early."

I say into the intercom, "I'm coming," and hop out of my seat.

"Who's early?" Lyla says, following me out the door, through the carport, and into the house, Pooty draped lazily over her shoulder. "Who's early?"

When I open the kitchen door, I find Julian and Colton

standing there chatting with Mom like that's a normal thing to do. Lyla lets Pooty down and goes over to a pile of mail on the table. It's one of her duties to look through it to see if there's any for the company. We haven't received official mail yet, but it's only a matter of time.

"Well, I can't wait to see you perform, Coco," Mom says.

"You can call me Julian when I'm in my boy clothes," he says, smiling real big. "Coco Caliente is just my drag persona."

And *OMG!* They're talking about *this* right here in our kitchen.

Lyla holds up a square bright yellow envelope. "Mom! This has my name on it."

"I see that," Mom says. "Go ahead and open it."

Lyla about rips the thing to bits. Julian and Colton giggle at her like she's the cutest little kid they've ever seen. *Ugh.*

"Oh, look," Mom says, peering over Lyla's shoulder. "It's an invitation to Chandler Martin's birthday party."

"Gross," Lyla says, dropping the tattered invitation on the table and picking up Pooty. "Boy birthday parties are the worst—all superheroes, video games, and fart jokes." She huffs off into the den.

I snatch up the invitation and slip it into my pocket because my junior talent coordinator just gave me an awesome idea.

"Julian is super-crazy good, Mom," I say, trying to sound calm and professional. But Colton is smiling at me and, well, you know. *Stomach. Blender. On High.*

Colton nods. "He's way better than some of those contestants on *RuPaul's Drag Race* and he's only thirteen."

Julian grins from ear to ear. Talented people like to hear a lot of compliments.

"Well, now I *really* can't wait to see you perform," Mom says. Like she didn't actually mean it the first time.

She puts a hand on Julian's shoulder and winks at him. "I just hope Coco has an easier time in heels than I do."

Mom laughs too loud, like it's the funniest thing she's ever said in her entire life. It's not, but it makes Julian and Colton chuckle.

Michael Pruitt Business Tip #362: Always have a proper waiting area for your guests with comfy chairs, a water cooler, magazines, and a NO PARENTS ALLOWED sign.

I move to guide Julian and Colton out of the kitchen.

"Okay, Mom," I say. "We've got research to do. Please hold my calls."

I don't know why I said that last thing, since I have my phone in my pocket, but it sounded cool and professional to say in front of Colton. He grins at me. So, you know, totally worth it.

15

THE RESEARCH

"I know what a death drop is, Michael," Julian says. "But my body won't bend like that."

I can't believe I only met Julian one week ago in my office and now he, Colton, and I are lying on our stomachs on my bed watching videos on my laptop. Sandwiched between them, I keep hitting Repeat on one of the gazillion videos we found on YouTube of drag queens doing death drops. Sometimes they call them a *shablam*. The one we're watching is from *RuPaul's Drag Race* and it shows a queen walking into the workroom for the first time and then all of a sudden dropping all the way to the floor on her back with one knee bent under her. Talk about pizzazz!

After the clip plays again, I look over at Colton. "What do you think?"

He shakes his head. "I don't know, Mikey. I mean, I know I said we need, like, a more spectacular end to Coco's routine, but death drops look kind of dangerous."

"See," Julian exclaims, rolling over on his back. Forbes

jumps up on the bed and goes to town licking Julian's face.

Colton points to the bottom of the laptop screen. "Look. Somebody even wrote *Do not try this at home* in the comments."

Colton turns over on his back, too. Forbes walks right across Julian's stomach to give Colton the same licky-face spa treatment he just gave Julian. Colton giggles, scratching Forbes behind his ears. I think it's cool that he likes dogs as much as I do. Especially Forbes. When I roll over on my back, Forbes lands on my lap with a heavy plop. We all stare up at the ceiling a minute before I break the silence.

"Why don't you think you can do it, Julian?" I ask. "Coco Caliente, Mistress of Madness and Mayhem, can do anything, right?"

Julian sighs. "I know. Coco is, like, amazing and all that, but . . ."

I look over at him. All the Coco Caliente confidence he normally has is gone from his eyes.

I give Forbes a scratch on the head. "But what?"

Julian turns his head in my direction. "I don't know if you've noticed, Michael, but I'm not one of those skinny queens in those videos."

"So?" I say.

Julian gives me a dramatic eye roll. "So? I'm a plus-size queen. You know, a big girl?" He sighs when I don't respond. "I'm fat, Michael."

His eyes go dark. He looks hurt. Like *I* called him fat. But

I honestly didn't mean to make him feel bad. When he's all dressed up as Miss Coco Caliente, he doesn't seem to care that he's a big dude in a dress.

"Sorry," I say. "You always seem so cool being who you are at school. And you ignore Tommy Jenrette and his jerk friends when they call you names in the cafeteria."

Julian stares at me. "Just because I ignore them doesn't mean I don't hear them. And it doesn't mean that it doesn't hurt. I act like they don't bother me so they'll get bored and stop. It's exhausting."

"Oh," I say. *Lame.* "How do you even do that? Ignore them and act like it doesn't hurt?"

Julian shrugs. "Like Lady Gaga says, *Don't be a drag, just be a queen.*"

And somehow, I get that. Julian is brave—like a heck of a lot braver than I am. Because he chooses to be brave. He chooses to be a queen.

"You're not *fat*," Colton says softly. "You're . . . well rounded."

There's a slight pause before we all start cracking up big-time—even Julian, his eyes sparking back to life.

"Girl," Julian exclaims, kind of loud and snort-laughing. "Miss Coco gonna roll over on you and crush your skinny butt flat as a fritter."

Colton looks over at me, flashing all his shiny white teeth. "Miss Coco gonna squash me like a bug."

That makes us all laugh even more.

When I catch my breath, I say, "Miss Coco gonna go all King Kong on your butt."

Julian and Colton stop laughing and the room is suddenly quiet. I glance back and forth between them. They both have super-crazy-serious looks on their faces.

"What?" I say, worried but not sure why. "What did I say?"

Julian props himself up on one elbow. "Michael, you don't *ever* compare a gorgeous Latina queen such as Miss Coco to a hundred-thousand-pound gorilla."

They both give me hard looks and I feel about one inch tall. Me and my big mouth. I thought we were all doing a thing—poking fun at Julian's size. Just like sometimes Trey and I make fun of how skinny Dinesh is and he laughs as much as we do. On *RuPaul's Drag Race* they call it *throwing shade*. But I guess I did it wrong or went too far.

Finally, like after a gazillion seconds pass, Julian's hard-as-stone face cracks. He throws his head back and snort-laughs loudly. Colton rolls over on his side, roaring with laughter and holding his stomach. Dang, they got me good.

"You guys suck," I say, shaking my head at them, but I can't help but grin a little.

Julian points at me, barely able to speak. "You should've seen your face. OMG. Hilarious!"

He rolls off the bed, still laughing, but manages to land on his feet. "I've got to pee."

I point to the door. "Down the hall."

Forbes jumps off the bed and follows Julian out the door.

For some reason Julian closes it behind him. Suddenly, lying here on my bed with the door closed, just me and Colton, feels *way* different than it did before with Julian and Forbes in the room. It feels like we're doing something wrong, which is weird, because we're not.

Colton finally stops laughing at me and we just lie there on our backs, both looking up. My ceiling looks like it has a gazillion white pimples on it, so your eyes can kind of get lost in the crazy patterns. There's only a couple of inches between my hand and Colton's hand, I guess, but it's like I can feel the heat of his skin. My heart is pounding so loud in my chest that I'm sure Colton can hear it. It's embarrassing.

"So why don't you sing anymore?" I say, trying to drown out my loudmouth heart.

Colton runs a hand through his hair. It's so thin and silky that it slips through his fingers and falls right back into place. His hair is just as cool as he is.

"It was just something I did for my mom," Colton says. "She taught me this song called 'True Colors.' It was her favorite. She asked me to sing it for her all the time."

"So where is she?"

As soon as I ask, I can tell by the way Colton's face goes blank that I shouldn't have. He doesn't answer.

"Sorry," I say. "You don't have to tell me if you don't want to."

Colton pauses. It just might be the way the light is shining down on his face, but his eyes look as glassy as marbles.

"It's okay," he says, turning his head in my direction. "She's in rehab in Summerville."

Wow. I wasn't expecting that and I don't have any idea what to say next. I don't think I've ever had a friend with a parent in rehab—not that I know of anyway. But I guess that's not the kind of thing kids usually talk about at school.

"Is that why you were in the guidance counselor's office the other day?" I say, hoping it's okay to ask.

Colton nods. "Miss Troxel is the only one at school who knows. She checks on me sometimes."

Colton's eyes look even glassier now. He holds the tears back, though. I don't know what to say, so I don't say anything. I feel like I should touch his hand or hold it or something, just so he knows he's not alone and that I care that he's sad. So I inch my fingers closer to his—*very* carefully.

I'm still not even sure if Colton is gay or not. If Colton's not gay, he might punch me for touching him. But I guess if he *is* gay, he might punch me, too, if he thinks I'm trying to put the moves on him—which I'm not. I mean, I'm only twelve. I don't think I even have any moves yet.

I finally decide I'm willing to chance getting punched if I can make Colton feel better about his mom being in rehab by holding his hand. Or at least just touching it. But it's taking, like, forever for my fingers to cross the two-inch ocean of comforter between us. My comforter has an underwater scene with fish and sharks and dolphins and stuff printed on it, so it's like my fingers are swimming over to Colton Island.

My fingers have almost made it, too. I can feel the heat of the Colton Island shoreline. But when I reach across that last little bit for it, a sharp snap of static electricity zaps our point of contact. Colton yanks his hand away, but I don't know if it's because of the electric shock or because I freaked him out by trying to touch him.

Julian comes barreling through the door, so I guess I'll never find out. Colton and I shoot up into sitting positions on the bed, and the ocean of comforter separates us again.

"Okay!" Julian exclaims. "Forbes and I discussed it, and he thinks I should at least give the death drop a try."

"Are you sure?" Colton asks, acting like the finger-touch-zap thing didn't even happen.

Julian nods, planting a hand on his hip. I've learned he does that when he's feeling Miss Coco confident.

He points a finger at me. "But only if we find a professional to teach me how to do it so I don't break my leg. Or my butt. Or anything in between."

I think for a few seconds and then I cross my arms, because that feels like the professional thing to do. "I have an idea."

16
THE EMERGENCY CLIENT MEETING

There should be meeting rooms at school where you can conduct professional business during lunch, like mini conference rooms. They could even serve lunch in them so the cafeteria wouldn't lose out on any lunch money. But our school district is not very business savvy. It's like they have other priorities. That's actually a great business idea, now that I think of it. I could sell my consulting services to the North Charleston School District to help them become more kid-entrepreneur friendly. I pull my *Amazing Business Ideas* notebook out of my backpack and write that down before I forget:

Anything School District Business Consulting

A division of Anything, Inc.

Michael Pruitt—President, Founder, CEO,

and Wicked-Good Kid Entrepreneur

It's Tuesday, and instead of sitting in the green zone with Trey and Dinesh like I normally do, I've called an emergency client meeting in the yellow zone, where most of my clients eat lunch. They're all crazy talented, but they're all kind of outsiders as well. Weird.

"Yo," Trey says, setting his food on the table. "Why are we sitting here?"

He looks at the others sitting around the table like they're aliens. But actually it's Trey who's the alien here. He's in their territory now. Stuart sits in his wheelchair at the head of the table. Brady is across from me, and Colton and Julian are on either side of me. Dinesh follows close behind Trey, giving the group the same confused look that Trey did.

"Sorry, dude," I say to Trey. "I needed to have an emergency client meeting. This is a super-crazy-busy time and there's a lot going on."

Even though Colton isn't technically one of my clients, he's like an unofficial adviser/helper/I-like-looking-at-him sort of person.

Dinesh shrugs like he's over the change in his lunch routine now and sits. Trey does, too. Those guys always have my back.

"Cool," Trey says. "Let us know if you need our help. Moms say we should always support the arts."

"I definitely need your help on something," I say. "So it's good that you're here."

Dinesh nods. "Count me in, too, Mikey. I might not have any talent, but I could tutor your clients if they need help with their schoolwork."

I shake my head at him. "Everyone has some kind of talent, dude. Even you."

As soon as Sadie arrives and takes a seat, I launch right into the meeting.

I clear my throat first, because that seems like the professional thing to do. "Let the record show that in attendance are Anything Talent and Pizzazz Agency official clients Sadie Cooper of the Amazing Sadie and Fifi . . ."

Sadie waves at everyone.

"America's Junior Comedic Sensation Brady Hill . . ."

"Um . . . I like it, but I'm not a junior," Brady interrupts. "I'm in seventh grade."

There's a little discussion about what the word *junior* means. I give a loud *ahem*, to regain control of the meeting. It works, because everyone quiets down right away.

"The Super Kid of Many Faces," I say a little mysteriously as I point at Stuart.

Everyone at the table widens their eyes, oohing and aahing at Stuart as he fist-pumps the air. I was especially proud of that one.

"And Miss Coco Caliente, Mistress of Madness and Mayhem," I say, gesturing to Julian.

The group claps respectfully, probably because they all know that Julian is my star client. He's what we in the biz call A-List. Julian does a little sitting curtsy, which makes everyone laugh—even Trey and Dinesh.

I figured since Julian has such a great stage name, it would be good for all my clients to have one. I stayed up super-crazy late last night coming up with them. I think it was totally worth it.

Noisy snickers draw our attention. Of course it's Tommy, Colby, and Trace passing by as they make their way to the red zone. I think I hear the words *freaks* and *queers* a couple of times. It's pretty obvious now that Tommy knows about my whole gay thing, but I still can't figure out *how* he knows. I try to focus on *my* business and not all *that* business.

"Let the record also show," I say, just realizing that Lyla isn't here to take notes to let the record show anything. Not that she would actually be taking notes if she were. "That also in attendance are Anything Talent and Pizzazz Agency Executive Advisory Committee members Trey Johnson, Dinesh Lahiri, and Colton Sanford."

I just made up the Anything Talent and Pizzazz Agency Executive Advisory Committee, like, half a minute ago, but I smile at its new members like I've been planning this announcement for months. It works, too, because Colton, Trey, and Dinesh all light up at the recognition.

"Wow, dude," Dinesh says, sitting up straighter. "Thanks."

"And finally," I say. "Let the record show that absent from this meeting because they go to entirely different schools are junior talent coordinator Lyla Pruitt and Charvi Lahiri, Mystic to the Stars."

I pause, giving them time to ooh and aah at the stage name I gave Charvi, which they all do.

"And Fifi, of the Amazing Sadie and Fifi, who's probably asleep right now dreaming about dog biscuits and squirrels."

Sadie nods real hard like what I just said is the gospel truth.

"First order of business," I say. "Trey, you said the other day that your mom's friend Manny is a professional drag queen, right?"

Trey nods as he pops a chicken nugget in his mouth. Our cafeteria loves to serve poppable food. I'm not sure why.

"Yeah," Trey says. "He's really good, too. Why?"

I look over at Colton and Julian. They smile back like they know exactly what I'm thinking.

"Could you get Manny's phone number or email address from your mom?"

Trey nods. "On it, dude." He doesn't need any explanation because that's just how best friends are.

"Thanks," I say, and then turn to Sadie. "Hey, so Fifi is a rescue dog, right?"

Sadie smiles. "Yep. When I turned seven, I wanted a puppy for my birthday, so my parents took me down to the animal shelter to pick one out."

"And you chose Fifi?" Dinesh says. "Was she even a puppy back then? She looks pretty old."

Sadie jerks her head around to look at Dinesh. Her long straw-colored ponytail sails through the air like a helicopter blade, missing Stuart's face only by a couple of inches.

"No, she wasn't a puppy," she says with a glare at Dinesh.

"But she looked so sad and lonely, and the people at the shelter said she'd been there longer than any of the other dogs. Nobody wanted her. But I took one look at her and just knew we were meant to be together. And when she looked at me, I knew she thought the same thing."

"Dude," Trey says to her. "No offense, but Fifi has, like, *never* seen you."

Sadie looks puzzled. As if she'd never thought about that.

As nice as this story is, it's taking way too much time away from important business stuff.

I clap once to get everyone's attention. "And the rest is show-biz history!"

Sadie seems happy enough with that ending to the Fifi story.

I point at her with a chicken nugget. "Can you and Fifi meet me at the Petcare store out by Northwoods Mall this Saturday at ten a.m.?"

Sadie nods a little hesitantly. "I guess so."

"Okay," I say. "I'm taking Charvi to her first audition this afternoon."

Dinesh glances up. "Where's her audition?"

"Prince George Nursing Home," I say.

Dinesh looks a little puzzled, but he doesn't ask any questions. See? Best friends. I was super-crazy excited when Dad said Pap Pruitt was doing well enough for me to go visit him after school today—which gave me a great gig idea for Charvi. You might say Pap is the inspiration for my action plan for Charvi. I can't wait for him to meet her.

"What about me?" Brady says.

I point to him. "I have some very important calls in about you."

Brady grins and goes back to eating, like that's good enough for him.

"So," I say, pausing to meet each of their gazes. "I was thinking you could all compete in the end-of-the-year talent contest. You know, representing Anything Talent and Pizzazz Agency."

Nobody says anything. They all just stare back at me like I'm Voldemort—except for Julian and Colton. They already know about this plan.

"But the tryouts are on Monday and the talent show is next Friday," Stuart says. "Are you sure we're ready?"

I throw my hands in the air. "Of course you're ready. And the big show is the last day of school, so how cool would it be if one of you won that hundred-dollar prize right before summer break?"

Brady and Stuart nod at each other. Sadie agrees, too. I think I'm selling this.

"I bet you all get into the show," I say, leaning in like that's a secret. It's not. "And as your agent, I'll take care of all the details. All you have to do is practice your acts and be ready for the tryouts on Monday."

I reach into my backpack and pull out three pieces of paper from my yellow notepad. I wrote out each of their contracts last night after supper.

"These are your standard boilerplate talent-agency agreements," I say, like it's no big deal. It is. "I just need you all to sign them before I can officially represent you."

"What does *TBD* mean?" Sadie asks, scanning her contract.

"To. Be. Determined," Julian says, snapping his fingers on each word.

I nod. "That's right."

"Shouldn't we get our parents to look at this before we sign it?" Brady says, pushing his wavy brown hair out of his eyes.

"My mom's a lawyer," Stuart says. "I could get her to look at them for us."

Okay, this is getting out of control. Just who do these people think they are anyway?

"Guys, guys," I say in a calming voice, with my hands up like I'm surrendering. I'm not. "It's no big deal. Signing it just means that you won't let anyone else represent you and that I make commission off any gigs that I get for you."

"What's a gig?" Dinesh asks.

"Um . . . a job, genius," Julian says.

Dinesh hangs his head, looking embarrassed. Colton elbows Julian.

"Ow, girl," Julian says, scowling back at him. But then he turns to Dinesh. "Sorry, dude," he says. "I didn't mean anything by it."

Dinesh kind of half grins. I think everything is okay again.

I clear my throat. "Signing this is just the professional thing to do."

"But how much is your commission?" Sadie asks, her ponytail following the turn of her head in my direction.

My phone vibrates in my pants pocket. *Perfect timing!* I don't see Vice Principal Grayson anywhere. Technically we're not supposed to have our phones out during lunch period. I finally spot Mr. Grayson dead center of the red zone, talking to Tommy and some other basketball players. Mr. Grayson lets them get away with just about anything because he's also the assistant coach of the basketball team. I slip the phone out of my pocket but keep it hidden under the edge of the table. When I flip it open, I see that it's the number I've been waiting for. It vibrates a second time.

"Hey, guys," I say quickly. "This is a very important business call that could be a life-changing big break for the Super Kid of Many Faces. But I can't really take it and represent him until he signs the contract. And I can't do the same for you guys until you sign, either."

The phone vibrates again. One more before it goes to voice mail.

They all look at Stuart with wide, wonder-filled eyes. Stuart looks terrified. Maybe I went just a tad overboard describing the call. But it works, because they all scramble around in their backpacks until they find pens. I wait until they have all signed. Trey looks at me, amazed. Colton smiles at me like he's proud of me and, well, you know . . . stomach-smoothie time.

I press the Call button before it vibrates a fourth time and cover the mouthpiece with my hand.

"Okay. Give me a minute and cover for me," I say, hunching over.

Everyone nods and looks around like spies as I slip out of my chair and under the table. I clear my throat.

"Anything Talent and Pizzazz Agency, this is Cheryl. How may I direct your call?"

Okay, so it wasn't my best fake-receptionist voice. I think I went too Southern and way too high. It sounded like I just sucked on a balloon full of helium and grits.

"Um, yes," the woman on the line says. "I'm returning a call from Michael Pruitt?"

She says it like a question. I don't know why. I mean, are you returning a call from Michael Pruitt or not, lady?

I go back into helium-and-grits-voiced-receptionist-Cheryl mode.

Michael Pruitt Business Tip #363: Once you commit to a business strategy, you stick with it. No matter how silly you sound.

"Yes, ma'am," I say, or Cheryl says. I'm getting confused. "Can I tell Mr. Pruitt who's calling?"

I can barely hear what the woman is saying because there's a lot of noise in the cafeteria—shrieks of laughter and lots of next-Friday-is-the-last-day-of-school shout-talking. And Trey is talking in his outside voice. I kick his leg to shut him up.

"Ow!" he yells from above. "Yo, what was that for?"

"Quiet, dude," I whisper-yell with my hand over the mouthpiece.

"I'm sorry, ma'am," I say into the phone in my super-professional Cheryl-the-receptionist voice. "I didn't catch your name."

"Bobbie Jo Martin," the woman says, sounding a little annoyed. "Mikey Pruitt, is that you?"

"Hold for Mr. Pruitt, please," I say in a hurry, my voice rising another octave at least.

Holding the phone to my chest, I count to five, then I raise it to my ear again. "Yes, this is Michael Pruitt."

"Mikey, aren't you at school?" Mrs. Martin says. "Does your mama know you're making prank calls at school?"

"Yes, ma'am," I say. "She knows. And this isn't a prank. I was calling about Chandler's birthday."

"Yes," she says. "What about it? Is your sister coming? Chandler would be so happy if she came."

"Yeah, sure," I say, my eyes peeled to a pair of grown-up-man legs edging closer and closer to our table. "Lyla will be there. I was wondering if you had booked any entertainment for the party yet?"

"Entertainment?" Mrs. Martin says. "What kind of entertainment? It's a bunch of eight- and nine-year-olds. They're pretty good at keeping each other entertained. Plus we have a Wii and Monopoly."

Wow. Wii and Monopoly? This lady *does* need my help.

"Well, I'm sure you've heard of Stuart Baxter, the Super

Kid of Many Faces," I say, mustering up some Miss Coco Caliente courage and confidence that I see Julian using all the time. "He's all the rage at nine-year-olds' birthday parties."

I'm not exactly sure what being *all the rage* is, but Mom says it all the time and she's always smiling when she says it. So I'm pretty sure it's a good thing.

"Stuart stays pretty booked up, but I'm his official agent, so I could probably work Chandler's party into his schedule since Lyla and Chandler are such good friends."

Dinesh sticks his head under the table. "Dude! Grayson's coming this way." Then his head disappears.

"What was that?" Mrs. Martin asks.

"Oh, nothing, ma'am," I say. "Just one of my associates. So would you like to book Stuart for the party?"

There's a pause. And then Mrs. Martin says, "Now what does this boy do exactly? Is it a magic show? Or does he make balloon animals?"

OMG! Adults always ask so many dumb questions.

"Don't worry, Mrs. Martin," I say, trying not to huff into the phone. "I promise you'll be amazed. Trust me. The first time I saw Stuart's act, it stayed with me for days."

Three days of hair washing to get all that Silly String out, to be exact. There was even some way up my nose. I thought I'd sneezed some of my brains out.

"He'll keep those kids entertained and out of your hair for hours," I add.

"Hmm," Mrs. Martin says. "I don't know, Mikey."

I don't have time for this. Mr. Grayson's legs have stopped a couple feet away and all the legs at our table go completely still. Not a good sign.

"And you say this Stuart has done other birthday parties before?" Mrs. Martin asks. "Like how many?"

I can't hear what Mr. Grayson is saying to my friends above because of all the cafeteria noise, but I have a bad feeling.

I lower my voice to nearly a whisper. "I can guarantee you, Mrs. Martin, that Stuart has been the main attraction at thirteen birthday parties."

Stuart is thirteen years old. So it's not like I'm lying or anything.

"And he was rewarded very well at those parties."

That's not a lie, either. Stuart is an only child and an only grandchild, so he always gets a ton of birthday presents.

"Oh? Well . . . how much does he charge?" Mrs. Martin asks.

Mr. Grayson's long legs bend at the knee. *Crap.*

"I could probably get him to do it for an even one thousand dollars," I say quickly.

Mrs. Martin either chokes or chuckles. I can't be sure which.

I keep going before she can say no. "And that's a real bargain. Don't tell anyone you're getting him at that price."

The vice principal is squatting now and we're face-to-face. *Double crap!*

There's a pause on the line. "I'll pay twenty dollars. And

make sure he's here by one o'clock a week from Saturday."

Once again my ask-for-way-more-than-you-expect-to-get strategy works.

"Yes, ma'am," I say into the phone. "He'll be there. And thank you for your business."

Mr. Grayson holds out his hand as I close the phone.

"Give me the phone, Pruitt," he says. "Now."

17

THE FREE SAMPLE

Mr. Grayson kept my phone until the end of the day and gave me the first-ever strike of my middle school career. No one is sure how many strikes Mr. Grayson gives before he calls your parents. It kind of depends on his mood, I think. But I don't care as much about the strike as the fact that he took my phone away. I don't know how the vice principal thinks I'm supposed to conduct business at school without it. What if Mr. Billy Shannon calls me back in the middle of math class? Or during a school assembly? Does Mr. Grayson seriously think I'm going to let that call go to voice mail? *No, thank you very much, Vice Principal Grayson, and have a nice day.*

As soon as I get my phone back, I call Dad and ask him if it's okay if I bring my friend Charvi to visit Pap this afternoon. He said he thought that would be fine since Pap has been feeling better. It's been almost three weeks since I've seen Pap and I haven't been able to tell him about the Anything Talent and Pizzazz Agency at all. I think it will cheer him up, because all he ever does is sit in a wheelchair in his room all day watching TV. And since he's blind, by *watching*, I mean his wheelchair faces the TV and he talks back to the characters on the shows like they're in the room with him. Pap Pruitt isn't crazy or anything, though. I think he's just lonely—which is kind of sad—so I try to visit him as much as I can. Dad didn't seem to mind at all that I wanted Charvi to go with us and he didn't even ask me why. Just tapped her address into the GPS and we were on our way.

Penelope guides us in the direction of the Battery, close to downtown Charleston. Penelope is what Dad calls the British lady GPS voice blaring through the minivan. Dad *loves* Penelope and talks back to her like she's a real-live person all the time. I think he has a crush on her, but she doesn't sound interested in him, like, at all.

"Turn right onto Ashley Drive in one-point-five miles," Penelope says, like she's bored out of her mind.

"Why, thank you, Penelope," Dad says in a terrible British accent.

Penelope doesn't ever say *you're welcome*, though. Or maybe she does in Dad's head.

They should have kid GPS voices. I think I would be great at that. During the summers, I sometimes go with Dad on his landscaping jobs and I've learned how to get around Charleston pretty well. And I wouldn't sound bored or British if I were giving directions on GPS. I would just sound like a real-live kid. Actually that's another great business idea:

I would be all, like, *Dude, turn right at the McDonald's up ahead and if you pass Chuck E. Cheese, you've gone too far, so don't do that, yo.*

And my dad would probably say, *But where's Penelope?*

And I would say, *Yeah, so, Penelope got fired for sounding bored all the time and—yo, dude, you just missed your turn! What's the matter with you? Pay attention and stop thinking about Penelope.*

Bored British Penelope guides us into a cool-looking neighborhood called Wagener Terrace close to the Ashley River, and right into Charvi's driveway. It's a pretty old house that's been fixed up to look like it might have when it was first built, like, a hundred years ago. You know, but better.

I'm surprised to see Dinesh sitting with Charvi in a swing on the big wraparound porch. I didn't even explain to him why I'm taking her to meet Pap at Prince George. I hope he's not mad about that. They hop up and run out to our minivan before Dad even has a chance to stop. Dad pushes the button to open the automatic door.

"What's up?" Dinesh says, piling in. "Hey, Mr. P."

Dad salutes Dinesh, but it looks goofy and not very official.

"Hey," I say, waving to Charvi as she gets in behind Dinesh.

Dad pushes the button and the door closes in super-slow motion.

"This is Charvi, Dinesh's cousin," I say to Dad.

"Nice to meet you, Charvi," Dad says. He looks over his shoulder as he backs out of the driveway. "Buckle up, you guys."

Charvi is dressed in jeans and a light blue T-shirt, with her hair pulled up in a ponytail. Dinesh looks like he's going to church, though, wearing khakis and a white button-down shirt. I guess he catches me eyeing his clothes, because he shrugs.

"I've never been to a nursing home before," he says. "I didn't know what to wear."

"Don't take this the wrong way," I say to Dinesh, "but what the heck are you even doing here?"

Charvi raises her hand. "Guilty. My mom didn't like the idea of me going off with you since she's never met you or your dad. No offense. So I asked her if I could go if Dinesh comes with me. She was cool with that."

"I totally understand, and am not offended at all," Dad says, pulling out into the street.

"Turn left onto Battery Way in point-seven miles," Penelope says.

"Brilliant. Thank you ever so much, love," Dad replies.

Dinesh and Charvi exchange a glance. Dinesh leans forward and whispers in my ear, "Dude, why is your dad talking like Dumbledore?"

I just shake my head. Parents can be super-crazy embarrassing.

***

When we arrive at Prince George, I'm surprised to find Pap Pruitt sitting in front of the TV, not in his room, but in the nursing home's common area. He must be feeling a lot better, which makes me feel a ton less worried about him. Pap sits by himself watching *The Andy Griffith Show*—his favorite—while other residents are grouped together at game tables, on sofas, and sprawled out in La-Z-Boy recliners like they're tanning under the fluorescent ceiling.

It's really bright in here, because just about everything is white—the walls, the ceiling, the floors. About the only other colors in the room are the fake green plants and the ugly brown furniture. I don't care what the staff of Prince George Nursing Home thinks, I can tell you right now that green, brown, and white *do not* go together. And I'm not even a professional decorator. Unless . . . maybe I am:

Anything Nursing Home Redecorating Service

A division of Anything, Inc.

Michael Pruitt—President, Founder, CEO,

and Queer Eye for the Old Guys

It could work.

Dad touches Pap lightly on the shoulder as we approach. "Hey, Dad."

You can't be too careful with blind, old people. You don't

want to sneak up on them and give them a heart attack or anything.

Pap Pruitt smiles at Dad's voice. "Sherwood."

Yeah. My dad has a funny name. But it only sounds funny to other kids my age. Adults act like it's no big deal. Weird.

"I brought Mikey, Pap," Dad says.

Pap Pruitt reaches in my direction, which is kind of freaky because I haven't made a sound yet. I think it's kind of cool how sometimes you can't even tell he's blind. Dinesh and Charvi look amazed, too. Like Pap just did a magic trick by sensing where I'm standing.

"Mikey," Pap says.

And that's all he needs to say. It's like he can have a whole conversation with you just by saying your name. Like just then I felt like he said to me, *Hey, there, Mikey. I'm so glad you came. Why has it been so long since your last visit? Is it because I've been sick? Or because this place creeps you out? I get that. It creeps me out sometimes, too. I'm just glad you're here now.*

Pap's wearing his favorite blue denim overalls and he looks even more ancient than the last time I saw him—not much hair left, and what he has is greasy and flaky. His skin is pale, with lots of brown spots that are much bigger than Colton's freckles. He's not wearing his dentures because he doesn't like them and says they're only good for eating.

Pap touches my chest and leans closer to me. "Who are your friends, son?"

Charvi and Dinesh look amazed again, this time that Pap

155

had figured out I brought friends without seeing them.

"This is my best friend Dinesh and his cousin Charvi," I say, touching Pap's shoulder.

Dinesh and Charvi both say hello and then I launch into telling Pap all about my new business, and how Charvi is one of my clients, and how I have four other clients, five if you count Fifi. And I tell him that Fifi is blind, too, which makes Pap smile. I also tell him all about the talent show next Friday and how if one of my clients wins, I'll make my first-ever commission. That makes Pap smile with his whole face.

He leans even closer to me. "All it takes is a dream and a prayer, right, Mikey?"

I nod even though Pap can't see me. "That's right, Pap. All it takes is a dream and a prayer."

I can't wait to come back real soon and tell Pap all about how successful Anything Talent and Pizzazz Agency is. Because the talent show is only the beginning of my plans.

"I'm proud of you, son," Pap says in a crackled whisper.

A pesky lump forms in my throat, because when your hero tells you he's proud of you, well, it doesn't get much better than that.

A tall, dark-skinned lady wearing a gray pantsuit walks over to us. "Wow, Mr. Pruitt. You have quite the fan club today."

That's Mrs. Prosser. She runs all of Prince George Nursing Home, so she's, like, super-crazy important and famous here. Dad shakes her hand, which looks very professional.

Pap turns his head in Dad's direction. "Did you bring me some chewing gum, Sherwood?"

That makes Charvi giggle a little, and Dinesh smiles. Pap Pruitt always asks for chewing gum—Wrigley's Juicy Fruit is his favorite.

Mrs. Prosser touches Pap on the shoulder. "Now, you know you can't have any chewing gum, Mr. Pruitt. You might swallow it."

She says it kind of loud. Like she thinks Pap will have trouble hearing her. I want to remind Mrs. Prosser that Pap Pruitt is blind, not deaf, but that doesn't seem like the professional thing to do right now.

"Mikey wanted to bring some friends to meet his granddad," Dad says to her. "Mikey, you remember Mrs. Prosser."

I don't know why adults always tell you that you remember someone whether you do or not. Usually, though, that's Dad code for *be polite and say hello to this person even if you actually don't remember her*. But what Dad doesn't know is that I was hoping to run into Mrs. Prosser today, so this is perfect.

"Hi, Mrs. Prosser." I stick my hand out to shake hers.

She smirks a little before she takes it, like she thinks I'm acting too big for my britches, but it's okay because shaking hands is always the professional thing to do.

Pulling one my business cards from my back pocket, I hand it to Mrs. Prosser. She eyes it like it's fake. Or maybe she's trying to figure out the whole *pizzazz/pizza* thing.

To distract her from Lyla's messy and unprofessional-looking correction on the card, I gesture to Dinesh and Charvi. "This is my best friend Dinesh and his cousin Charvi Lahiri, Mystic to the Stars."

Both Mrs. Prosser and Dad look surprised at that.

"Wow," Mrs. Prosser says, inspecting Charvi up and down, like she is super-impressed to be meeting a real mystic. "How interesting. Have you worked with any stars that I might have heard of?"

Charvi and Dinesh look at me, panicked. But it's okay. I got this.

"Charvi's number one client at the moment is Coco Caliente, Mistress of Madness and Mayhem," I say confidently.

Julian would be proud.

"Oh," Mrs. Prosser says, crinkling her face. "Is she one of the Avengers?"

"Um," I say. "Yeah. Sure. Right."

Dad glances away and shakes his head a little. *Busted.*

"I brought Charvi to interpret a dream that Pap told me about last time I visited," I say, changing the subject quickly.

Pap turns his head in my direction with a puzzled look twisting his face. "You remember that, Mikey?"

His voice is sandpaper rough. Like he's been chewing on rocks since we got here—which would probably be hard to do without his dentures.

"What dream?" Dad asks.

Mrs. Prosser glances at my business card again and then crosses her arms. I don't know if that means she thinks I'm joshing, or if she's super-crazy interested. But she doesn't leave, which is kind of the whole point.

"Pap said he's been having a dream about Grandma Clara," I say to Dad.

Pap's eyes go moist and hazy on a dime. Dad always said he never saw two people more in love than his mom and dad. He said Pap was never the same after Grandma Clara died, and that's when his health started going downhill.

Charvi steps forward right on cue. Dinesh pulls a chair over and positions it in front of Pap. Sitting, Charvi takes Pap's wrinkled and knotted hands in hers. Dad and Mrs. Prosser actually take a step closer, like they don't want to miss the show. I should probably charge them to watch Charvi in action. And I bet Pap Pruitt would pay good money to have his dream interpreted, but . . .

Michael Pruitt Business Tip #364: Sometimes you have to give away free samples to make the big sale.

"Tell me about your dream, Mr. Pruitt," Charvi says, closing her eyes and breathing in deeply.

Dinesh looks over at me, grins, and nods. Probably because he thinks this was a brilliant idea I had. He's right.

Pap clears his throat. "Well, now, let me see, sweetheart. I remember seeing my Clara in a beautiful garden full of all her favorite flowers—roses, daisies, tulips, azaleas. She called them all her babies." Pap chuckles a little before continuing.

"Our front yard used to be one big old flower garden."

Pap coughs into his shoulder. The cough goes on a lot longer than usual, which worries me. It doesn't sound so good at all.

He finally stops and clears his throat. "I fenced the flower garden in to keep the critters out and Clara would spend hours out there tending to it, teaching the kids how to plant and prune and such."

I look up at Dad. He covers his mouth with his hand and his eyes have misted over. Grandma Clara died before I was born. I never knew she was a gardener. She's probably the person who taught Dad how to be such a great landscaper.

"In my dream, Clara is young and beautiful," Pap continues. "Just like the day I met her. She waves at me and I want to go to her, but I can't."

Charvi's eyes are still closed tight, like she can see everything Pap is describing to her on the inside of her eyelids. She hasn't let go of his hands, either. "Why can't you get to her, Mr. Pruitt?"

Mrs. Prosser leans in, her face soft and her eyes glassy.

"There's a black wrought-iron fence that goes all the way around the garden. About ten feet high. There isn't any gate, though. So I keep walking around the fence. Around and around the garden looking for a way in. A way to my Clara. But there ain't one."

Pap's eyes are swollen puddles now. He reaches into the pocket of his overalls and pulls out one of the handkerchiefs

Lyla and I gave him. That's all he ever asks for around Christmas, or his birthday. Just new handkerchiefs. Oh, and some Juicy Fruit gum. Pap wipes his eyes and blows his nose.

I can tell Mrs. Prosser is trying hard not to cry. She twists her mouth and scratches her nose with the back of her hand—both dead giveaways that someone is trying not to lose it. She probably thinks it would be unprofessional. She'd be right about that.

Charvi finally opens her big brown eyes and smiles at Pap. "Thank you for sharing your dream with me, Mr. Pruitt."

He smiles and wipes his eyes. "Call me Pap, sweetheart. Any friend of Mikey's is a friend of mine."

"Can I call you Pap, too, then?" Dinesh asks.

Everyone laughs as Pap nods over at him. "Sure you can, son."

"I think your dream is beautiful," Charvi says. "I believe that your wife is trying to tell you that she's okay. She misses you, but she's doing just fine. And that you shouldn't be sad or worried about her."

I look over at Dad. He's grinning from ear to ear, but his eyes are all shiny. Mrs. Prosser beams at Charvi like she's the baby Jesus.

Pap's face softens, and he gives Charvi a sweet but sad smile. "But I can't get to her. I can't get to my Clara because of that fence."

Charvi puts a hand on Pap's shoulder. "You built the fence, Pap. Just like you built the fence around Clara's flower garden.

And only you can tear it down to get to her. She's waiting for you. It's okay to let go."

Something clicks to life in Pap's hollow eyes. Like he understands what Charvi means, which is good, because I sure don't. How is Pap supposed to tear down a dream fence? And what's he supposed to let go of?

Charvi pats his hand like she did when she finished interpreting Julian's dream at the open-call auditions. That must be her cue that the show is over. Dad puts a hand on her shoulder and squeezes, like *Thank you*.

Mrs. Prosser wipes her eyes with the back of her hand. "Well, that was simply lovely, Charvi."

Mrs. Prosser scans the room, her gaze landing on a sad-looking lady sitting in the corner of the room alone. The woman looks a lot older than Pap.

"Mr. Pruitt," she says to Dad. "If you're not in a hurry, would you mind if I borrowed Charvi for a few minutes? There's someone else I'd like her to meet."

"Of course," Dad says, seeming a bit confused.

And I guess I'm giving two Charvi Lahiri, Mystic to the Stars, free samples away today. But as long as Charvi's okay with it, so am I. Because in my whole life, I don't think I've ever seen such a peaceful look on Pap Pruitt's face.

18

THE SIZZLE REEL SMACKDOWN

"Last looks, people," I yell out, wishing I had a megaphone.

I learned about *last looks* on Google yesterday. When you're directing America's Junior Comedic Sensation in his first sizzle reel, it's something you say right before you start taping. I also learned that a sizzle reel is kind of like an audition, but on video.

Julian rushes over to Brady, fiddling with his hair and tugging his Iron Man T-shirt down at the hem. "Can't we do this after I have time to go to the Gap? This boy needs a complete wardrobe makeover."

Brady rolls his eyes at Julian. "I'm, like, right here. I can hear you."

It's Thursday and we're on the front lawn of the school during second lunch period getting some video on Brady for his sizzle reel for *Later Tonight with Billy Shannon*. Colton holds my mom's iPhone up, pointing it at Brady. I told Mom what I needed her phone for and she understood. But she made me promise that I wouldn't use the phone inside the school and that I would take good care of it, because it's brand-new and I guess they cost, like, a gazillion dollars. We're lucky I was able to get her to let me borrow it today. My flip phone doesn't do video so well. Or, like, you know . . . at all.

Brady glances down, touching the red-and-gold Iron Man mask on his chest. "What's wrong with my clothes, anyway?"

Julian slaps Brady's hand away from the shirt, tugging at the hem again. "Nothing, if you plan to sit around all day playing video games."

"What's wrong with sitting around all day playing video games?" Brady whines.

Julian steps out of the shot, clapping his hands like a teacher trying to get our attention. "Hush up. Michael is working."

"Thank you, Julian," I say. I look at Brady. "Ready?"

He nods and his high-wattage performance smile pops into place, stretching out his whole face.

I crouch down a little. I don't know why, but it seems like the professional-director thing to do. I hold up a finger. "*Aaand* action!" I point to Brady.

"Hello, Mr. Shannon," Brady says, without any of the whine in his voice. "I'm Brady Hill and I'm a comedian, just like you. And one day I hope I'll have my own late-night show like you. But right now I'm stuck in the seventh grade at North Charleston Middle School in South Carolina."

So far I'm directing the heck out of this thing. Colton

stands right beside me doing a super-crazy-good job of pointing Mom's phone at Brady and holding it still. The red in his hair is almost blinding in the full sun as it beats down on us. Brady doesn't look the least bit bothered by the heat, though. That's called professionalism.

"Middle school is the worst, am I right?" Brady says. "You don't get to have the fun of elementary school or the freedom of high school. It's like the middle child of schools."

Brady grins and pauses like people are laughing. There are a few kids milling around, but no one is paying us any attention. Julian is definitely not laughing. He has his hands over his eyes like he's watching a scary movie. Colton and I glance at each other. Nope. Neither one of us is laughing, either. Maybe the laughing people are in Brady's head. I think he's just nervous and still getting warmed up. When he realizes that we aren't laughing, he launches right back into his routine.

"And what's the deal with square pizza in the school cafeteria? Everywhere else you go, pizza slices are triangles. Pizza Hut, Chuck E. Cheese, Little Caesars—all triangles, like pie. I mean, when one of your parents makes an apple pie, they don't cut you a square piece, do they? If my mom gave me a square slice of apple pie, I'd probably check her medications."

Colton and I both giggle a little, nodding to each other. Brady is right about that. I look over at Julian. He doesn't smile, not even a little. Actually he crosses his arms, frowning at Brady like he's thinking, *Step it up, dude—you're blowing this.* Man, Julian is a tough audience.

Brady smiles bigger and starts using his hands more, like Billy Shannon does when he's doing his monologue at the beginning of *Later Tonight*.

"The other day in science class, we learned about atoms," he says. "But me? I don't know. I just don't trust atoms. That's right. I don't trust them one little bit."

Brady pauses just for a second like a professional comedian would. He even glances around, looking at different people in an imaginary audience.

"You want to know why I don't trust atoms?"

Colton and I are already giggling, which is a good sign. We nod at Brady.

Brady throws up his hands. "Because they make up *everything.*"

That makes me and Colton laugh out loud. Colton's hand dips a little and I grab it to hold the iPhone in place. We're both pointing it at Brady with my hand on top of his for, like, three whole seconds before I pull mine away. I don't want Colton to think I'm a creeper. But he glances over and flashes me one of his famous stomach-in-the-blender smiles, so I guess he doesn't.

Brady is on a roll now and goes right into the next joke.

"In math class yesterday, I was looking at my textbook and I thought to myself—this is the saddest book I've ever seen. I mean, no textbook is sadder than a math textbook. You want to know why?"

"Why?" Colton asks, chuckling.

Brady lights up at the audience interaction. "Because it's full of problems!" He throws his hands up again and they land on his hips.

Colton and I are laughing so hard now we must sound like a whole audience on the video. That one even makes Julian smile. Just a little. He at least uncrosses his arms and starts fanning himself.

"You know, North Charleston Middle is a very diverse school," Brady says, looking more serious now. "We have kids from all different backgrounds and cultures." Brady counts off on his fingers. "We have black kids, white kids, Indian kids, Middle Eastern kids, Asian kids—heck, we even have some elf kids."

Colton and I glance at each other with raised eyebrows like, *Whaaat?* I don't have any idea where Brady is going with this one, but I have to just trust his comedic genius. That's part of being a good talent-and-pizzazz agent.

"That's right, folks, *elf kids*. And everyone at North Charleston does the same thing after school, except for the elves," Brady says, real serious-like. "All the other kids have to do their homework. But elf kids have to do their *gnome-work*."

That gets the biggest laugh yet from me and Colton. I *did not* see that one coming. *Gnome-work*. Now, that's smart *and* funny. Even Julian can't help himself from laughing out loud.

Brady holds both hands up and waves at us, slowly backing away. "Thank you. Thank you very much. You've been a great audience."

He heads off to the right and out of the shot. Colton hits the red button on the iPhone, stopping the recording.

"How was that?" Brady asks, running back over. "I figured I should end on the biggest laugh. That's what other comedians do on *Later Tonight*."

"You were super-crazy good, Brady," I say, slapping him lightly on the shoulder. "So funny."

Colton hands me the iPhone, pushing his blinding reddish-brown hair off his forehead. "It was great, Brady. I laughed a lot."

"Thanks, Colton." Brady looks at Julian for his verdict.

Julian tugs at the front of his T-shirt and then fans himself with both hands. He gives Brady a little grin. "You had a slow start, but you brought it home."

Brady looks pleased enough with that. "So, Mikey," he says. "Do you think the video has enough *sizzle*?"

"I think so," I say. "You might want to get a couple of short clips at home. You know, making fun of your mom or your dad or both. That's always good for a laugh. Email them to me and I'll edit them in and then send the sizzle reel on to Billy Shannon's booking office."

"Wow," Brady says, his face as bright as a mall Christmas tree. "I can't believe I'm going to get discovered on *Later*

Tonight. And then one day I'll have my own show like Billy Shannon. I think I'm much funnier than Billy, anyway."

"Maybe don't say that on the sizzle reel," I say.

"Yeah, don't get a big head just yet," Julian says.

I spot Trey and Dinesh coming out the front entrance of the school and heading our way.

"How did it go?" Trey asks, dropping his backpack on the ground.

"Great," I say proudly. "Brady killed it."

"He murdered it," Colton adds with a little laugh.

"That's so cool." Dinesh pushes his glasses up the bridge of his nose. "Hey, Charvi is psyched about her gig at the nursing home."

I nod. "Me too. I think she will really help some people."

It's not a *real* paying gig, though. It's more like a volunteer position. After Charvi talked with some of the residents at Prince George about their dreams, Mrs. Prosser asked her if she would like to come by every other Saturday to visit. She said it was good for raising the residents' spirits. I thought about pushing for Mrs. Prosser to pay Charvi one thousand dollars per visit, but Charvi was so excited about the idea of helping out and putting smiles on so many faces that I didn't play hardball. She's even going to start this weekend. I might not get any commission from Charvi's nursing-home gig, but it'll help get her name out there, which will help me get her paying jobs in the future. So I'll just consider this one a marketing expense in my action plan for Charvi Lahiri, Mystic to the Stars.

The front doors of the school burst open and some guys from the basketball team charge out in a noisy rumble. Of course Tommy Jenrette leads the pack, and of course his gaze locks in on us immediately. *Crap.*

"Hey, guys," I say to my friends, looking away from Tommy. "We should go back inside."

Julian fans himself with a spiral-bound notebook now. "Yes, honey. Miss Coco is not about this heat."

"But we still have, like, ten minutes of lunch period left," Colton says, his freckled face twisting in confusion.

Colton doesn't realize that Tommy, Trace, and Colby are walking right up behind him. Colton has his hand on his hip like Lyla does sometimes, and Tommy is staring at him.

"Is this your new girlfriend, Gay Mikey?" Tommy says, sneering at Colton.

Trace and Colby laugh like Tommy is America's Junior Comedic Sensation instead of Brady. He isn't. Trust me. Julian rolls his eyes at them as Brady stands motionless. Dinesh and Trey look down, probably wishing they could make themselves invisible.

Tommy bumps Colton with his shoulder kind of hard, causing Colton to stumble forward and lose his balance. Then he's falling. Landing on one knee and a hand. Luckily we're on the grass and not the concrete, but my blood boils just the same. I don't know exactly what I plan to do. Tommy is much bigger than me and has muscles. But Tommy just can't do that to Colton and get away with it, either. I hesitate a moment too long, though, and it's not me but Julian who gets all up in Tommy's face.

Julian points a finger at Tommy's chest, forcing air through his nostrils like a fire-breathing dragon. "What is your problem, you psycho, redneck Neanderthal?"

"Whoa," Trey says, almost like a prayer.

Brady and I help Colton back to his feet. He has some dirt on his jeans and a grass stain on his hand.

"Are you okay?" I ask him.

"Are you okay?" Tommy says, mocking me in a high, whiny voice. "Jesus, what a big fruit basket you all make." He points to me, Colton, and Julian one at a time. "You, your little sissy girlfriend, and this he/she, illegal tub of lard."

"Uh-oh," Dinesh says in a whisper.

We haven't known Julian long, but I think Trey, Dinesh, and I realize that Julian is braver than all three of us put together, especially when he's wearing a dress, but even now when he's not. He might not have as many muscles as Tommy, but he's just as tall and probably weighs more.

"Julian?" Colton says, because we all can see the way Julian's face has hardened into something pretty scary looking.

"Yo, Julian," Trey says calmly. "Don't do it, bro."

Tommy slings his thick mop of brown hair out of his eyes.

"What's he gonna do? Take a Weed Eater to my yard while his dad mows it?"

The next few seconds pass in slow motion, like a dream. I mostly remember the blood—spewing out of Tommy Jenrette's nose, covering Julian's fist, and some even splattered on the red-and-gold Iron Man mask on Brady's shirt. Then it's like *WWE SmackDown*. Well, the North Charleston Middle School version of *WWE SmackDown*. Colby and Trace tackle Julian, wrestling him to the ground, which is no easy task because of Julian's size. Julian yells, slaps, and kicks, trying to get out from under them. Colton, Brady, and I jump on top of the pile, yelling at Colby and Trace to get off Julian, which would be kind of hard for them to do since we are all on top of *them*. Tommy runs around holding his gushing nose and letting curse words fly with no bleeping like they have on *RuPaul's Drag Race*.

Trey and Dinesh are trying to pull us all apart while yelling something about the gray sun, which doesn't make any sense. It takes me a minute, but what they're saying finally clicks in my head.

Vice Principal Grayson is coming.

I guess it registers with everyone at the same time, because all of a sudden the sizzle reel smackdown is over and we all scramble to our feet. Mr. Grayson's approach doesn't stop Tommy from cursing at Julian, though, calling him every mean name in the book that has anything to do with his size, his being gay, or the fact that he's Mexican. I scan the ground for Mom's new iPhone before Mr. Grayson reaches us. If he confiscates her phone, I'm toast.

Tommy catches me searching right when I spot it close to his feet. We look at each other for a frozen second, him holding his bloody nose and me ready to sprint. I make the first move, but before I even get close, Tommy slams his foot down on the phone. The sound of it shattering under the heel of his shoe is muted and unspectacular, but my heart drops to my stomach anyway. Mom is going to kill me. Brady's sizzle reel footage is gone. And with less than two weeks of school left, I'm pretty sure I just got my second strike from Vice Principal Grayson.

19

THE MIDDLE SCHOOL
JUSTICE SYSTEM

Tommy, Julian, and I sit silently in a row of chairs lined up in front of Mr. Grayson's messy desk like we're facing a firing squad. I'm in the middle and don't like being this close to Tommy. With his head tilted back, he holds a gauze bandage the school nurse gave him to his nose. Apparently Mr. Grayson decided the three of us were the most to blame for the fight. Tommy and Julian, maybe. But why me? I don't say a word, though. It's something I've learned the hard way in my career.

> Michael Pruitt Business Tip #365: During tense business negotiations, never be the first one to speak, or you'll lose the upper hand.

"He hit me for no reason, Coach," Tommy says with a slight pout in his voice.

I'm glad Tommy was the one who just lost the upper hand, but I would've been happy, too, if it had been the vice principal. I guess Mr. Grayson sat me in the middle to keep them apart, but Tommy and Julian act like I'm not here anyway.

Julian points at Tommy. "He pushed Colton Sanford down on the ground. Colton didn't even do anything. It was a hate crime."

Julian folds his arms over his chest.

"Fat freak," Tommy mumbles.

"That's enough," Mr. Grayson barks.

Julian and Tommy both go silent. Mr. Grayson exhales through his nose and runs a hand over his shiny bald head. I don't know why. Maybe he likes to pretend he still has hair. He looks directly at me. Why is he looking at me?

"What was your role in all this, Pruitt?" Mr. Grayson asks.

I knew he was trying to pin this on me. The vice principal has never liked me for some reason. Maybe he's a homophobe with good gaydar.

I shrug. "All I did was try to get Trace and Colby off Julian after they tackled him."

The way Mr. Grayson looks at me with cold eyes and little teeth showing like a ferret makes me wonder if I need a lawyer. There really should be lawyers for kids who are sent to the vice principal's office, to make sure they get a fair trial. Especially when the vice principal is a suspected homophobe, and the assistant basketball coach, and your drag-kid client just gave the captain of the team a bloody nose. I would probably be a super-crazy-good lawyer. I could even start my own firm to help kids who get into trouble at school:

Anything Middle School Legal Services
A division of Anything, Inc.
Michael Pruitt—President, Founder, CEO, and Law Stuff Expert

Mr. Grayson grabs Mom's smashed iPhone from his desk and holds it up. "Was the fight over this, Pruitt?"

"No, sir," I say, shaking my head like there's no tomorrow. "That's my mom's phone. I just dropped it and then . . ."

I glance over at Tommy. He shoots me a warning glare that would make Voldemort pee himself.

"Then, um—uh," I stammer, trying to avoid Tommy's hard gaze. "I guess I accidentally stepped on it during the fight."

Tommy gives a little nod. I feel about two inches tall telling that lie—especially to save Tommy Jenrette's butt just because I don't want him to pound my face in. Julian doesn't say anything because he didn't see anything. He was too busy trying to breathe under a pile of boys to catch Tommy smashing the iPhone with his foot.

"Well," Mr. Grayson says. "I'm sure your mom will be anxious to hear about the condition of her phone. Why don't we give her a call right now? I'm sure we have a home phone number here somewhere."

"No," I say a little too quickly. "She's at work. She teaches at North Charleston High."

"I'll send her an email, then," Mr. Grayson says, like he's disappointed he can't call Mom right now and rat me out.

"What about him?" Julian says, pointing at Tommy again with a whole load of Miss Coco sass in his voice.

As a future lawyer, I would advise him to keep his mouth shut right now. There must be something seriously wrong with Julian the way he keeps pointing the finger at Tommy. It's like he's not scared of Tommy at all. Does he not know who he's dealing with here? The psycho dude who duct-taped Stanley Rogers inside a trash can behind the school and left him there for three hours before the janitor found him? The same guy who gave Ty Erickson such a legendary wedgie in the locker room that the kid walked like an overweight duck for a week? Maybe Julian hit his head too hard on the ground when he was tackled. Maybe he doesn't remember all that. I sure as heck do.

Mr. Grayson sighs, drumming his fingers on the desk. "Colton Sanford said he didn't see who pushed him. And Jenrette is the only one sitting here with a bloody nose. So, Vasquez, you're suspended for one day."

Julian's eyes widen, and he looks like his whole head is going the explode. "What the—"

"Watch it, son," Mr. Grayson says, pointing a finger at Julian before he curses. "One more word and you'll be suspended for two days. I'm going easy on you because I don't have all the details."

Julian clamps his mouth shut, but his eyes are yelling at the top of his lungs.

Mr. Grayson eyes me and Tommy. I can't tell what he's thinking, though. I know he doesn't want to suspend his star basketball player.

"You two," he says. "Detention today after school. Right here in my office."

Tommy huffs, but he doesn't say anything, which is probably smart. That might force Mr. Grayson to do something worse to him.

I raise my hand. I don't know why. Maybe because I'm afraid if I speak out of turn, I'll get more than just detention.

Mr. Grayson rolls his eyes. It's very unprofessional. "What, Pruitt?"

"Sir, what exactly am I getting detention for?" I say as politely as I can. "I mean, I have to understand my punishment so I can explain it to my parents."

Mr. Grayson's eyes plow into mine. I get the feeling he thinks I'm sassing him, but I'm not. Okay. Maybe I am, just a little. I break his hard gaze and stare down at his basketball of a belly.

"Um, never mind," I say, swallowing the lump in my throat.

"That's what I thought," he says. "Now, all of you, back to class. Mrs. Taylor will give you a note."

Tommy is the first one out the door, huffing all the way.

Julian and I take our time. I feel so bad for him. He doesn't deserve suspension. Tommy had it coming. He started the whole thing. The middle school justice system is super-crazy unfair. It's not until we're in the outer office waiting at the counter for Mrs. Taylor to give us a note that I finally get a good look at Julian's eyes. They're dark and maybe a little wet. The Miss Coco sparkle, sass, and pizzazz are gone.

I touch his arm to get his attention. "Hey. Are you okay?"

Julian looks at me like he's in a trance. He shakes his head slowly. "My dad is going to kill me."

20

THE MURDERY DETENTION

After school, Tommy and I sit in Mr. Grayson's office quietly serving out our detention sentence. Tommy hasn't said a word and he hasn't looked at me, either, which is all just fine by me. I do worry a little bit that he might be sitting over there plotting to murder me. Mr. Grayson left a while ago, and I hope he comes back soon. The door is open so Mrs. Taylor can keep an eye on us and hopefully come to my rescue when Tommy decides it's time for my life to be over.

With his chair pulled up close to the corner of Mr. Grayson's desk, he's hunched over a notebook, drawing something with one of Mr. Grayson's blue pens, but I can't see what it is. His thick dark hair hangs down, hiding his brown eyes from me. His nose is a little pointy, but not in a bad way, and his lips are full and round. Actually Tommy would be a good-looking guy if he weren't such a jerk. But the jerk part kind of ruins his whole look.

I pretend like I'm reading *Wonder*, but I've already finished it. It was just the only book I had in my backpack. I'll bet

Tommy hasn't ever read it. It's all about being kind to one another. That doesn't sound like something he would be too interested in.

But I can't take the silence anymore. Besides, maybe if I get him talking, he'll stop thinking of all the ways he can murder me. Who knows, maybe I can get him to confess to starting the fight. I wish I had a phone to secretly record our conversation for evidence.

"What are you drawing?" I ask, trying to keep my voice light but steady. Like it's no big deal that we're in here alone together.

It's the only thing I can think of to say and at first I don't even know if he hears me. Finally he glances over and sighs. He holds up the notebook and—*OMG!*—it's the coolest drawing of Hogwarts I've ever seen. It looks just like it does in the movies, except it's all done in blue ink.

"That's pretty good," I say, and I'm not even lying.

I'm no art critic, but I could probably be one if I wanted to. I bet art critics don't make much money, though, so I probably wouldn't start a whole new division of Anything, Inc., just to go around looking at people's drawings and saying what I like and don't like about them. I can do that for free. Like charity work.

Tommy gazes at the drawing for a second, and then looks back at me. "You think so?"

I nod and sit up a little straighter. "It looks like a scene from one of the movies—maybe *Deathly Hallows: Part 1*. And I like the way you have Hedwig sitting in that window." I point to the Hedwig spot. "That was a nice touch."

"Thanks," Tommy says, his face twisted like he thinks I'm pulling his leg. Or maybe he's just not used to saying the word *thanks* and it tastes nasty on his tongue. He dives back into his sketch, but at least now he looks a little less murdery to me.

"I guess you like to draw, huh?" I say. Lame question. *Duh.*

He doesn't respond, but keeps drawing with his left hand. I never noticed before that Tommy is left-handed.

"You're talented," I say, leaning back in the chair. "And I should know because I'm a talent agent in real life."

In real life? That was a pretty dumb thing to say. Of course, *in real life.*

Tommy scratches his head with the cap end of the pen. "You mean that little freak-show thing you were having in your garage the other day? I thought you guys were just playing around."

"Technically, it's a carport, not a garage," I say, slumping down in my chair. "And why do you have to be so mean all the time?"

I meant to just think the question, but the words tumbled right out of my mouth before I could stop them. That happens to me a lot. I wonder if there are support groups for that. Like Speakaholics Anonymous. I'll have to google that later.

Tommy leans back in his chair, staring blankly at me. "I'm not mean. I just like having fun."

I slip my book inside my backpack and cross my arms. "Well, news flash, being mean to people isn't very fun for the people you're being mean to."

Tommy doesn't say anything, but he keeps staring at me. Finally he goes back to his drawing. "Whatever, Gay Mikey."

"And why do you keep calling me that?" I ask with a little huff.

"It's just a name," he says. "And you *are* gay, right?"

I glance down at the floor, hoping it will open up and swallow me whole. I think about all the different responses I could throw out.

Why, yes, Tommy Jenrette, I'm a proud gay kid. I'm here and I'm queer. Get used to it.

But then I realize for the first time that I'm not all that proud of it. Even though I'm definitely the other two things— gay and a kid. I guess I don't have any business joining the Pride Club, after all. Maybe Trey was right about me being the worst gay ever.

I could say, *What the heck are you talking about, Tommy Jenrette? Why would you say something like that? Of course I'm not gay. Gay people suck. I like girls. Girls rock. I want to, like, kiss them and everything. There's nobody not gayer than me.*

But being a coward and saying nasty things about other people like you seems a lot worse than just not being proud of who you are. I guess I could just say, *I don't know if I'm gay or not, Tommy Jenrette. And it's none of your business, anyway, so thank you very much and have a nice day.*

Even though I do know. "Who told you?" I say, which was not even in the running for my possible responses.

Tommy puts the pen down and holds up his drawing, inspecting it like he's trying to decide if he thinks he might be a talented artist or not. And he seriously is, as much as I hate to admit it. I'd be lying if I said I hadn't already thought of ways I could promote him as an artist *if* he was one of my clients. And, you know, a nice person and all.

"You just did," he says. "I was guessing because I never see you with any girls." *Crap*. Tommy Jenrette has better gaydar than I do. That doesn't seem fair at all. I shift in my seat and the chair creaks. These metal chairs make your butt go numb fast. I think that's why Mr. Grayson has them in his office. So kids' butts will go numb and they'll be super-crazy uncomfortable.

"I guess there's no use in asking you not to tell anyone," I say.

He kind of half chuckles. "If you keep hanging around that fat Mexican kid, trust me, everyone will figure it out."

My neck goes hot. "Don't call him that."

Tommy looks over at me. "What? Fat or Mexican? 'Cause last time I checked, he was both."

I don't know what to say to that. Julian is Mexican, and he even called himself fat. And there isn't anything wrong with either of those things. But the way Tommy says it makes it sound like there is. But I don't say anything and that feels

184

wrong and not like something a friend would do. Which makes me wonder—*Are Julian and I friends?*

Tommy holds up the drawing to me again. "You seriously think I have talent?"

"Sure," I say, shifting my numb butt in the seat again. "Everyone has *some* kind of talent. You have two kinds— playing basketball and drawing. Maybe you should spend more time working on those and less time shoving kids like Colton around. Or calling people freaks, losers, and he/she. Or saying *gay* like it's a bad word."

I figure if Tommy's going to murder me anyway, I might as well say what I want to him first. But he doesn't murder me. Not yet. He just shoots me a blank stare, without saying a word. Like he might actually be thinking about what I just said. But I guess that's not very likely.

"You should take an art class in high school next year," I say.

Tommy sighs like talking to me is draining all his energy. "My dad would never let me do that. He says I have to focus all my time on basketball."

"Oh," I say. "I thought you loved playing basketball."

Tommy closes his notebook and puts Mr. Grayson's pen back into the pencil cup on the desk. "I like it okay. But I'd rather draw."

Just then I realize that this is the longest conversation I've ever had with Tommy Jenrette. Actually it's the only time we've ever been alone, which is probably why he's talking to me at all. Trace and Colby aren't around for him to try to impress—if you can call being a jerk impressive. But I've learned at least two things I didn't know about Tommy—he's a crazy-good artist and he'd rather draw than play basketball but his dad won't let him. Oh, and he's left-handed and he thinks being mean is *having fun*, which makes no sense at all.

Mr. Grayson sails in through the door. He's changed into navy shorts and a white polo shirt and a whistle hangs from his neck. "Okay, gentlemen. That'll be all. Jenrette, get to the gym. You're late for practice. Pruitt, your mom is here to pick you up."

Great. Punishment—round two.

Tommy pops up out of his chair with a sudden burst of energy. He rushes out the door before I can tell him that he left his notebook with the Hogwarts drawing on the vice principal's desk. Mr. Grayson doesn't notice it, either. So, as I pack up the rest of my stuff, I grab the notebook, slip it inside my backpack, and hurry out the door.

21

THE TRAITOR

Michael Pruitt Business Tip #366: Don't get grounded for destroying your mom's brand-new iPhone when one of your clients has a big audition at the Petcare store out by Northwoods Mall.

I spend Saturday morning in my office at the world headquarters of Anything, Incorporated, waiting for my junior talent coordinator to get back and give me a full report on how the Amazing Sadie and Fifi did at Petcare. There's only one more week of school and it's going to be super-crazy busy, so I'm making notes on my legal pad while I wait for Lyla:

> Monday—talent-show tryouts!
> Tuesday—Julian death-drop rehearsal with Manny.

I make a mental note to google *kid life-insurance policies*. Then I write down:

> Wednesday—math final exam.

I'll get Dinesh to help me study for that. He *loves* math. Weird.

Thursday—language-arts final essay due?

I put a big old question mark by that one because I don't even know what I want to write about. But Mr. Crowder said it could be on anything we want, because he's cool that way.

Friday—The Big Show!!!!!!

Then I remember something else important and write it down:

Next Saturday—the Super Kid of Many Faces
world premiere at Chandler Martin's b-day party.

Stuart is so excited about his upcoming gig, you'd think he *was* getting paid a thousand dollars, which is what I told him I was going to ask for. I forgot to tell him that Mrs. Martin only agreed to pay twenty bucks.

I add one more thing to my list:

Figure out a way to get Tommy's super-crazy-good
drawings back to him without getting punched in the face.

I'm getting nervous about the talent-show tryouts on

Monday because Mr. Arnold, the drama teacher who heads up the show every year, has high standards. He's almost like a real-live show-business professional. He's usually the star of all the Lowcountry Community Theater shows and he does interpretive dance with his troupe every year at the Spoleto Festival. I saw him dance one year at the festival. The dancing was weird, but Mr. Arnold was pretty good. But I, like, *never* need to see him in tights ever again—*No, thank you very much, Mr. Arnold, and have a nice day!*

I hope all my clients have been practicing because Mr. Arnold doesn't let just anyone go through to the big show. He's kind of like Simon Cowell that way. He's even made kids *and parents* cry before. But I think that's just part of being a professional in show business. I'll probably need to learn how to make people cry if I'm going to be a good talent agent. Maybe Mr. Arnold can teach me.

Dad and Lyla have been gone a long time, so I hope nothing went wrong with Sadie and Fifi's audition at Petcare. I should've been there. It's very unprofessional that I missed the whole thing. It was my idea, after all. But Lyla jumped at the chance to go in my place when Dad offered to take her. It's not fair that I was grounded for the weekend, just because Tommy Jenrette smashed Mom's phone yesterday. Like I had anything to do with that. But Mom is all about *taking responsibility for our actions,* and I guess my action of taking Mom's iPhone to school came with the responsibility of getting it safely back home. Although I didn't sign anything that explained all that, so the grounding is probably not even legal. I pointed that out to Mom, but the look she gave me told me I should probably just let it go.

Forbes lies at my feet, staring up at me with his time-to-close-up-shop-go-outside-and-play-ball look.

"Sorry, Forbesy," I say, reaching down to give him a scratch on the head. "I have to work today. I'm waiting on an important email, buddy."

He rests his furry head on the concrete floor with a prolonged whiny grumble. Poor Forbes.

Thankfully Brady's sizzle reel didn't die with Mom's phone. Dad found it hiding somewhere in *the cloud* and downloaded it onto my laptop. I edited in the stuff that Brady sent me and sent the final video link to Miss Allie Rosen at *Later Tonight with Billy Shannon* twenty whole minutes ago and I still haven't gotten a response. I mean, I know it's a Saturday, even in New York, but I think it's unprofessional of Miss Rosen not to at least let me know that she got the email. I mean, if you work for someone as important as Mr. Billy Shannon, weekends must be just as busy as weekdays. I'll bet his staff works every single day of the week and they probably think he's a jerk to make them do it. But I think he's just a smart businessman. I mean, it's Saturday here in North Charleston, South Carolina, too, and you don't see me out in the backyard playing ball with my dog, do you?

I hit the Refresh button on my email, but no new messages come through.

Very unprofessional.

I had to reschedule the rehearsal planned for today with Julian and Manny the drag queen—who's going to teach Julian how to do the death drop—because of my grounding. I need to be there to make sure they get it right. And so that Julian doesn't actually, like, you know, die. Plus with Gabby and Lyla as his backup dancers, I need to make sure they don't try to steal the show. Backup dancers can do that, you know. I'm sure Mrs. Beyoncé Knowles-Carter knows all about it. Google taught me her whole name when I searched for *things gays should know*. Google never lets me down. I should probably buy stock in it when my clients make me, like, a gazillion dollars in commission.

Reaching down into my backpack, I pull out Tommy Jenrette's notebook. It kind of feels hot in my hands. I wonder if he realizes yet that he left it in Mr. Grayson's office. I don't know why I took it. I guess I just wanted to see if the Hogwarts drawing was a one-time thing or if he had any other good ones. I start thumbing through the notebook, being careful not to crinkle or smudge the pages with my fingerprints.

The Hogwarts drawing was definitely *not* a one-time thing. I stare down at a picture of Harry Potter and Ron and Hermione that is *amazing*. They look like real people, not like the actors in the movies, though. Better than that. After several pages of super-crazy-good Harry Potter drawings, there's a bunch more of superheroes—Iron Man, Black Panther, Superman, Aquaman, Thor. I would never have thought that Tommy Jenrette had so much talent and pizzazz. Or, like, any pizzazz at all.

I flip past the superheroes and find faces of people I recognize from school. Most of them are kids I see hanging out with Tommy and the drawings are so good, it's easy to recognize them. There's one of Colby and Trace playing basketball and a funny one of Mr. Grayson where his head is twice as big as his body. One shows all the guys that Tommy hangs with at lunch sitting around a table stuffing square pizza in their mouths. All I can say is *wow*. If Tommy were my client, I'd try to get him a gallery showing to sell a bunch of his art. I'd bet people would pay, like, a hundred thousand dollars for each one. My commission from that would be enough to reprint my business cards *and* get an iPhone. And, like, a house or two.

A ping sounds through my laptop speakers. Looking over at the screen, I see that my email inbox shows one new message, and for a second I just about pee myself. But it's *not* from *Later Tonight with Billy Shannon*. It's from Colton. I know because the email address is colton.sanford@ncms.edu. It would be pretty weird if it was from anyone else—especially *the* Billy Shannon. I double-click on the message and the email pops up.

Mikey,

Sorry you're grounded this weekend. Have you heard from Julian? I know he was suspended from school yesterday, but I haven't seen him around his house. Hope he is okay.

C U Monday.

Colton

I'm about to hit the Reply button, when the door swings open. I turn in my chair and find Lyla standing there holding Pooty.

"We're back," she says, sounding bored as usual.

Her dark curls bounce along with her as she shuffles over to the metal chair by my desk. She's wearing one of her favorite Hello Kitty T-shirts with jeans and sandals.

"What the heck took so long?" I say with a huff.

Forbes watches Pooty out of the corner of his eye the whole time. When Lyla sits, Pooty curls into a ball in her lap and stares down at Forbes like he's a big fluffy bowl of cocker-spaniel-flavored Meow Mix. Forbes whines and scoots under my desk. Poor Forbes.

"We went to see Pap Pruitt on the way home," Lyla says, pushing her hair out of her eyes. "Charvi was there, interpreting dreams. All of Pap's friends like her a lot, but I think it's pretty dumb that she doesn't get paid for it. How come you didn't get her any money for that gig?"

I cross my arms, ignoring the dig at me. "How was Pap?"

Lyla sighs, petting Pooty real slow. "Not too good. He was in his bed and he didn't say much."

That worries me. Pap is always sitting in his wheelchair when I see him, never lying in the bed. I wonder if he's getting worse. I was hoping he might even be able to come out to the big talent show and see me finally succeed at one of my business ventures.

I shake the worrying thoughts about Pap out of my head because it's too hard to think about that. "How did it go with Sadie and Fifi at Petcare?"

"They got the job," Lyla says with another bored sigh.

"Yes!" I say, pumping my fist in the air. "I knew it."

Hang in there, Pap. It's all starting to happen. You are going to be so proud of me.

"The animal shelter was doing pet adoptions in front of the store, like you said they would be," Lyla says.

She kisses Pooty on top of his head. *Ew.*

"Once Sadie and Fifi started their act, more people came over to look at the dogs and go into the store."

Lyla stops like that's the end of the story.

"And?" I say, egging her on.

"And the manager came out to see what all the fuss was about," she says. "I thought he was going to yell at Sadie and Fifi to go away, but he didn't. He stood there and watched them for a while. Then he asked Sadie if she wanted a job doing tricks with Fifi in front of the store every Saturday. He said it'd be good for business. And because Fifi came from the animal shelter, it would help more of the dogs get adopted, too."

I. Am. A. Genius! I sit there waiting for the good part. But Lyla just strokes Pooty and swings her legs.

"Lyla," I say. "How much are they paying her?"

Lyla sighs. "I did like you said. I told the manager that he would have to pay Sadie and Fifi at least five thousand dollars a day to perform outside the store."

She pauses again. I don't know why she has to make me pull it out of her. Must be part of her human-demon-doll personality.

"So? What did the manager say?" I ask, throwing my hands up.

Lyla doesn't look at me. She kisses the top of Murder Kitty's head again. "He said he'd give her thirty bucks a Saturday. But I told him we could only accept dollars."

I jump up out of my seat, spooking Forbes, who scrambles from under the desk and goes running out the door. Pooty poots.

"That's amazing," I say, another first bump with the air. "My strategy worked again and you handled it perfectly."

I can't stop grinning at her because even though my little sister can be a huge pain in the butt sometimes, right now I'm super-crazy proud of her.

"Yeah, about that," Lyla says. "I think I deserve the commission on Sadie and Fifi's gig at Petcare."

And we're back.

I stand there staring at her, my grin fading fast. She didn't even know what a *gig* was a week ago and now she's trying to take credit for Sadie and Fifi getting one.

"What? Why would *you* get the commission?" I say, and then point at my chest. "I'm the Amazing Sadie and Fifi's agent, not you."

Lyla shrugs. "Sadie said she and Fifi have been thinking about making a change for a while now."

"A while?" I say, my voice cracking. "They've only been with the agency for a week!"

"She said she thinks you have too many clients and that you give Julian all your attention. She didn't like it that you didn't show up today."

I feel like cartoon steam is about to shoot out of my ears. "Didn't you tell her that I'm grounded and that's why I couldn't be there?"

Lyla looks up at me as innocent as the baby Jesus himself. "I think maybe I forgot to tell her that part. But she was so happy that I got her a gig that pays thirty dollars a day, she wants me to manage them now. And so does Fifi."

Lyla swings her legs and strokes Pooty's back like this is a normal conversation. It's not. This is what Pap would call a hostile corporate takeover, only it's *not* going to happen.

Not today, Satan, not today.

I take a deep breath, trying to stay calm. I even sit back down in my chair like a professional boss would.

"Fifi is a dog," I say slowly, rubbing my eyes because that

seems like the professional frustrated-boss thing to do. "So how do you know what she wants?"

Lyla gazes at me with her blank demon-doll eyes. "Because she signed my contract."

I stare at her. "Your what?"

Lyla reaches under Pooty's fat stomach and into the pocket of her jeans. She pulls out a crumpled-up piece of paper and hands it to me. Well, I guess I kind of snatch it from her. I straighten it out on my desk. It's some ratty old Petcare receipt. Written on it in Lyla's purple pen scribble is:

I want Lyla Pruitt to be my agent.

Sadie signed her name at the bottom of the receipt and there's a muddy paw print beside it. *Wow.* You can't trust anybody in this business. Not even a blind, three-legged pit bull.

"I didn't authorize this," I say, holding the receipt out to Lyla. "I should fire you right here on the spot."

Lyla stands and cradles Pooty up to her shoulder. "Even if you could, then the agency would lose a client. The Amazing Sadie and Fifi will follow me wherever I go." She walks over to the door and opens it real slow, she and Pooty both looking back at me and—*OMG!*—I just realized they have the same eyes! Why haven't I ever noticed that before?

"And who knows," the traitor says with a smirk, "some of your other clients might want more attention, too."

Pooty hisses at me over her shoulder and they're gone.

22

THE EPIC DISASTER

Monday at school, it seems like everyone's in a bad mood, which is weird because it's the last week before summer break. Colton hasn't smiled at me all day, and Dinesh is grumbling because he thinks he bombed his social studies final exam this morning. But *bombing* for Dinesh would be like getting an A minus. Trey is bummed because his crush, Heather Hobbs, forgot his name and called him Terry, and Julian is moping around the yellow zone of the cafeteria like a zombie right now. I wonder if it has anything to do with his suspension last Friday, or his ghosting us over the weekend. I guess he could just be nervous about the talent-show tryouts after school today.

I'm still ticked about Lyla stealing the Amazing Sadie and Fifi right out from under me. The only reason I haven't fired her is because she might go off and start a competing agency. Plus it would look bad if Anything Talent and Pizzazz Agency lost a client so soon. At least this way I can say that Sadie and Fifi are still on my agency's roster, even though Lyla is their agent and not me.

Dinesh, Trey, and I eat lunch at our regular table in the green zone. I feel a little bad that most of my clients are sitting way over in the yellow zone. At least they're all at the same table. Stuart, Sadie, Brady, and Julian. Colton's over there, too. Maybe I should have sat with them. Or maybe I should go and invite them to come sit with us. Yeah, that sounds like the nice, human thing to do. But that would require crossing through the red zone, so, *no, thank you very much and have a nice day.*

I still have Tommy's notebook in my backpack and I feel like I'm carrying around a bomb that could go off at any minute. He's not going to like that I took it, and he might even punch me in the face if he knows I looked through it. I know Tommy's been searching for the notebook. I just saw him coming out of Vice Principal Grayson's office and now—OMG!—he's headed right for our table. Dinesh spots him, too.

"It's Tommy Jenrette," Dinesh says in a panicked whisper. "Act cool and don't look him directly in the eye."

That's solid best-friend advice, right there.

Tommy stops, standing at the end of our table. We don't look him directly in the eye, like Dinesh said. I keep my gaze directed at his chest, not an inch higher. I'm not sure if we're acting cool or not, but I kind of doubt it.

"Hey," Tommy says.

To me, I think. But I'm not looking him in the eye, so I can't be sure.

"Why are you staring at my chest?" he asks.

Yep—definitely talking to me.

"Nice pants, Tommy," Dinesh says, his eyes locked on Tommy's waist. "Are those from Old Navy?"

"Huh?" comes Tommy's headless response.

Trey looks over at me, shaking his head like Dinesh and I are the most ridiculous people he's ever met. We probably are.

"Sorry," I say, directing my gaze far away from Tommy's chest. Like all-the-way-to-the-front-office far away.

I only caught a glimpse of him and he's standing there with his hands on his hips, resting his weight on one side like the cool kids stand. I've tried that in the mirror, but it never looks right on me.

"Dude," he says, waving a hand in front of my face. "I'm over here. Did you go blind all of a sudden?"

"That's a cool belt," Dinesh says to Tommy's belt. "Also Old Navy? Are they having a sale?"

Dinesh sounds like a baby seal, nervously laughing at his own lame attempt at a joke. Like he just told the funniest joke in the whole entire seal kingdom.

I slowly lift my gaze all the way up to Tommy's face. He's staring at Dinesh with his thick, grown-man-looking eyebrows all bunched together and his mouth twisted.

"I don't know where my mom buys my clothes, okay?" Tommy looks back at me, his bushy eyebrows parting ways. "Hey, Mikey."

Wow. He said *hey* and didn't even put the *gay* in front of my name, so that's something, I guess.

"Yeah?" I say, trying with all my might to hold his laser-sharp gaze.

He squints his left eye at me, like a middle school pirate. "Did you see what happened to my notebook on Thursday? I thought I left it in Coach Grayson's office, but I just checked and it wasn't there."

I stare at him, silently wondering what I should say. I could tell him that I picked up his notebook, took it home, and looked at all the pictures inside. But then he might punch me right in the face. Or I could lie and say, *Why, no, Tommy Jenrette, I don't have any idea where your notebook is, so thank you very much and have a nice day!* But then what would I do with it? Keep it forever? I make a quick decision and go with it.

Michael Pruitt Business Tip #367: A good businessperson should always be quick and decisive. Except when it comes to firing your board-approved, human-demon-doll junior talent coordinator. That's a lot trickier and riskier. You know, Murder Kitty hexes and all that.

I shift nervously in my seat, pushing my hair out of my eyes. "Um . . . uh . . . yeah."

Okay, so not as quick and decisive as it sounded in my head.

"Um . . . uh . . . yeah . . . what?" he says, mocking me.

I clear my throat, looking over at Trey and Dinesh for some bro support. But Trey pretends like he's reading the nutrition label on his juice box, and Dinesh is still staring at Tommy's belt like an undercover Old Navy secret shopper.

"I mean, yes," I say, looking right in his eyes like I'm not supposed to be doing. "I saw that you left it on Mr. Grayson's desk, so I put it in my backpack for safekeeping. I was just waiting to run into you today to give it back. So this is, like, so cool. This, that you're here now so that I can do that. So . . ."

I sound weird and I'm repeating words for no reason, so I shut my mouth. Reaching into my backpack, I pull out the blue notebook and hand it over to him. He looks at my hand like I have gay cooties and might have infected his notebook.

"Oh," he says, his face tightening. He shifts his weight to the other side, like he's nervous. "You didn't look inside, did you? Because it's private. And that would be, like, illegal or something."

Tommy would make a terrible lawyer because just looking at something is not illegal. I don't think so anyway. No, I'm pretty sure. But this is another quick decision I don't hesitate to make. I shake my head faster than I knew it would shake.

"No," I say. "I would never go through someone's private stuff. Like I said, I just wanted to make sure you got it back safely. You're such a wicked-cool talented artist, those drawings could be worth a lot of money. You should be more careful about where you leave that lying around."

Tommy squints at me like he's trying to decide whether to believe me or not. I pray he does because, as unimpressive as my face is, I like it just the way it is.

"So you honestly think I could make money with my drawings?" he asks.

I look at Trey and then Dinesh. They both stare back at me with their mouths hanging open. They don't have any idea what I'm about to say any more than I do. But I guess I wait too long, because Tommy shakes his head.

"Never mind," he says, rolling up the notebook like a baseball bat. "They're just stupid pictures. Well, thanks or whatever, I guess, for getting it back to me."

Tommy glances around, nods once, and then he's gone. *Finally.*

Trey exhales like he'd been holding his breath the whole entire time Tommy was here. "You totally looked through his notebook, didn't you."

But he doesn't say it like a question, because he knows me too well.

"Well, *duh*," I say, leaning over the table. "And the weirdest thing is that he's a super-crazy-good artist."

Dinesh leans back, crossing his arms. "No way. Tommy Jenrette?"

"Yep," I say.

Trey pushes his tray forward. "So, a jerk like that is a killer ballplayer and a super-good artist?" He shakes his head. "That's all kinds of not fair."

Colton and Julian walk up to the table and sit on either side of me.

"What's up?" Dinesh says, nodding at them like he approves of them joining us.

"Hey," Julian says, his voice small and tight.

He rests his chin in his hand, staring at nothing on the table. Then he sighs. A very dramatic sigh. Like a diva sigh.

I look at Colton. "What's wrong?"

Colton kind of grimaces, nodding to Julian. "Julian has some bad news."

Dinesh and Trey lean forward at the same time. Those guys *love* bad news for some reason. Or at least they love to hear about other people's bad news. I think we all get a little bit of that from our grandmas, but Trey and Dinesh got an extra dose.

"Don't tell me you're not ready for the tryouts today," I say.

Julian shakes his head, slumping in the chair. "My dad lost his crap when I got suspended last week," he says. "I'm grounded for a month. I can only come to school and stay at home. And he said, *No exceptions.*"

I can't feel my face. My fingers start tingling and I think I might pass out. Is he saying that my star client can't perform at our first major gig? Julian was my best shot at the one-hundred-dollar grand prize. Brady's still working out his new material and I haven't even heard it yet. Charvi doesn't go to school here, so she can't even be in the talent show. And

Stuart has his first gig at Chandler Martin's birthday party on Saturday and says he needs to focus all his attention on that. He's going in a new Iron Man direction and still has to fine-tune his new act. And I'm not even sure the Amazing Sadie and Fifi are still my clients. Plus they're traitors. If they win, Sadie might pay Lyla the commission on the prize money and not me. And Mom and Dad are planning to bring Pap Pruitt if he's well enough. What if Pap comes all the way out here to see the big show and none of my clients win? This is an epic disaster.

"Mikey," Colton says, finally snapping me out of my panic. "What are you going to do?"

When I look up again, they're all staring at me. Trey, Dinesh, Julian, and Colton. "What am I going to do?" I don't think I meant to repeat out loud what Colton said, but I need a second to think. I glance around the cafeteria, like I'll find the answer that way. Tommy Jenrette is staring at me from across the room. *Creepy.*

But I guess Tommy's creepy stare helps, because I get a brilliant idea and focus on Julian again. "So your dad said you could only be at school and your house, right?"

Julian nods, sitting up a little straighter.

"Well . . . the tryouts are *technically* here at school. And I could talk to Mr. Arnold about giving you a spot as close to dismissal time as possible so you won't get home much later than usual."

All four of them nod at me like, *So far so good, but keep going, dude.*

"And we have to rehearse the death drop with Manny tomorrow in your garage, but *technically* that's part of your house, right?"

More hopeful nodding. Now I just have to bring it home.

"And the talent show is Friday. So that's also *technically* here at school during the school day."

Julian's eyes widen. "So *technically*, I won't be breaking the rules and I can still compete in the talent show."

I lean back, relaxing my shoulders and feeling a little proud that I just solved my client's problem. That's why I get paid the big bucks. Or at least I will one day.

"That's right," Colton says, eyes sparkling at me. "Wow. You're very good at getting around the rules, Mikey."

I give Colton a casual shrug. "Yeah, Mom says I'm, like, a pro at it."

And there it is. My next brilliant business idea:

Anything Bend-but-Don't-Break-the-Rules
Consulting Services
A division of Anything, Inc.
Michael Pruitt—President, Founder, CEO, and Pro–Rule Bender

23

THE TRYOUTS

I sit at the end of the fifth row in the auditorium after school that day—Julian, Brady, and the Anything Talent and Pizzazz Agency Advisory Committee filling the seats to my left. Stuart's wheelchair is parked in the aisle on my right. Even though he's not trying out for the talent show because of the super-crazy-important birthday party gig he's preparing for, he came to support his agency, which I think is a very nice thing to do.

Sadie stands over by the wall as Fifi naps at her feet. You'd think Fifi would be going crazy with all the noise of the kids in the auditorium, but she looks like she can't be bothered with all that. Sadie hasn't said anything to me yet about the whole Lyla brainwashing/client-stealing/selling-your-soul-to-the-devil thing, but the fact that she didn't come over and sit with us tells me that she probably feels like a big old traitor—which she should. Because she is.

Michael Pruitt Business Tip #368: People and blind, three-legged pit bulls can be very disloyal.

The drama teacher, Mr. Arnold, a tall, skinny man with a curved flattop and dark eyes under thick, round glasses, passes around a clipboard getting everyone's name, email address, and talent description. Dressed today in his usual crisp khaki pants and a perfectly pressed button-down shirt, Mr. Arnold is usually a stickler for the rules. But he was wicked cool about letting Julian audition first when I told him that Julian's dad is super-crazy strict and expects him home right after school. Which is all totally true by the way, so you know, *rules officially bent but not broken.*

Mr. Arnold slowly walks up the aisle, inspecting students and making marks on his sign-up sheet. He stops by Stuart's wheelchair.

"Baxter, I don't see your name on the sign-up list," Mr. Arnold says, staring Stuart down through his big thick glasses.

Mr. Arnold has a hard look in his eye when he says it, like he'd rather be in his tights dancing onstage at the Spoleto Festival right now than dealing with a bunch of show-business amateurs. I know the feeling. Not about dancing in tights at the Spoleto Festival, but the other thing.

"Are you not trying out?" he asks Stuart, clutching the clipboard to his chest like one of us might try to steal it.

"Um, no, sir, I'm not." Stuart smiles politely. "Just here to support my friends."

Mr. Arnold gives him a slightly suspicious nod as he peers down our row over the top of his glasses. "Is that so?"

Dinesh and Trey wave at Mr. Arnold like the nervous dorks they are, but he ignores them, zeroing in on Julian instead.

"Vasquez, you're up first," he says, glancing down at the sign-up sheet. "But you didn't write down what your talent will be."

I want to correct Mr. Arnold and tell him that if you have real talent like my clients, you always have it. And it's not something that *will be* for just ninety seconds on the auditorium stage of North Charleston Middle School. And being a big-time official talent agent, I should know. But I decide to keep my mouth shut because it probably wouldn't be very smart to tell a real show-business professional how to do their job.

Julian looks down the row at me with eyes that scream, *What the heck should I say?*

"Julian dances," I respond to Mr. Arnold in my strong professional voice, because it's true. And that seems like the right thing to say. And the right voice to say it in.

Better to wait and surprise Mr. Arnold with the full-on Coco Caliente, Mistress of Madness and Mayhem experience at the talent show. Pap Pruitt always says it's better to ask for forgiveness than permission, so I guess we know where I got my rule-bending-but-not-breaking talent from.

Mr. Arnold nods. "Do we have your music?"

"Yes, sir," Julian says, pointing down to the first row. "I gave it to Miss Troxel."

Mr. Arnold seems pleased enough with that and walks away. He climbs the stairs to the stage—and with his long dancer legs doesn't take much time at all—and walks over to a microphone stand in the center.

Mr. Arnold leans into the mic. "Okay, middle schoolers, quiet in five . . . four . . . three . . . two . . ."

His voice gets softer and softer as he counts down. And it works, because the crowd noise dies down as he does. *Cool trick.*

"Welcome to the auditions for the North Charleston Middle School end-of-year talent show," Mr. Arnold says, all proud, like he created all talent shows. "Or I should say the talent *contest* this year, because we have a cash prize of one hundred dollars, graciously donated by the Arts Boosters."

Mr. Arnold steps back and claps like the Arts Boosters people are here and he's thanking them. But they're not here and no one else claps, except Miss Troxel in the front row.

"Not everyone here will make it to the live show this Friday," Mr. Arnold continues. "We only have fifteen spots to fill and there are . . ." He counts down the sign-up list with his finger. "It looks like around thirty or so people trying out today."

Wow. Julian, Brady, and Sadie and Fifi need to get into the top fifteen to represent the Anything Talent and Pizzazz Agency and for me to have any chance at earning my commission. I did fill in their information on the sign-up sheet myself after all. And Julian would never have tried out for the talent show if it hadn't been for me. And he wouldn't get to go first today either. I think I've earned every penny of my commission already.

Mr. Arnold gives everyone a real big dose of teacher-grade stink eye. "*Please* remember to keep it to a *tight* ninety. I *will* cut you off if you go over."

Man, he is really serious about his job, which is super-crazy professional of him.

"And no foolishness, people," he adds. "I am *not* having it today."

He points from one section of the auditorium to the next, giving us a silent stare for, like, a whole minute. Like he's putting a no-foolishness spell on everyone.

"First, we have Julian Vasquez," Mr. Arnold finally says, waving Julian up to the stage. "Vasquez?"

Everyone in our row claps like crazy, but no one else in the auditorium does. We all have to stand to let Julian out and it takes a while for him to make it to the end of the row.

"Today, Vasquez," Mr. Arnold says, sounding annoyed—which I think is kind of rude because Julian is a big dude and it takes a little longer for him to get by us.

Julian finally wedges his way free from our row and kind of slow jogs heavily down the aisle to the steps of the stage.

"Earthquake!" someone yells from the back of the auditorium.

If I had any hair on the back of my neck, it would be standing at attention right now. *What the heck? Who the heck?*

Julian hangs his head and slows his jog to a near stop. He looks hurt and embarrassed, and that's a look you don't see very often on his face. He usually doesn't let cracks like that bother him. But I guess with everything going on with his dad, his Miss Coco defenses are down today. Some people laugh and snicker at him and I hate them for it. Most everyone turns in their seat to see who the jerk was that yelled out and I'll give you one guess. *Ding, ding, ding!* You guessed it—Tommy Jenrette. He stands back there behind the last row with Trace and Colby and they're all laughing hysterically. My blood boils and I shoot Tommy a death glare. And when his gaze meets mine, he actually stops laughing. *Wow.* That must have been a Hermione-grade glare I shot him, because it worked *some* kind of magic on him.

Mr. Arnold grabs the microphone stand, pulls it close, and barks their names. "Jenrette. Brown. Williams." His voice booms through the auditorium like the voice of God. "Do you have some business in here? Are you auditioning for the talent contest?" He doesn't give them a chance to answer. "I didn't think so. Out. Now."

Mr. Arnold points to the rear exit as Trace and Colby snicker all the way out the door. Tommy follows them, still not laughing anymore. Trey and Dinesh both look over at me, shaking their heads, as if to say, *Jerks.* Julian lumbers up onto the stage looking a little like he just got punched in the mouth. Our row gives him a last round of applause to let him know we have his back. And it makes me feel super-crazy good inside that Trey and Dinesh are clapping the loudest.

I glance over at Colton, holding up my crossed fingers. He

shows me his also-crossed fingers and smiles. *Blender time!*
I should do a commercial showing how good blenders can
whip up a stomach smoothie in no time flat.

Julian leans over to say something to Mr. Arnold, but we
can't hear him.

"No," Mr. Arnold says into the microphone like he's an-
swering the audience and not Julian. "Your backup dancers do
not have to audition, too. You are the featured performer. If
you get in, they get in."

Mr. Arnold walks off to the side of the stage where a chair
waits patiently for his arrival. Julian stands up there, looking
seriously nervous, and suddenly I'm worried he's going to
chicken out altogether. He shakes it off, though—like, he literally shakes his arms, legs, and head. Finally he nods down to
Miss Troxel in the front row, and she starts his music. One of
Beyoncé's fast, thumpy songs blares through the auditorium.

Julian goes through his routine as Julian Vasquez, Thirteen-
Year-Old Middle Schooler, and not as Coco Caliente, Mistress
of Madness and Mayhem. And without the extra pizzazz of
a wig, a dress, high heels, makeup, and a shablam ending, it
doesn't have the same *wow* factor. I start to panic. Julian *has* to
get to the live show—he just has to. Pap's coming if he's well
enough and I think Coco's my best shot at winning.

Stuart turns to me. "Is that all he does? Why is he pointing
so much?"

I don't answer him. Stuart has never experienced the real
Coco Caliente, so I'm sure he doesn't understand why Julian

is my number one client just going by what he's seeing right now. I glance down our row. Trey is thumbing through a new book, Dinesh is playing a game on his phone, and Brady is studying his new jokes on index cards. They're not even paying attention to Julian. Not a good sign. Colton looks as worried as I feel, nibbling on the tip of his index finger. The song doesn't end fast enough for me, and when it finally does, I let out a lungful of air that I feel like I've been holding since Thursday.

"Thank you, Vasquez," Mr. Arnold calls out over a smattering of semi-polite applause.

I give an extra few claps and whoops to try to make Julian feel better, but I can tell by his sagging face and slumped shoulders that he knows it wasn't his best performance. Let's just hope it was enough to get him into the live show. He doesn't come back to our row, though; he heads straight for the exit. Julian's mom is supposed to pick him up outside and get him home before his dad finds out about this. So I don't worry that he's out in the lobby having a diva meltdown or anything. At least I hope not.

We have to sit through some pretty boring acts while we wait for Brady and Sadie and Fifi to be called. Heather Hobbs thinks she can sing. She can't. It's a good thing God made her smart. Taylor Hope sings, too, but she's actually good. Dustin Parks juggles. He drops three tennis balls, but who's counting? Melissa Chambers recites one of Shakespeare's sonnets like she's getting ready to tongue-kiss the audience. *Ew.* And when did memorizing and reciting become a talent? Heck, even I can do that. Chad Charles does a hip-hop dance that's so good I wish he was my client. It doesn't hurt that Chad Charles is super-crazy cute. But not as super-crazy cute as Colton.

Finally Mr. Arnold says into the microphone, "The Amazing Sadie and Fifi? Please come on up and make it fast, people."

Mr. Arnold must think Fifi is a *people*, too. But he soon sees he's wrong when Sadie guides blind, three-legged Fifi up the stairs. For a second I wonder if Mr. Arnold is going to tell Sadie she can't use a dog in her act because Fifi doesn't go to school here, but he doesn't.

Sadie pulls a few chairs out onto the stage as Fifi sits patiently, *staring* out at the audience waiting for Sadie's commands. There's a restless rumble from kids in the audience, but everyone quiets down when Sadie goes to the front of the stage and nods to Miss Troxel. Music plays through the speakers—a slow song, which surprises me. I would have told Sadie to go with a fast, happy song. But she chose Lyla over me, so *your loss, Sadie. Thank you very much and have a nice day!*

Sadie starts with the whole Fifi-jumping-back-and-forth-over-her-as-she's-down-on-all-fours thing, but then she starts getting real fancy on the chorus of "Wind Beneath My Wings." Why the heck did Lyla tell her to use that old song? But then I glance over at Miss Troxel and Mr. Arnold and— *OMG!*—they both look like they're about to cry. So that's why

Lyla chose that song. Sadie does a lot of tricks that I've never seen her do before and I wonder if Lyla had anything to do with that, too. Sadie has Fifi run through a maze of chairs following the sound of her voice, and Fifi doesn't bump into *any* of the chairs.

Dinesh looks over at me. "That was seriously good, dude."

And I have to admit, it *was* good.

After a couple more new tricks, as the strings of the song sail out through the speakers, I'm starting to wonder if Lyla is a better agent for Sadie and Fifi than me, after all. That's *if* she had anything to do with this new routine. Maybe I wasn't giving the Amazing Sadie and Fifi the attention they deserved. I feel kind of bad about that now. And I wonder if Brady, Stuart, and Charvi have felt the same way—like I've been too focused on Julian.

When Sadie and Fifi bow after the last trick, just about everyone waiting to audition is on their feet clapping—including all of us. If Sadie and Fifi were still my clients, I'd probably be standing on my seat, yelling as loud as I can. But I don't. I just stand and clap politely because that feels like the professional thing to do.

"Well done, Cooper," Mr. Arnold says with his mouth close to the microphone so we can hear him over all the applause. He wipes his cheeks with the back of his hand. "And your little dog, too."

Miss Troxel blows her nose—super-crazy loud—as Sadie guides Fifi down the steps and back over to the wall. She looks at me and I give her two thumbs-up because it's also the professional thing to do. That makes Sadie smile, and I'm sure if Fifi could see me, it would make her smile, too.

Mr. Arnold touches the frames of his glasses, lifting the sign-up sheet closer to his eyes. He kind of slow reads/mumbles to himself, but he's close enough to the microphone that we all can hear.

"Soon to appear on *Later Tonight with Billy Shannon*, America's Junior Comedic Sensation, Brady Hill?" Mr. Arnold plants the hand holding the sign-up sheet on his hip. "What kind of foolishness is this? Do not try my patience, people. Do. Not. Try. Me. Not. Today. Hill? Are you ready, Hill?"

Brady pops up out of his seat and scoots down our row to the end of the aisle a lot faster than Julian did. Stuart high-fives him before Brady heads up to the stage.

"Okay, people, settle down," Mr. Arnold says, pointing to a group of kids who are getting a little loud. "Thompson, don't make me come out there. Settle down, I said."

More Mr. Arnold stink eye. Only when Greg Thompson and his friends settle down does Mr. Arnold take the microphone off the stand and hand it to Brady.

"Hey, everybody," Brady says into the mic as he walks to the edge of the stage. He casually slides one hand into the pocket of his jeans like he's super comfortable onstage and does this all the time. "My name is Brady Hill and I do comedy." He pauses. "Or as Mademoiselle Archer likes to call it, *teaching French.*"

Mademoiselle Archer is our French teacher. And she has a lisp. It's very noticeable when she speaks French, so you know, *not* funny, Brady. The response from the audience is mixed. Some people laugh out loud. Others cover their mouths and giggle. And some just look kind of shocked, like Miss Troxel and Mr. Arnold. *Oops.*

"And how about Mr. Arnold, everyone?" Brady says, pointing to the drama teacher standing on the side of the stage.

A few people clap like they were forced to. Mr. Arnold smiles nervously. I grab the armrests and hold on tight. I'm starting to think that maybe it would be a good idea if Brady keeps his comedic insults focused on anyone other than our teachers.

Brady nods to the crowd as if *everyone* in the auditorium is clapping and not just, like, four people. "That's right. Mr. Arnold is our favorite drama queen."

And—*OMG!*

Several people gasp at the same time, including me. "*Teacher* . . . I mean drama *teacher*," Brady says. He slaps himself on the forehead like he's such an idiot and he obviously meant to say drama *teacher* and not drama *queen*. At least he has the *idiot* part right.

Mr. Arnold's nervous smile melts into a frown. No, he's way past frowning. He's on to *scowling* at Brady. And his stink eye has morphed into a death glare.

Trey leans over to me. "This is bad, dude."

"I know," I whisper back sharply.

Colton leans in, too. "Do something, Mikey."

218

Do something? What the heck am I supposed to do? What does an agent do in a time like this? Go up there and drag the client off the stage? Or trust him to get this train back on the tracks. So I choose the second one, hoping I'm right.

"And Miss Troxel," Brady says. He points down to the front row, where a nervous-looking Miss Troxel sits. "Our awesome guidance counselor. Let's hear it for Miss Troxel, everybody."

Again, a few people clap, but like they were ordered to and not like they actually want to. I hold my breath and grip the armrests even tighter.

"You know, I heard a rumor that Miss Troxel has a new boyfriend," Brady says.

I don't think he has any clue whatsoever that his routine is tanking and making some people downright angry. Mr. Arnold's mouth tightens into a thin line—like this is Brady's last chance to turn this thing around. But it looks like he's going to jump off a cliff instead.

"Yeah," Brady says, smiling down at Miss Troxel, whose whole face is twisted in confusion. "Turns out, though, she's been dating this guy for years! And you can tell who he is just by looking at her." Brady holds the mic close to his mouth. "His name is Colonel Sanders."

Brady pauses with a stupid grin on his face, waiting for people to lose their minds laughing. But they don't. Just a few muffled snickers here and there. Others groan—including me.

He points down at poor Miss Troxel, whose usually pasty-white skin has turned splotchy-red. "Looks like he's been giving her a great discount at KFC, am I right?"

Stuart looks over at me, shaking his head real slow-like.

"Whoa," Trey says in an ominous whisper.

"Oh no, he didn't," Dinesh says.

"Oh yes, he did," Colton and I say at the same time.

Brady taps the microphone. "Is this thing on?" He gives a little nervous laugh. I think it's finally sinking in that he's bombing.

That's as far as he gets before Mr. Arnold snatches the microphone from his hand, guiding him pretty forcefully off the stage.

"What did I say about foolishness, people," Mr. Arnold says into the mic. He walks back to the center of the stage. "Do. Not. Try. Me."

Brady walks down the steps and up the aisle toward our row, looking confused and deflated. And I feel as bad as he looks. I think I just failed my second client.

Michael Pruitt Business Tip #369 (learned the hard way, like, just now): Always review and approve your comedy talent's new material before letting them try it out in front of real-live people like your plus-size guidance counselor and your maybe-gay drama teacher.

24

THE SHABLAM

"Hit Refresh again," I say.

"I just did," Lyla whines. "It's not there yet."

It's the day after the talent-show tryouts—also known as the day of Manny the drag queen's shablam class in Julian's garage. Lyla sits in one of the metal folding chairs in front of the stage with my laptop balancing scarily on her swinging legs. I have her watching the school website, where Mr. Arnold will be posting the final list of kids who made it into this Friday's talent show. It should be up any time now. In fact, he said it would be there by four o'clock and according to my flip phone, he's already five minutes late. Very unprofessional.

"Hit it again," I say, irritated but trying not to lose my temper because that only makes Lyla *more* of a pain in the butt. *"Please,* Lyla."

Manny the drag queen has been teaching Julian how to do the death drop for, like, the last gazillion minutes. It was pretty scary to watch at first. I thought Julian was going to break a leg or his back or his butt. But thankfully he has a lot of natural padding and now at least he knows how to do it, even if it still looks kind of messy and clumsy. Manny says Julian just has to *commit, papi* and go for it. And even though he's sort of dressed in boy clothes right now, Manny's a real-live professional drag queen. So he probably knows what he's talking about more than I do. *Probably.*

"Where are my backup dancers?" Manny barks from the stage. He and Julian stand there, sweating and panting.

Lyla sets my laptop on the chair beside her and stands. "Sorry. I have to go use my talent for someone who appreciates it," she tells me.

Was that supposed to be a burn? *Lame.* She joins Gabby onstage. The two of them stand in a starting position a few feet behind Julian, who's still bummed out about not doing his best at the talent contest tryouts. He doesn't think he's even going to make it to the live show, but I told him not to give up hope because, as his official agent, that's my job. Giving him pep talks, I mean. Not giving up hope.

Colton gives Gabby and Lyla a couple of last-minute instructions. I didn't have any idea that Colton could dance or that he could come up with a whole dance routine on his own and teach it to other people. On *RuPaul's Drag Race*, they call that *choreography*, which is just a fancy word for teaching someone how to do a dance that you come up with all on your own. Colton said he spent summers helping his mom in her dance studio in Columbia before she started having *problems*, lost all her clients, and had to close the business. He got kind of sad when he was telling me about that part, so I didn't ask a lot of questions. But he must have learned a lot watching his mom work all those summers because he's super-crazy good at choreography.

I knew Gabby was like a professional kid dancer, but I was surprised at how fast Lyla picked up the steps. That's what Colton calls them. *Steps.* And they went over the steps so many times when we first got here that I feel like I could probably do the steps pretty good myself. Maybe I should start a new business with Colton. We could be partners. Colton could teach other kids how to dance and I could handle the business side of things because creative people like Colton aren't usually good with all that stuff. Maybe we start with one studio here in North Charleston and then branch out all over the world. We could call it:

Anything Dance Studio of North Charleston and Beyond
A division of Anything, Inc.
Michael Pruitt—President, Founder, CEO,
and Business-Stuff Manager
Colton Sanford—Creative Director, Head Choreographer,
and Wicked-Cool-Smiling Expert

All of a sudden I realize I haven't been bossing anyone around for, like, thirty minutes. So I stand up and walk over to the edge of the stage.

"Okay, people," I say in my strong professional-boss voice.

"Let's get a move on. We don't have all day and time is money." That's what Dad says sometimes to his workers when they're out on a landscaping job.

Everyone stares at me from the stage. Manny looks at me like I was speaking a foreign language and not one of the two he understands—English and Spanish. He walks over to the edge of the stage right in front of me and leans down, giving me a hard look full of smoky black eyeliner, a silver hoop nose ring, and ruby-red lips.

"Listen to me carefully, little boy," he says, pointing a finger in my face. "Right now, this is *my* house and *I'm* in charge. So why don't you go sit down and let me do my job, capisce?"

Colton, Julian, and Gabby stand behind him looking like they're holding their breath and afraid for my life. I want to remind Manny that this is a *favor* he is doing and not an actual *job*. Because I don't have any money to pay him with and I hope Trey told him that when he set this up.

I clear my throat and stand up straight. "Okay, then. Good work, everyone. Great job on the choreography, Colton. And, Julian, just *commit, papi!*"

No reaction. From anyone. I think they're all scared of Manny, except Lyla, that is. She gazes up at him like he's Hello Kitty in the flesh. And he kind of looks like Hello Kitty with his cutoff blue overalls and that pink bow glued to his shiny bald head.

"I'll just go back over there to my seat and check to see if Mr. Arnold has posted the talent-show list yet. He's late, you know. Very unprofessional of him." I nod at Manny. "Mr. Manny, please continue."

Manny doesn't say anything, but he does give me a crooked smile. Well, a *sort of* smile. Then he turns back to Julian, Gabby, and Lyla, counting them off with sharp claps.

I think I handled that pretty well.

Michael Pruitt Business Tip #370: Always keep a firm hand with your subordinates, but it's helpful to give them praise and a little room to do their own thing once in a while. The results just might surprise you.

While everyone onstage is dancing to the beat of Manny's clapping and counting, I hit the Refresh button again for the umpteenth time.

Refresh.

Nothing.

Julian is going to be so bummed out if he doesn't make it into the show.

Refresh.

Nada.

Colton's wicked-cool dance routine will go to waste.

Refresh. Refresh.

Zip.

Mom and Dad are planning to pick up Pap Pruitt from Prince George and bring him to the big show on Friday, as long as Pap doesn't get sick again. He's really had a hard time lately with his diabetes and his heart condition. But I want him to be there when Anything Talent and Pizzazz Agency wins the big prize so bad because I know he'll be super-crazy proud of me. Heck, it might even make him feel better and get well faster.

Refresh. Refresh. Refresh.

Ding, ding, ding!

There it is. Right there on the home page of the school website like Mr. Arnold said it would be. My heart races as I scan down the list of fifteen acts.

Taylor Hope. *Duh.*

Chad Charles. *Double duh.*

Heather Hobbs. *What?!*

The Amazing Sadie and Fifi. *Whatever.*

Dustin Parks. *Really, Mr. Arnold? He dropped three balls!*

Now I feel like my stomach is doing a shablam because I don't see Brady's or Julian's name and I'm getting closer to the bottom of the list. So I speed up. Like ripping off a Band-Aid, I read the rest of the names real fast, but I still don't see them. Then my eyes land on the last name on the list and I finally let out the breath I didn't realize I had been holding in.

Julian Vasquez. *Whew! That was close.*

I'm seriously bummed that Brady didn't make the cut, but it was pretty clear that he didn't make any friends on the judging panel with all his new material making fun of teachers and staff. Rookie mistake, though. He can still bounce back, with my guidance and direction.

I shoot up out of my seat, carrying my laptop to the edge of the stage. I clear my throat, but no one pays attention. So I do it a whole lot louder. Finally Manny spins on his platform-heel boots.

He claps on every word. "What. Is. It. Little. Boy? What. Do. You. Want?"

I can't help grinning from ear to ear because I know that it doesn't matter what Manny the drag queen thinks. Right now I'm the most important person in this garage and he doesn't scare me anymore. I hold the laptop up and turn it so they can see the screen. Colton's eyes widen, but Julian's grow dark and fearful—until he sees the last name on the list.

I look him straight in the eyes and say the words that all professional talent agents like me are born to say.

"You got the gig."

25

THE WICKED-COOL MASK

The last week of school continues to slog by, one dumb final exam after another. I think I do pretty good on my social studies exam. Math, not so much. In homeroom on Friday morning, everyone's talking about their plans for the summer, starting with Memorial Day cookouts and pool parties on Monday. It's a half day of classes and then the talent show takes place in the auditorium after the last exam period. Everybody seems pretty excited about it. Except Brady because he didn't get in, and the athletes because they think it's dumb and hate that the whole school is required to go. I guess they think we should end the school year with some kind of sports event, but to that idea I say *no, thank you very much and have a nice day.*

But ever since Dad told me last night that Pap Pruitt's blood pressure shot way up yesterday and he won't be able to come today, I'm finding it hard to get excited about anything—the big show, the last day of school, Julian's death drop, any of it. I wanted Pap to be there so badly. I wanted him to see the Anything Talent and Pizzazz Agency succeed. I wanted to make him proud.

I glance over my shoulder at Colton. He sits at his desk digging a fingernail into the wood and not talking to anyone. He actually looks kind of down, too. I wonder if he's worried about a final exam today. Or maybe he's worried about Julian's performance at the gig later. I glance back to the front of the class. Poor Mrs. Campbell gave up trying to settle everyone down a while ago. An older white lady who's been at North Charleston Middle School since they built the place, she's barely managed to keep us in our seats today. Right now she's at her desk, reading a book and hardly even paying attention to us. So I slip out of my seat to talk to Colton.

I kneel beside his desk so Mrs. Campbell doesn't see me. "Hey. What's up?"

Colton gives me a half smile—not the full-on freckles, sparkly white teeth, stomach-blender treatment.

"Hey," he says with a sigh, his shoulders slumping.

We just kind of stare at each other for an awkward second or two, waiting for the other to say something. He doesn't, so I do.

"I'm getting really nervous about the talent show," I say. "Julian has some stiff competition and he said he's been having trouble perfecting the death drop."

He nods. "I know. He really has to bring it."

More fingernail digging into the desk. Something's up, but I'm not sure if Colton wants to talk about it.

"My mom got out of rehab yesterday," he says, holding my gaze like he wants to see how I will react.

It sounds like good news, but Colton doesn't look super-crazy excited about it.

"That's great, right?"

He shifts in the seat. "My grandma and I went to pick her up, but when we got there, they said she'd already left *with a friend.*"

Colton shakes his head on those last three words, like his mom has done this kind of thing before.

"I shouldn't be surprised, though," he says, his shiny reddish-brown hair hanging down over his eyes. "When she was using drugs, she always made promises she didn't keep. Most of the time I felt more like the parent." He stops digging into the desk with his fingernail. "I was just kind of hoping, since she's been in rehab getting better, that she'd be here for the talent show today." He glances over at me and pushes his hair out of his eyes. "I really wanted her to see the dance I choreographed. Grandma left her three messages about it last night. But she also laid into Mom for taking off like that without telling us, so I doubt she will want to face Grandma anytime soon."

I don't know what to say to him. I don't actually know what it's like to have a mom or dad who has problems like Colton's mom does. And my parents would never leave me or not show up to something I'm a part of. I never really thought about how lucky I am that way. I also realize that Colton's been hiding a lot of sad stuff behind that wicked-cool smile of his. Like a mask. I guess you just never know what's going on with someone, even if they seem okay and wear a mask that's nice to look at.

"I'm sorry, Colton," I say, because it's all I can think of. *Lame.*

Colton waves a hand in front of me like he's waving his mom right out of his head. "It's okay. I'm used to it."

I want to hug him, because that seems like the good-friend thing to do. But we're right in the middle of homeroom. And if we hugged, all the kids would think that's super gay—which is funny because of the whole me-being-gay thing. I'm still not 100 percent sure about Colton, though. My gaydar needs a tune-up. Or a jump start. There should be a place where you can go to have that done. Like a gaydar service station or something.

"Pap Pruitt can't come today," I say, because I can't think of anything else to say.

Colton's eyebrows scrunch up. "Is he okay?"

I shake my head. "He's really sick. He's had diabetes for a long time. It even made him blind. Now he's having problems with his heart."

Colton sighs a little. "I'm sorry, Mikey. I know you wanted him to be here."

I nod. "I did. He's my hero. I just wanted to make him proud."

"Mikey Pruitt." Mrs. Campbell's sharp voice slices through the air. "Back to your seat."

Colton gives me the wicked-cool mask smile. The one I now know doesn't always mean everything is okay.

"Busted," he says.

I smile, too. "Yep. See you at the rehearsal before the show."

"Oh," Colton says, sparking back to life a little. "I forgot. Julian's mom and abuela are bringing his wardrobe during the rehearsal period. Do you think Trey and Dinesh could help them load everything in? I'll be busy helping Julian with his makeup."

"Bringing his *whole* wardrobe?" I stand so Mrs. Campbell thinks I'm going back to my seat. "But we already decided which dress Coco will wear. The red sparkly one."

"He said he needs options depending on *his mood*," Colton says, using air quotes on those last two words.

I roll my eyes super-crazy slow as if to say, *Divas, am I right?* That makes Colton laugh. I like the sound of his laugh. I wish he felt like laughing all the time.

"I guess his dad still doesn't know about the talent show?" I say, starting to move away so Mrs. Campbell doesn't yell at me again.

Colton shakes his head. "And Julian hopes he never finds out."

"I don't know," I say. "I kind of think it would be good for Mr. Vasquez to see Julian perform. Like in front of an audience, you know? Then he might get it."

That gives me a great idea. At least I hope it's a great idea.

"Now, Mikey," Mrs. Campbell says, using a sharper tone than before.

"Yes, ma'am," I say over my shoulder.

"Hey, Mikey," Colton says, his mouth curling up on one side. "I'm sure Pap Pruitt is already wicked proud of you."

What he said kind of makes my eyes itch, but I'm afraid if I talk any more about Pap Pruitt, my eyes will do a whole lot more than just itch.

I just nod, smile, and wave at him like some kind of dork. "See you at rehearsal." *Lame.*

But Colton waves back and shoots me the full-on stomach-blender smile. So, you know, totally worth it.

26

THE VERY UNPROFESSIONAL
REHEARSAL

I should start a new business where I go around to middle schools all over the country supervising and organizing their year-end talent shows. I could call it:

Anything School Talent Shows R Us
A division of Anything, Inc.
Michael Pruitt—President, Founder, CEO, and Talent-Show Guru

I've always wanted to be a guru of something. And Mr. Arnold should be my first client, because the rehearsal period before the talent show is a complete disaster. Nobody knows what's going on, or what the order of the show will be, and there's no catering table or private agents' lounge or anything. It's very unprofessional and I'm super-crazy disappointed in Mr. Arnold because, being in show business, he should know better.

Miss Troxel is helping all she can, but backstage it's like

a zoo where all the animals have been let out of their cages. Only Taylor Hope and Dustin Parks have been able to rehearse onstage and that leaves thirteen acts to go before the show starts in, like, thirty minutes. I'm not great at math, but it seems like we're screwed. My board of directors showed up late with Lyla, and she didn't even have her dance costume on. I sent her and Mom to the girls' bathroom down the hall to change. Lyla rolled her eyes at me, so I'm going to write her up as soon as I get back to the office. *Document, document, document.*

"Hey, bud."

I turn to find my dad standing there, looking a little lost. His eyes are red and puffy. I'm not sure if that's because he's been crying or because he spent the night at the nursing home with Pap. He probably didn't get much sleep.

"Hey, Dad," I say, shoving my hands down in my pockets, like some kind of defense mechanism against bad news.

Dad has his serious look. And that's a look I don't see on him a lot.

"What's wrong?" I ask cautiously. "Is Pap okay?"

Dad doesn't shake his head no, so that's a good sign. But he doesn't nod yes, either.

"I stopped by to check in on him on the way here," Dad says. "His blood pressure is still high and he's pretty weak. Mrs. Prosser said she would call if there's any change."

I nod and swallow back a huge lump in my throat.

"He wants you to know that he wishes he could be here and that he's rooting for you," Dad says with a weak smile. "He said to tell you that whether your clients win or lose today, you're already a huge success as far as he's concerned. And he's proud of you."

Another huge lump. Another swallow. Because it's like I hear the words for the very first time. Pap already thinks I'm a success. He's already proud of me. Now that I think about it, he's told me he's proud of me, like, a gazillion times. So have Mom and Dad. Maybe Pap isn't the person I've been trying to impress all this time. Maybe it was me. Maybe what I really need is to be proud of myself.

Dad puts a hand on my shoulder. "I'd better go find your mom and get seats."

All I can do is nod. No idea where my voice went. But Dad must get it, because he pulls me in for a huge bear hug and then leaves.

"Where do these go?" Trey asks. He's helping Dinesh carry a big trunk with a handheld steamer balancing on top.

Dinesh grunts, switching hands on the trunk handle. "Why did he bring so much stuff? He can only wear, like, one outfit, right?"

I take a deep breath and try to get my head back in the game, because I know that's what Pap would want me to do.

"He said he wanted options," I say, giving them my divas-am-I-right? slow eye roll. "Just put it over there by the wall."

I follow them, pulling out my flip phone to check the time

236

and to see if I missed any calls. I left Mr. Vasquez a message a while ago at his car dealership. *Thanks, Google!* I just hope he gets it in time.

I glance back at Trey and Dinesh. "I don't think he's going to get to rehearse if he's just now deciding what to wear."

Fifi barks somewhere in the chaos and I see that she and Sadie are running through their routine on the stage. It looks super-crazy good. I know I should be rooting for Sadie and Fifi, too, and I guess I am, *kind of,* but I just want Julian to win. Julian's mom and abuela walk into the backstage area with Gabby trailing them. Gabby already has her dance costume on and I think that's very professional of her, unlike Lyla showing up without hers on.

"Don't forget the big box of wigs in the back seat, boys," Mrs. Vasquez says to Trey and Dinesh with a nervous smile. "And the bag of shoes, too."

Trey and Dinesh nod politely, heading back out. I can hear them grumbling a little as they walk away, though.

Mrs. Vasquez fiddles with Gabby's hair. "Sorry we're late."

Abuela turns, wringing her hands as she scans the backstage area. "Where is Julian?"

"In the bathroom with Colton, putting on his Coco Caliente face. He brought most of his makeup to school in his backpack."

"Smart boy, that one," Abuela says. She relaxes a little and pats my arm. "Always thinking."

Mrs. Vasquez looks around, nervously wringing her hands like Abuela was just doing.

"Is everything okay?" I ask her. "You guys seem nervous."

"I just hope my husband doesn't find out about this," Mrs. Vasquez says. "He's never seen Julian actually perform as Coco before. Especially in public." She shakes her head. "As good as Julian is, I know his father is not ready for that."

And—*OMG! I hope she's wrong about that.*

Abuela pats Mrs. Vasquez's arm, nodding. "My son is sometimes too much like his father—stubborn and set in his ways."

Mrs. Vasquez covers Abuela's hand with her own and smiles at me. "Don't get us wrong, Michael. My husband loves his son very much. They used to be so close, before Julian started playing *dress up* in my clothes."

Abuela covers her mouth and chuckles at that. "He was so cute and sassy, even back then."

"I had a few drag queen friends of my own when I was young," Mrs. Vasquez sort of whispers to me. "I was a bit of a party girl before I met Julian's father."

There's a mischievous twinkle in her eye that I haven't seen before. But I still don't think now would be a good time to tell Mrs. Vasquez about the message I left her husband, so I'm glad when Gabby pipes up.

"Where's Lyla?" she asks.

And speak of the devil, Lyla walks up in her dance costume.

"Hey, Gabs," she says with a casual wave like she's not late at all.

Gabs?

They're dressed like identical twins in short, sparkly red-and-white dresses with big purple bows pinned in their hair. Julian *finally* chose the song "Born This Way" by Miss Lady Gaga for the routine. It's a song about being proud of exactly who you are and how God made you because you were, well, you know, *born that way*. It makes perfect sense in my heart. I just wish it did in my head.

"Mom and Dad are getting seats in the auditorium before they let all the students in," Lyla says. "When are we going to rehearse?"

"Here's the rest of it," Trey says, huffing behind me.

I turn as he and Dinesh walk up, dropping the box of wigs and bag of shoes on the floor with a thud. Julian and Colton are coming right behind them.

"Careful with that," Julian barks.

And—*OMG!* Julian looks like a scary clown-ghost with all his makeup on while still just wearing black sweatpants, a T-shirt, and no wig.

"Miss Troxel said she doesn't have my music," he says to me in a sharp diva-like tone. "Did you give it to her?"

"Yeah, I gave it to her," I say. I'm a little annoyed that he's questioning me—his agent.

I gave it to her, right?

"We need to rehearse, Mikey," Lyla whines. "On the stage with the lights and music and everything. Before the show."

Gabby nods. "Lyla's right."

Colton looks at me with raised eyebrows. "They do need to go through the routine. Will there be time?"

How should I know?

"Fifi," Sadie's voice calls out backstage. "Where's my dog? Fifi? Girl?" She comes over to us. "Have you guys seen Fifi? She was right beside me and then she was just gone."

"Um, no," I say. "Maybe you should ask your *agent*."

The hurt look in Sadie's eyes makes me wish I could suck the words right back into my big fat mouth.

"Harsh, dude," Dinesh says quietly beside me.

"I'm sorry, Sadie," I stammer. "I'm sure Fifi—"

"Michael," snaps Julian the scary clown-ghost. "Where. Is. My. Music?"

I sigh. *How should I know? I gave it to Miss Troxel. Right?*

"Excuse me," Mr. Arnold says, walking up to us wearing a headset microphone. But he doesn't say it like he's asking us to excuse him. More like he's saying, *Excuse me, what the heck do you think you're doing?* And he's staring right at Gabby and Lyla.

"Who are these children and why are they wearing these inappropriate costumes?" he says to me.

I think he says it to me, anyway. Maybe he can sense that I'm the real boss around here. I get that.

"Mr. Arnold," I say. "This is my sister, Lyla, and Julian's sister, Gabby. They're Julian's backup dancers. Remember he told you at the tryouts that he would have backup dancers."

Mr. Arnold shakes his head. "Oh no, ma'am."

And, no, I don't know why Mr. Arnold just called me, a twelve-year-old boy, *ma'am*. And, no, I don't know why his head is going from side to side like it's about to come off his shoulders and shoot up into the rafters.

He points a finger at me. "It is clearly stated in the rules that I posted online with the final list of contestants that only North Charleston Middle School students are allowed to participate in the talent show. And I'm positive that these two little girls do not go to school here."

"Rules?" Julian says. "What rules? Michael, you didn't tell us about any rules."

Mrs. Vasquez exchanges words with Abuela in Spanish. And now everyone is looking at me—Sadie because Fifi is missing, Julian because Miss Troxel can't find his music, and Gabby and Lyla because it sounds like Mr. Arnold is not going to let them dance in the show.

"What?" Mr. Arnold says. He glances away and touches his finger to the earpiece of the headset. "What do you mean he has the flu?"

We're all quiet, waiting for Mr. Arnold's head to finally blast off into outer space. "Yes, I know what the flu is, *Miss Troxel*. But he's supposed to be here." He listens. "Well, what am I supposed to do now? Who's going to emcee the show?"

Now even Mr. Arnold is staring at me because I guess he just lost his emcee and doesn't know what to do. Everyone is looking at me for answers. Julian. Mr. Arnold. Sadie. Colton. Gabby and Lyla. Even my best friends, Trey and

Dinesh, because they're a couple of busybodies who love when there's all kinds of trouble going on and want to see how everything turns out.

I close my eyes and repeat over and over in my head:

WWPD?

WWPD?

WWPD?

What would Pap do?

Pap may not be here in person tonight, but I know he's here in spirit.

Finally, a wave of calm blankets me from head to toe.

Michael Pruitt Business Tip #371 (learned just this second): Being a super-successful talent agent is all about one thing: solving problems.

I turn to face Dinesh. "Charvi's supposed to be here, right?"

Dinesh pushes his glasses up the bridge of his nose and nods real fast. "Yesterday was her last day of classes, so she came to support the agency."

"Good. Take Sadie and go find Charvi," I say. "Maybe she'll be able to sense where Fifi is."

"But she interprets dreams," Dinesh says.

Sadie grabs Dinesh's hand, pulling him away. "It's worth a try. Let's go."

"Trey," I say, pointing at his chest because that seems like the professional thing to do at a time like this.

Trey stands at attention, shoulders back and chin up. "Yes, my dude."

"Go out front, find Brady, and get him back here right now."

"On it," Trey says with a dorky salute, and he's off. Because when you're a best friend, you don't require a lot of explanations. If your buddy needs something, that's good enough.

I turn to Mr. Arnold. "Mr. Arnold, Brady can emcee the show because he's America's Junior Comedic Sensation and he's hilarious, and I guarantee you that he won't insult anyone. Especially not you and Miss Troxel. He's real sorry about all that. And it was actually my fault anyway because I'm his agent and I didn't review his new material before he tried it out in public. My bad."

Mr. Arnold eyes me suspiciously, but he knows he doesn't have a whole lot of options right now. "Fine. But there'd better not be any foolishness, Pruitt. Do. Not. Try. Me."

I nod at him and then walk over to Mrs. Vasquez. "Mrs. V. You know what the flash drive with Julian's music looks like, right?"

She nods. "Yes, of course I do."

"Will you go down to the front row and help Miss Troxel find it?" I ask.

"Yes," she says with a determined look. "I can do that."

There's a ruckus coming from the auditorium, so I guess the doors are opening. Students pour in, noisily finding seats.

I scan the audience and spot Mom and Dad. They see me and wave. I don't wave back. That would be middle school suicide if someone like Tommy Jenrette saw me. I just act like I've never seen those people before in my life because that seems like the smart thing to do. Thankfully, someone pulls the stage curtain closed. It's a lot darker backstage now.

For some reason I whisper to myself, "All we need is a dream and a prayer."

I take a deep breath in and exhale slowly. It's like I can feel Pap right here with me, cheering me on. I smile.

Mr. Arnold claps his hands twice. "Okay, people, I'm sorry that we ran out of time and all of you didn't get a chance to rehearse onstage, but nevertheless we go live in five minutes. Five minutes, people, and *do not try me*."

"What about my backup dancers?" Julian paces around us and looks like he's about to cry. "Gaga has backup dancers. So does Beyoncé. And Ariana. Coco Caliente *needs* backup dancers. What are we going to do, Michael?"

Julian is definitely losing his Coco Caliente confidence, so I have to do something fast. I glance over at Gabby and Lyla, who are off pouting by the back wall. I can't fix everyone's dreams today. Gabby and Lyla are young. They'll have another shot. But this is probably definitely Julian's last chance to perform as Coco Caliente, Mistress of Madness and Mayhem, in front of the entire student body of North Charleston Middle School and to show all the haters what a drag-kid superstar looks like. And I got him here. I'm not going to let him do it

244

halfway. Pap always says, *If something is worth doing, it's worth doing right.* And as much as I'm sure I'm not ready for this, I have to do it for my client. And for Pap, too.

I look over at Colton. "Are you ready to be the wrong kind of middle school popular?"

Colton might already have guessed my plan, because he smiles at me bigger than he ever has before and my stomach goes right back into that blender. On High. Stomach-smoothie time.

"That's already kind of my thing," Colton says. "So, sure."

I turn to Julian. "We're going to need to borrow some of your clothes. And, Abuela, Julian told me you make all of his Coco outfits. Did you bring your sewing kit?"

She nods, looking confused. "Of course. I never go anywhere without it."

A look of surprise covers Julian's face for a moment or two, but finally he lets out a big sigh. His face softens and a mischievous grin spreads across his face. "Come on, girl. Let's do this."

We all follow him over to his wardrobe trunk, and weirdly enough, I'm not even a little embarrassed that Julian just called me *girl.*

27

THE NORTH CHARLESTON MIDDLE SCHOOL END-OF-YEAR TALENT CONTEST

Taylor Hope nails her song.

Chad Charles's hip-hop dance routine is good enough to be in a movie or on television, and I don't even mean that just because he's so cute.

Dustin Parks doesn't drop any tennis balls and gets one of the biggest rounds of applause yet.

The competition is super-crazy tough and I'm starting to get a little worried for Julian. What if the audience doesn't get it? Or if they just don't like him? Or if they're mean because Julian will be wearing a dress, a wig, and high heels onstage? Heck, the other students might not even recognize him. He's full-on Coco Caliente, Mistress of Madness and Mayhem, now. I can't even see Julian anymore when I look at him. And in the end, he went with the sparkly red dress and the blond wig with pink and purple highlights just like we'd always planned. *Divas, am I right?*

I'm just trying to keep us all out of Mr. Arnold's sight before we go on. He might call this all *foolishness* and say we are *trying him*. So we stand on the opposite side of the backstage area taking turns peeking through the curtains at the audience. I scan the crowd for my special guest, but I don't see him anywhere yet.

"She found it!" Mrs. Vasquez hurries over to us, looking a little flushed but thankfully smiling. "You *did* give Miss Troxel the flash drive, Michael. It was on the floor under her chair."

Whew! Thank you very much, Mrs. Vasquez, and have a nice day!

Julian straightens his wig. "Sorry I yelled at you, Michael. I should have trusted you."

I shrug like it's no big deal, but secretly it is. "That's okay."

Mrs. Vasquez's face twists in confusion as she scans me and Colton up and down, and who could blame her. We're dressed *way* different than we were when she saw us earlier. Eventually she gets it and a smile explodes on her face.

"Don't they look great?" Abuela says, smiling at me and Colton. I think she's really proud of her last-minute handiwork, and she should be.

"You both look adorable." Mrs. Vasquez takes Abuela's hand. "We're going to sit with Gabby, Lyla, and your parents." She faces Julian and smooths out the sleeves of his dress with her free hand. "Good luck, mijo. You look beautiful. I'm so proud of you."

"Thanks, Mom." Julian grins from ear to ear.

He's so tall in the high heels that he has to lean way down to air-kiss his mom on the cheek. While he's down there, he gives Abuela one, too.

Brady's voice booms through the auditorium speakers. "Coming up next, we have a very talented performer, folks. She's seventy-seven years old, she's blind, and she has three legs."

There's some nervous laughter from the audience, and who could blame them with that setup?

"I'm just kidding, folks." Brady pauses a beat. "She's only eleven in dog years!"

The audience laughs a little less nervously now.

"Crap," Colton says, slinging his bright red wig hair over his shoulder. "It's time for Sadie and Fifi, but they haven't found Fifi yet."

"Yes, they have," Julian says, pointing to the stage door. Dinesh and Charvi lead Sadie and Fifi over to us. Fifi sniffs everyone, her tail going ninety miles an hour.

"You found her!" I say to Dinesh. "Where was she?"

But he just stares at Colton and me with his mouth hanging open like we're aliens from another planet.

"Wow, my dude," he says to me. "Or should I say, my *dudette*?"

I roll my eyes at him. "Don't even start."

"No," Dinesh says, taking a step back to inspect us. "You both are actually kind of pretty."

I don't know whether to say thank you or what to that, so I just act like I didn't hear him.

248

Sadie doesn't give Colton and me a second look. "Charvi was amazing. She sensed where Fifi was hiding."

Charvi also doesn't seem all that surprised at seeing me and Colton in makeup, short dresses, and wigs. Weird.

"She wasn't hiding," Charvi says. "I just sensed that Fifi might have needed to go to the bathroom."

"She sniffed her way to the courtyard," Dinesh says with a crinkled nose. He waves a hand in front of his face. "And, man, did Fifi have to *go*." He gives me another look and shakes his head like he still thinks I'm pretty. "I'm going to go find Trey and my parents and sit down. I can't wait to see where all this is going."

Brady's voice interrupts our little reunion with Fifi.

"But don't feel bad for Fifi the blind pit bull because she only has three legs," Brady says from the stage. "I mean, that's one more than we have, am I right?"

There's actually a decent amount of laughter from the audience.

"Fifi already has a *leg up* on all of us," Brady says to more laughter.

Now even Mr. Arnold is chuckling from the other side of the stage.

"You guys are on," I whisper to Sadie. This should be Lyla's job as their new agent, but that's what you get when you go with someone inexperienced and unqualified. "You ready?"

"Yeah," Sadie says, kneeling and scratching Fifi's head, I guess for good luck. "Hey, Mikey, I'm sorry about the whole

249

wanting-Lyla-to-be-my-agent-instead-of-you thing. I think I might have made a mistake. I mean she's pretty smart for a kid, but she can be kind of intense sometimes. Do you think you could be our agent again?"

Michael Pruitt Business Tip #372: There are times to make people sweat a little before you forgive them and take them back, but right before they go onstage to possibly win a hundred dollars for your talent agency is not one of those times.

"Sure, Sadie," I say with a smile. "That would be wicked cool."

"The Amazing Sadie and Fifi," Brady calls out, stepping back and waving Sadie onto the stage.

Colton, Julian, and I peek through the curtains, watching the crowd go crazy when Fifi waddles out onto the stage. Mom and Dad smile and clap from the third row. Julian's mom, Abuela, Gabby, and Lyla sit beside them. Trey and Dinesh are sitting in the fourth row with their parents, Manny and Stuart on the end of the aisle. The auditorium is packed. Every seat is taken and some parents and teachers stand lining the walls. That's called *standing room only*. It's a real show-biz thing. But I still don't see my special guest anywhere.

"I wonder where my grandma is," Colton whispers beside me, lines of worry etched in his face.

"Wait, isn't that her standing over there by the back door?"

Julian whispers, pushing strands of his blond wig out of his face. "Who is that woman with her?"

"Oh yeah," Colton says, the muscles in his face relaxing. "I see her now. And that's—my—my—"

I think I know what Colton is trying to say. I put a hand on his shoulder. "Is that your mom?"

But he doesn't answer me. He just stares out through the curtain, his eyes growing cloudy.

"She came," Colton finally says, his voice cracking a little. "She actually came."

I don't know what to say. My throat closes up and my eyes itch real bad. So I don't say anything, and that seems okay.

Colton and Julian step away from the curtain, but I keep watching Colton's mom. Her hair is pulled back into a loose ponytail, and she stands with her arms wrapped around her stomach. She's wearing jeans and an orange hoodie with the Clemson Tigers logo on it. She stares out into the audience as Sadie and Fifi wrap up their routine and Miss Bette Midler plows into the big dramatic high part of "Wind Beneath My Wings." The performance wasn't quite as good as their audition. Fifi was slow and a little sluggish after all the excitement of being lost. She tripped a couple of times. But I hope it was good enough for the judges.

I'm about to pull the curtain closed when I spot a big man standing just inside the center door of the auditorium, arms crossed tight and high on his chest, and—*OMG!*—it's Julian's dad. He came. He must have gotten my message. I let the curtain fall into place.

"Michael?" Julian says with his arm around Colton. "What is it? You look like you've just seen a ghost."

I don't know what to say. Should I tell him that his dad is here right before he performs or wait until after? And should I tell my client that I'm the one who invited his dad? I don't want to get in his head and ruin his concentration right before he goes onstage. But I guess I waited too long.

"Jesus, Mary, and Joseph," Julian says, peering out through the crack in the curtain above me. "What's my dad doing here?"

I step back from the curtain. "I, um—" I say. "I called and invited him."

Julian's gaze is ice-cold. *"You did what?"*

Sadie and Fifi take their bow and the curtain closes in front of them. Sadie's smile isn't as big as it usually is after they perform, and neither is Fifi's. I think they both realize the performance wasn't their best. I feel bad for them, but I'm more worried about my star client having a meltdown right now. Julian wasn't expecting his dad to meet Coco today. I hope I didn't make a huge mistake thinking it would help their relationship if Mr. Vasquez saw Julian perform and how talented he is. But my news has knocked the wind out of Julian's sails. He stares up into the rafters in a daze.

I touch his shoulder to get his attention. "Julian. Look at me."

He stares at me like he's in a trance.

"Coco," I say, snapping my fingers in front of his face because that seems like the smart thing to do at a time like this. *"Coco Caliente.* Are you in there?"

It takes a few seconds, but finally Coco's mascaraed eyes light up like she can hear me from somewhere deep inside Julian's fear.

"That's *Julian's* father out there, not yours. Because you are Coco Caliente, Mistress of Madness and Mayhem, and Miss Coco isn't afraid of *anything.* Coco is the baddest drag kid in all of North Charleston Middle School."

Colton cocks his head at me. "Are there many other drag kids in North Charleston Middle School?"

"America, I mean," I say quickly. "In all of America. Heck, the entire world!"

"Thank you, Sadie and Fifi," Brady says from the stage. "Let's hear it for them one more time, folks."

The sound of applause kind of wakes Julian up. His eyes light up as if they're all clapping and yelling for him. I think applause is like chocolate cake with ice cream for drag queens.

Julian stares into my eyes. "You're right, Michael. I'm the baddest drag kid in the entire universe."

And we're back!

"You've got this," Colton says to Julian, grabbing both his hands.

I nod in agreement. "We know you can do this. We believe in you. You just have to believe in yourself."

"Why be a drag when you can be a queen?" Julian says.

"Yes!" I exclaim. "Why be a drag when you can be a queen!"

I think he nods just a little bit, but it's hard to tell under all that blond, pink, and purple hair.

"Go out there and show him how amazing you are. And make your dad see you. Make him see that you matter."

I don't know where all that came from, but I think it sounded wicked cool and professional. I think that was my first-ever official talent-agent pep talk. And I think I kind of rocked it.

Michael Pruitt Business Tip #373: Make sure there are reporters or a documentary movie crew around when you give a super-crazy-good inspirational pep talk to your star client.

Brady's voice breaks through the speakers again. "And finally, our last performer is about to come out, and folks, let me tell you, you're not going to want to miss this one. So I hope you already went to the bathroom because you might just pee your pants when you see this act."

"Hill," Mr. Arnold whispers from behind the curtain as he makes his way over to our side of the backstage area. "Do *not* try me."

"Vasquez? Vasquez!" Mr. Arnold says, coming over to us. "You're up next."

When Mr. Arnold finally gets a load of me, Colton, and

Coco Caliente standing there in our costumes, I think he might pass out.

Mr. Arnold wags a finger up and down in front of us. "What kind of foolishness is this?"

Brady's voice sounds again, echoing backstage. "Please welcome Coco Caliente, Mistress of Madness and Mayhem."

Something sparks in Julian's eyes when he hears Brady announce him, and a determined look hardens his face. Colton and I grab Julian by the hands, scooting around Mr. Arnold and hurrying out to the center of the stage. We must pull a little too hard because Julian wobbles in his high heels and I think he just might topple over before the curtain even opens. Mr. Arnold follows us, whisper-yelling at us the whole way about the school board and his job and the PTA. But the curtains open, stopping him in his tracks.

And there we stand for God and everybody to see—Coco Caliente, Mistress of Madness and Mayhem, and her backup dancers in all our drag glory. The music doesn't begin right away and I start to panic a little as I scan the audience. At first glance of all the shadowy faces, I feel dizzy—like I'm going to pass out. As the students, parents, and teachers get a good look at us, the room goes quiet, except for the few people who gasp out loud. Then come the giggles and snickers.

My eyes begin adjusting to the dim lighting and I can see a lot of the faces staring back at me are frozen in shock or disgust. I can't tell exactly which. Mr. Grayson, who stands by the wall near the front, has a sour look on his face. Mrs. Campbell, my homeroom teacher, stands beside him with her hand covering her mouth. I spot Tommy, Trace, and Colby near the back, and of course, they're laughing their butts off. Well, Trace and Colby are—Tommy not so much.

Lyla is grinning like crazy, and Mom, Dad, Mrs. Vasquez, and Abuela are all smiling at us. Dad giggles a little bit, but I know it's not in a mean way. I imagine if Pap could see me now, he might giggle, too. Pap always told me to just be myself. It finally sinks in. And suddenly, I'm not scared. I'm not ashamed. Not even a little bit. I straighten my wig and plant my hands on my hips like Colton and Julian.

So I guess this is it. Whether I'm ready for all of North Charleston Middle School to know I'm gay or not, now they do. I mean, I know that just because you're wearing a short sparkly dress, a wig, and gobs of makeup it doesn't mean you're gay, but let's face it: In middle school, it pretty much does.

We wait for Julian to give Miss Troxel the cue to start the music, and for a second I think he might have forgotten. But then I see that he has locked eyes with Mr. Vasquez, who looks like he can't believe what he's seeing. The rest of the house-lights die down, sending Julian's dad off into total darkness, thank goodness. The audience is getting restless, but they're still mostly quiet. That is until a voice rings out from the back of the auditorium:

"Look. It's Gay Mikey and the he/she freaks."

It didn't sound like Tommy Jenrette's voice. Maybe it was

Colby or Trace. A few kids laugh, but most of the audience members shush them and the heckler. Like, *a lot* of them do, which is actually kind of cool and helps me to relax a little bit.

Colton and I stand in our starting positions behind Julian, hands on our hips, still waiting for him to give Miss Troxel the cue. I wonder if the hecklers got into his head. Maybe he's chickening out. I couldn't blame him if he did.

Finally Julian looks down. Takes a deep breath. Crosses himself like his abuela does sometimes. Then, looking at Miss Troxel in the front row, Coco Caliente, Mistress of Madness and Mayhem, nods once.

And, baby, we were born this way.

28
THE PERFORMANCE

All I can say is that I'm super-crazy glad that Julian didn't make me and Colton wear high heels.

I don't know how Julian does all that dancing, shaking, and twirling in those heels without busting his butt. The routine goes by in a blur. I don't even know if I'm any good or not. I'm more concerned about how short my dress is. I've watched Lyla and Gabby do the steps so much that I'm dancing on autopilot. I think my dress flies up once and I wonder what kind of underwear I have on, because I can't remember putting any on this morning. But I'm sure I did. I hope they were the blue briefs and not the white ones. Mom says white can be so unforgiving.

I know Colton matches me step for step, but I can't see much of him. I only see Julian. Or I should say—Coco. Because she's dancing and lip-synching her pizzazz off in front of us. The audience is so dark I wonder for a second if they're even still there. They could have all up and walked out right after we started and I wouldn't even know. And I can't hear *anything* other than the thumping dance mix behind Miss

Lady Gaga belting out "Born This Way." She's actually a great singer. I wonder if she needs an agent.

But I can't think about new clients right now. I just can't wait for the song to be over and I'm praying that Coco nails her finale. I know it's coming—the end, that is. It feels like a runaway freight train heading straight for us. The end of this song. The end of my life as a *not*-gay kid at North Charleston Middle School. The end of Julian's life altogether if Coco screws up the shablam. The end of Julian's drag-kid career if his dad hates the performance.

I shake my hips because that's what I'm supposed to be doing at this part of the dance. I never knew I had hips that would shake, but I guess I do. Maybe I'm better at this being-gay thing than I thought. But I don't think being gay is just about shaking your hips, loving Beyoncé, and calling other gay guys *girl*. It just now clicks in my head that both Pap Pruitt and Julian Vasquez gave me the exact same advice. *Be yourself.* Maybe I was a good gay all along just by being Michael Pruitt. Weird.

And here it comes. The end of the song in—

Five.

Coco moves into position. My heart pounds in my chest like it's trying to get out of her way.

Four.

Colton and I dance a few steps back to give her plenty of room.

Three.

I spot Lyla and Gabby dancing in their seats.

Two.

Mrs. Vasquez covers her eyes. Actually Trey and Dinesh do, too. Mom and Dad are hunched forward in their seats. Lyla must have told them all what's coming.

One.

Julian yanks his wig off and hurls it up to Jesus. And then it just happens. Julian lands hard on the stage floor with his left leg bent under him, lying flat on his back with his arms splayed out. The music stops. Colton and I freeze on our last pose—one knee bent, one hand on a hip and the other raised straight up in the air. Julian could be dead for all we know because he's not moving. And for a couple of seconds that seems like forever, there is complete silence in the auditorium. Then the most wicked-cool thing ever happens. Just about everyone in the audience bolts up out of their seat all at once—clapping, cheering, whooping, foot-stomping, and whistling. The auditorium erupts with noise—a super-crazy-good kind of noise.

I look out at the faces in the audience. I can't be sure, but it looks like Mrs. Vasquez and Abuela are crying. Mom and Dad are cupping their mouths and yelling my name like crazy people. Gabby is screaming out her brother's name. Lyla is standing in her seat, clapping so hard she looks like she's going to topple over. Trey and Dinesh pound their fists into the air. Charvi and Sadie stand by the wall jumping up and down and clapping. Fifi barks at the wall. And the craziest thing of all is that I spot Tommy Jenrette in the back row, standing and clapping and not yelling insults at us. Just clapping. He's too far away for me to be sure, but I'm almost positive there's a smile on his face.

Julian sits up on the stage floor, looking a little startled by the crowd's response. Colton helps him to his feet, because getting off the floor in heels and a dress after you just landed a death drop isn't easy. Finally Julian is on his feet. He straightens his dress and reaches down to pick up his wig. Then he bows to another surging thunderclap of applause. I can tell he's looking over to the side to see where his dad is and what his reaction is, but I don't see Mr. Vasquez anywhere. Julian looks back into the audience and just smiles real big with his Coco Caliente face, waving to the crowd like the amazing queen he is.

Colton takes my hand in his and—*OMG!*—I'm holding hands with a boy. Onstage. In a dress. In front of the entire student body of North Charleston Middle School. I'm sure I'll freak out and vomit all over the stage any second now. But the most amazing thing happens. I don't freak out. I don't vomit. I just stand there holding Colton's hand like it's no big deal. I'm not embarrassed at all. Not even a little bit. And I guess my gaydar finally kicks in, because I'm pretty sure now that Colton Sanford really *like*-likes me. That makes me smile bigger than I think I've ever smiled in my entire life.

Julian walks to the side of the stage, waving the entire time like a Miss Drag America contestant as the curtain begins to close. Colton pulls on my hand, leading me in the same direction. The applause, hollering, and whistling follows us all the way to the backstage area.

When we reach Mr. Arnold, I brace for a what-was-all-that-foolishness and an I-told-you-not-to-try-me lecture. But he doesn't say anything like that. He stands there, towering over us like a giant beanstalk with a hand covering his mouth. He doesn't even look mad at all. There's actually a tear running down his cheek. Weird.

"Vasquez," Mr. Arnold says, clearing his throat and batting away the tear with the back of his hand. "That was . . . you were . . ." He sighs real big, shaking his head. "You are amazing."

Mr. Arnold pulls Julian into a hug, just about knocking him off his high heels. I did *not* see that coming. They're both quiet for a few seconds, just hugging each other as the noise from the audience finally dies down. Colton looks over at me with that wicked-cool smile of his and I realize that he's still holding my hand. I also realize that I honestly don't want him to let go.

Mr. Arnold finally looks at me and Colton, his eyes moist. "You boys were wonderful, too."

Colton squeezes my hand. All my insides turn to goo.

"Oh no," Mr. Arnold says, looking panicked.

"What is it, Mr. Arnold?" Julian asks.

"The emcee that canceled was supposed to sing a song

now while the Arts Boosters judges choose a winner," he says. "They need a few minutes to deliberate."

The idea comes to me in no time flat, which is why I'm so good at this talent-agent thing.

I look over at Colton and stare into his eyes. And it's like he can read my mind, because after a couple of seconds, he smile-nods.

"I'll take care of it, Mr. Arnold," I say, standing up a little straighter because that seems like the professional thing to do.

Mr. Arnold glances down, noticing that me and Colton are holding hands, but he doesn't say anything. "Okay, Pruitt. You steered me right with Hill as the emcee, so I'll trust you once again. Don't let me down and do not—"

"—try me," Colton, Julian, and I all say.

Mr. Arnold smiles and then hurries to the other side of the stage.

I look at Colton and squeeze his hand. "You ready?"

He gives me one of those wicked-cool smiles of his. "Ready."

I finally let go of his hand, even though I don't want to. I walk over to the center of the stage, leaning into the heavy blue curtain.

"Brady."

He stops in the middle of his joke about atoms and sticks his head through the split in the curtains. His cheeks are flushed and his bushy hair looks wilder than usual.

"Hey," he says. "What's supposed to happen next? I'm dying out here."

"No, you're not," I say, giving him a thumbs-up. "You're doing great."

I give him his orders—I mean instructions—and he nods that he understands. Colton joins me center stage behind the curtain.

"Ladies and gentlemen," Brady says. "We have a special treat for you while our judges make their final decision."

I look over and wink at Colton. I have never winked at anyone in my life and I feel like a total goober doing it. I know if Trey and Dinesh saw me I'd never hear the end of it. But Colton just winks back as I leave him and walk offstage.

"Singing 'True Colors,'" Brady says, "specially dedicated to his mom, who is here today, is Colton Sanford!"

The curtain opens to polite applause and the crowd quickly falls quiet. Brady hands Colton the microphone as he walks to the side. Julian and I stand on the edge of the stage just behind the curtain watching Colton. At first, nothing happens. Colton just stands peering out into the auditorium, his eyes searching the half-lit crowd. I know he's looking for his mom. I guess he finds her because a smile finally spreads across his face and his shoulders relax as he holds the microphone up to his mouth.

There's no music for Miss Troxel to play. Nobody plays a guitar or a piano or anything. There's only Colton's small but steady voice pouring out of the speakers and filling the auditorium. That's called a cappella. And Colton sounds amazing. His voice is high and clear, like a real-live angel. I don't think I've ever heard a voice so beautiful. Not even Lady Gaga or Mrs. Beyoncé Knowles-Carter. It's one of those sad/not sad songs that he sings. It talks about being discouraged and afraid. And Colton sings his heart out for his mom:

> But I see your true colors,
> Shining through
> I see your true colors,
> And that's why I love you

I peek around the curtain and spot my mom with her head resting on Dad's shoulder. Shiny tears reflecting the stage lights streak her face. Trey and Dinesh sit staring up at Colton with their mouths hanging open. Lyla is smiling. Colton's mom and grandma stand near the back of the auditorium with their arms around each other's waists. They're too far away for me to see their faces, but I bet they're crying, too. How could they not be? The song ends way too soon for me. I could listen to Colton sing all day. And I wouldn't even want to make any commission off his performance or anything.

The only thing missing in this perfect and beautiful moment is Pap.

29
THE WINNER

Nobody stands up for Colton when the song is over like they did for Julian. But they do clap like crazy for a gazillion minutes. I clap, too—so hard I think I might break my hands.

Beside me, Julian cups his mouth with his hands and yells Colton's name right in my ear. There's a couple of whoop-whoops from the audience. I'll bet that was Trey and Dinesh. The curtains don't close, so Colton walks offstage and over to us as the applause dies down. I want to say something to him, tell him how incredible that was, but I can't get any normal human words out. I just nod my head, smiling. He smiles back at me like he understands.

Mr. Arnold walks out onto the stage, taking the microphone from Brady. "Thank you, Hill," he says. "How about a big round of applause for Brady Hill, everyone."

The crowd goes crazy clapping and hollering. Brady takes a long bow before leaving the stage. He was amazing, even though he didn't get paid for the gig. It's okay, though.

It was great practice for him for *Later Tonight with Billy Shannon*.

Mr. Arnold holds up an envelope to show the crowd. "I have the final results, everyone. And please help me thank the Arts Boosters for donating our one-hundred-dollar cash prize this year."

People clap, but not like they did for Colton or Julian or even Sadie and Fifi. Colton grabs Julian's hand and Julian grabs mine. Holding Julian's hand doesn't feel the same as holding Colton's and it doesn't give me blender-stomach, but it feels nice.

"Can I have all the contestants back on the stage, please?" Mr. Arnold says, waving us all out.

Everyone files onto the stage, forming a messy line. Colton and I stay behind, giving Julian this moment all to himself. We're only backup dancers, after all. Coco Caliente is the star. Julian has transformed back into full-on Miss Coco mode, with his wig in place, his head held high, and striking a confident hand-on-hip pose. The audience settles quietly, waiting for the big moment.

Mr. Arnold opens the envelope, pulling out a white card. "Our second runner-up today is . . ."

He looks out at the audience and then back at the row of contestants.

"Chad Charles," Mr. Arnold says into the mic.

The audience claps and yells and whoops for Chad and his wicked hip-hop dance moves. All the contestants clap, too, because that's the professional thing to do. Chad steps forward as Miss Troxel appears onstage to hand him a small gold trophy.

"Congratulations, Charles," Mr. Arnold says. "And now, the first runner-up is . . ."

He looks at the audience, then back at the contestants.

I think Mr. Arnold loves having this much control of the room.

"Taylor Hope," Mr. Arnold says.

Some girls in the front row squeal. They must be Taylor's friends. Everyone else claps super loud as if to say that they agree with the judges' decision. Taylor was by far the best singer in the competition. Miss Troxel gives Taylor a slightly bigger gold trophy than the one she gave Chad.

"Well done, Hope," Mr. Arnold says. "Very well done, indeed."

Colton looks over at me, worry creasing his eyebrows. I'll bet he's thinking what I'm thinking. Either Julian or Sadie and Fifi won, or else neither of them even made the top three. It wasn't Sadie and Fifi's best performance, but the Arts Boosters of North Charleston Middle School just might not be ready for a drag kid either—even though I'm pretty sure the rest of the world is judging by the crowd's reaction to Julian's performance. Now I'm getting worried, too.

I peek around the curtain into the audience. Mrs. Vasquez and Abuela have their eyes closed. Lyla and Gabby hold hands, eyes closed, too. As if closing your eyes will make bad news not so bad. Colton takes my hand and squeezes it. I squeeze his back. It feels like the most normal thing ever.

Mr. Arnold flips the card over. "And the winner of the North Charleston Middle School end-of-year talent contest, who will receive a one-hundred-dollar cash prize . . ."

He looks at the audience. Then back at the contestants. He would probably go to commercial if this were a live television show.

Mr. Arnold looks back at the card like he already forgot the name of the winner. Then a big smile crosses his face. "Coco Caliente, Mistress of Madness and Mayhem!"

I can't feel my face. Or my feet. Or my hand, which Colton is squeezing the life out of. I look over at Julian. His hand covers his mouth. His eyes are full of tears and mascara runs dark down his cheeks. All of North Charleston Middle School is on their feet clapping and cheering for him. He's being swarmed by the other contestants. Miss Troxel can barely get to him to give him the huge trophy. Mr. Arnold pushes his way through to give Julian an oversize check printed on cardboard. I hope the bank will cash that thing, because I need my commission.

"Would you like to say anything, Caliente?" Mr. Arnold says, quieting the crowd with outstretched arms. He hands the microphone to a trembling Julian.

Julian's voice is shaky at first. "Thank you." Then it gets a little stronger. "I want to thank the Arts Boosters. And my abuela. And my mom." He looks around the auditorium, but his gaze never lands anywhere in particular. "And my dad, too. He doesn't understand all this . . ."

Julian chuckles, running a free hand up and down in front of him, from his wig to his heels. Most everyone in the audience laughs along with him. Colton and I sure do.

"But he's still my dad," Julian says. "I'm still his son. I'm still the same Julian he taught to swim and ride a bike and to play tennis and to make churros. And I just want him to be proud of me."

I peer around the curtain again. I hope Mr. Vasquez is out there somewhere and that he didn't get mad and leave already.

"But I need to thank the person who took a chance on me," Julian says, looking down. "The person who believed in me. Who guided me and gave me great advice. And who reminded me that I can do anything. And that I matter."

Julian looks over at me. "My agent, Michael Pruitt of the Anything Talent and Pizzazz Agency."

Colton slaps me on the back as another lump forms in my throat. And then a super-crazy-weird thing happens. People in the audience start clapping. Because of what Julian said about me.

"Come on out here, Michael," Julian says, waving me to center stage.

Colton pushes me and I kind of stumble toward the center

of the stage until I meet Coco in the middle. And more people clap even harder—for me.

Michael Pruitt—President, Founder, and CEO of Anything, Inc.

Trey and Dinesh are on their feet going crazy. Mom and Dad, Mrs. Vasquez, Abuela, Gabby, and even Lyla are all standing up and clapping, too. Sadie, Stuart, Brady, and Charvi all yell my name. Fifi barks at the ceiling. And the weirdest thing is, I spot Tommy Jenrette in the back row— standing and clapping. He even nudges Trace and Colby, making them stand up, too, even though they look like they really don't want to, but they clap politely.

Julian looks over at me. "Thanks, dude."

He hugs me tight. But he doesn't hug me like a client hugs their agent. He hugs me like a real friend would and that feels good. I almost forget that I didn't change after the performance, but now I remember that I'm standing out here in front of all of North Charleston Middle School in a dress, a wig, and wearing makeup—again. But I realize something wicked cool. I don't care. Not even when Julian grabs my hand and holds it up between us like I just won a boxing match.

It just might be the best moment of my life so far—so many people clapping and standing and yelling my name, Julian's big old trophy and cardboard check that I helped him win, my family and friends all here to share in my first huge business success. The only thing that could make it all better would be if Pap Pruitt were here. I wish he could see me now.

He'd be the most proud of me for being myself, and for not caring what anyone else thinks. And then I realize something else wicked cool. It doesn't matter what all of North Charleston Middle School thinks, or my parents, my friends, Colton, or even Pap Pruitt. Because I'm proud of myself. And that's better than the longest standing ovation in history, which I'm pretty sure this is.

The thought makes me smile so hard my cheeks hurt. Julian hands me the trophy. I raise it high in the air to more cheers, applause, and thunderous joy.

I whisper, "This is for you, Pap."

30
THE BIG TIME

The lobby outside the auditorium is packed with parents chatting with teachers, students saying goodbye to each other for the summer, and one plus-size drag-kid talent-contest winner being swarmed by people wanting to congratulate him. I stand back, giving Julian room to be the center of attention and the good kind of popular. He deserves it. People who never would have talked to Julian during the school year now act like he's their best friend. Weird.

Heather Hobbs asks Julian how he styles his wig to give it those swooping wings on each side. Taylor Hope wants to borrow the red sparkly dress to perform in at a beauty pageant she has coming up. Chad Charles begs Julian to teach him some new dance moves. Manny's speaking to Julian in rapid-fire Spanish, I guess telling him how good the death drop was, because Julian nailed it. Even Mr. Arnold wants his picture taken with Coco Caliente, Mistress of Madness and Mayhem. Actually just about everyone wants a selfie with Miss Coco. And Julian is loving every minute of it. *Divas, am I right?*

I look over to find Mom, Dad, and Lyla walking toward me. Dad grabs me and hugs me tight. I'm glad I changed into my jeans before we came out, otherwise I'm sure my underwear would be on full display right about now.

"Big day for the company," he says. "Your clients were amazing."

Mom slips an arm around my shoulder. "Where did you learn to dance like that? I wish Pap could have seen that. He used to be quite the dancer himself. Maybe you got that from him, too."

Mom's eyes grow glassy. Dad's even glassier. And I get it. They're trying to prepare me for what's to come. Pap won't be around much longer. I've known that for a long time. But I don't want to cry in front of all my friends, so I look away fast.

I spot Colton, his mom, and his grandma talking to Sadie and Brady. His mom has her arm around his shoulders, just like mine does. She has the same reddish-brown hair as Colton, and even the same wicked-cool smile. Colton has his arm around her waist real tight like he doesn't want to let her go. He glances over and catches me staring at him. But he doesn't call the stalker police or anything. He just smiles and waves.

Stomach smoothie anyone?

"Oh yeah," Dad says. He play-punches my shoulder and gives me a cheesy dad grin and—*OMG!*—he caught me staring at Colton. "Now, who is that handsome young man over there?"

"Ew, Dad," I say. "That's my friend. Colton."

Lyla is hanging on to Dad's leg and swinging back and forth. "Is he your *boy*friend?"

"Lyla," Mom says. "Stop being nosy." She points at Dad. "You too. Behave."

"Thanks, Mom," I say, pulling her closer to me.

I can't believe she kind of–sort of scolded Lyla and basically told Dad to mind his own business, which I want to do, like, all the time, but it never seems like the smart thing to do.

Dad holds up his hands in surrender. "Sorry. Sorry. All I was going to say is that Mikey might like to ask his *friend* Colton to join us for ice cream before we head back over to Prince George to check on Pap. I know he'll want to hear all about the show."

Okay. So that's not the worst idea Dad's ever had.

"Maybe," I say. "I'll ask him. But his mom and grandma are here and he hasn't seen his mom in a while."

"Invite them along, too," Mom says. "We'd love to meet them. But only if you want to, honey."

Before I can respond, I spot Julian's dad making his way through the crowd. He's so tall and wide it's hard to miss him. Mrs. Vasquez and Abuela are following close after him and—*OMG!*—he's heading straight for Julian. I'm beginning to wonder if I made a huge mistake inviting him here.

"I'll be right back," I say to Mom and Dad, and hurry over to head off Mr. Vasquez.

I don't want him to ruin this moment for Julian and I guess

I'm willing to sacrifice myself to prevent that because that seems like the good-friend thing to do.

Colton must have the same idea because he's also on an intercept course with Mr. Vasquez. But we're too late. Mr. Vasquez rushes up and the crowd around Julian parts, giving his dad a close-up look at his son standing there in full drag. In public.

Crap.

I don't hesitate or think, which always seems to be my downfall. I just push my way through the crowd, stepping in front of Julian and facing Mr. Vasquez, who's got to be, like, four times my size, at least. Colton stands right beside me, helping me block Julian from his father. We both put our hands on our hips and widen our stance, just like our pose from the "Born This Way" dance routine.

Julian puts a hand on my back. "It's okay, Michael."

I look over my shoulder. "No, it's not okay."

"Michael, don't," Mrs. Vasquez says from somewhere close by.

I face Mr. Vasquez and point my finger at him.

"That is your son," I say, with a kind of scary edge in my voice. "And you're his father."

Okay, it wasn't quite the burn I was hoping for. Those are just basic facts. I try again.

"There's nothing wrong with him," I say. "He's a super-crazy-cool person, he's more talented than most of the kids at this school, he's loyal, he's honest, he's funny, and if he were my son, I would be wicked proud of him. And he's my friend."

"And mine," Colton says, crossing his arms over his chest.

Trey slips away from his mom a few feet away and slides in next to me. "Mine too." He sizes up Mr. Vasquez and swallows hard. "Sir."

"He's my friend, too," Dinesh says, standing next to Trey. His mom and dad stand behind him like bodyguards, which I think is pretty cool of Mr. and Mrs. Lahiri.

Stuart drives his wheelchair right over Mr. Vasquez's shoe to get near us. "And mine."

"Ours too," Sadie says, leading Fifi in and standing beside Colton.

Fifi growls at Mr. Vasquez, but she's looking in, like, a whole different direction.

Mr. Vasquez looks at each of us, one by one, but his face is kind of blank and I can't really tell what he's thinking.

"Julian's my friend, too, Mr. Vasquez," Charvi says, joining Sadie's side.

Brady walks up to us, clueless as usual. "Yo, what did I miss?" He eyes Julian's dad suspiciously. "Well, whatever this is, count me in."

Mr. Vasquez shakes his head and sighs. And a second later, even Lyla joins us.

She crosses her arms, peering up at him just as serious as

she can be. Like David facing down Goliath. "Mister, do you know how lucky you are to have Julian for a son?"

Wow. There may be hope for my sister, after all.

She points a thumb over her shoulder in my direction. "If not, I'm sure my mom and dad would be glad to trade you Mikey for Julian."

And we're back.

"Yeah, Daddy," Gabby says, planting herself beside Lyla. "You should be proud of Julian. He's amazing."

For a few seconds, I don't have any idea what's going to happen. We all stare up at Mr. Vasquez. His hard, crackled face and almost-black eyes are hard to read. Mrs. Vasquez stands behind her husband, shaking her head like she's watching a terrible car crash and can't look away. A small crowd has gathered around us. I notice a tall woman with short dark hair wearing red-framed glasses standing just a few feet away from us, watching the whole thing.

Finally Mr. Vasquez's face softens a bit. "May I please speak to my son?"

He asks so nicely that we're all caught off guard. And we don't know whether to let him by or not. But I feel Julian behind me, pushing through our line of defense. He stands in front of his father, facing him like a talented, proud drag kid with a ton of pizzazz would.

Mr. Vasquez scans Julian up and down, from his wig to his high heels. He rests a hand on Julian's shoulder, like the way my dad does to me sometimes.

He looks Julian in the eye and leans in close. "You *are* my Julian. You *are* my son. And I *am* proud of you. I don't want you to doubt that ever again. I'm sorry for the way I acted. I thought I was protecting you. The world is full of cruel people. I worry about you." He nods down to Julian's dress. "I might not understand . . . this," he says with a slight chuckle. "But I will learn, mijo. You will teach me, yes?"

Julian's face is tight and his eyes wet. I can tell he's trying to hold back tears as he nods at his father. Tears slide down his cheeks anyway. Mr. Vasquez pulls Julian into a hug—wig, dress, high heels, and all. Mrs. Vasquez wraps her arms around them both.

Colton and I exchange a what-the-heck-just-happened? look.

Mr. Vasquez finally steps back and does something else I didn't see coming. He grabs Julian's wig, yanking it right off his head, and—*OMG!* For a second I think that he fooled us and this was his plan all along. Just to get close enough to Julian to *snatch him bald,* as Pap Pruitt likes to say. But before Julian has a chance to react, Mr. Vasquez pulls the wig down on top of his own head and poses with one hand on his hip and the other straight up in the air the way Miss Coco does.

"How do I look, mijo?" he asks Julian, looking pretty silly and unprofessional.

We all wait, holding our breath to see how Julian reacts. Coco Caliente was just de-wigged right here in the lobby of North Charleston Middle School in front of everyone, after all. It could go either way.

Julian takes a step back, planting a hand on his hip and looking his dad up and down. "Um, we have some work to do, honey. I mean, Dad."

Mr. Vasquez laughs and throws an arm around Julian. "Let's go home, mijo."

Julian waves goodbye to us as he lets his wig-wearing dad lead him, Gabby, his mom, and his abuela out of the building and—*OMG!*—it hits me. This was just like Julian's dream, and the way Charvi interpreted it was exactly what just happened. That is way cool and a little creepy. I'll need to double her rates. Well, once I get her a paying gig, because you can't double *free*.

Trey and Dinesh fist-bump me before they leave, because that's how straight boys tell you that they're your friend and they love you.

I turn to Colton. "Hey. So, my mom and dad want to know if you and your mom and grandma want to come have ice cream with us."

Colton's eyes light up like a Christmas tree. "That'd be great! I'll go ask them."

As soon as Colton darts away, Tommy Jenrette walks up and stands right in front of me. *Crap!* Just when I thought this day was perfect. Tommy shifts his weight from one side to the other. He looks super-crazy uncomfortable.

"Hey," I say, because it's the only thing I can think of.

Tommy nods, nervously glancing around the room. "Um . . . hey." He finally looks directly at me. "You guys were so funny in the show." He cracks a smile. Like a real, non-jerk smile.

I relax a little, sliding my hands into my pockets. "Thanks."

I notice Trace and Colby standing close to the door, watching us suspiciously.

"So, I figure you looked through my notebook," Tommy says.

I tense up a little, but I guess he wouldn't kill me in front of all these people. "Yeah, I did. Sorry."

Tommy rocks back and forth on his heels, shaking his head. "It's okay."

"I really do think you're wicked talented, Tommy," I say. "You should keep drawing."

Tommy half-smiles back at me and grunts, but not in a mean way. "You're, like, the first person to ever tell me that I'm talented in something other than basketball." His cheeks go a little red. "Thanks."

Okay, this did not go like I thought it would.

"I was kind of jealous watching all of you in the show, doing what you love to do," he says, sliding his hands into his pockets and still rocking on his heels like he's nervous. "This talent-agency thing of yours is pretty cool."

I'm surprised by what he says, but it gives me an idea. This might be the dumbest idea I've ever had, but I hope not. I reach into the back pocket of my jeans and pull out one of my business cards.

"Why don't you come by my office tomorrow," I say in my

professional voice. "Let's talk about your future as an artist. Maybe I can help."

A huge smile spreads across Tommy's face as he takes the card and looks at it. He chuckles—probably because of the whole *pizza* thing. That's fair.

"Really?" he says. He slings his brown mop-top hair out of his eyes. "You would do that? For me?"

He probably says it because he's been such a jerk to me all these years and he can't believe that I would ever want to help him.

Michael Pruitt Business Tip #374: Sometimes you should swallow your pride and help people not just because it's the professional thing to do, but because it's the *right* thing to do.

I nod. "Sure. Why not?"

Tommy pockets the card and gives me another big non-jerk smile. "Cool. I'll see you tomorrow." And he takes off toward Trace and Colby.

I head over to my parents, but the tall lady with the red-framed glasses who was watching us earlier heads me off. She holds out her hand to me like a professional business-person would. "Hi there. I'm Sara Dimery with CTA."

CTA sounds familiar, but my brain is exhausted right now. I guess I look at her like I don't know what that is, because she explains.

"Creative Talent Agency," she says.

And—*OMG!*—a real-live talent agent. Not that *I'm* not a real-live talent agent. But, like, you know, *wow*.

"Oh, um, well, yeah." Because that seems like the professional thing to say. I finally shake her hand because it was hanging out there forever. "Michael Pruitt, with . . . um . . . ATAPA." I hope I got the letters in the right order.

Her face crinkles like she doesn't know what language I'm speaking. "So, I understand that you are Julian's agent."

I open my mouth, but my voice fails me. I scold myself internally: *Okay, pull it together, Pruitt. None of this foolishness now. Do. Not. Try. Me. Not today, Satan. Not today.*

I clear my throat and drop my voice about a gazillion notches. "Yes, I am. Very nice to meet you."

She smiles at me. *Finally.*

"I was very impressed with your client today," says Sara Dimery of *the* Creative Talent Agency *also known as CTA*. "He has a certain something. A certain . . . a certain . . ."

"Pizzazz," I say, helping her out.

Her grin widens. "Exactly. I can tell you know what I'm talking about."

"All the best talent agents know pizzazz when they see it," I say with a confident nod.

Sara Dimery of CTA laughs but not in a mean way. Just like we're talking at a party and I said something super funny.

"I'm in town visiting family and came to see my niece sing in the show," she says. "Taylor Hope?"

"Yes," I say, casually sliding my hands into my pockets. "That's her name."

She laughs again, reaching into her purse. "Here's my card," she says, holding a business card out to me. "There's a casting call for a new reality competition show for the Good-Flix network. It's called *America's Next Drag Kid Sensation*. I think Coco Caliente would be a perfect fit for it. I would love for Julian to audition." She leans back, raising an eyebrow at me. "*If* you think that's the right next move for his career after winning the North Charleston Middle School talent contest, that is."

She gives me what seems like a flirty smile. That must be a New York thing. But Sara Dimery of CTA is definitely climbing up the wrong tree. You know, because of the whole me-being-gay thing. Plus I'm only twelve.

I dig around in my back pocket and thankfully find the one business card left there. I pull it out and hand it to her.

"That sounds interesting," I say, trying to act like it's not that interesting at all, even though it's super-crazy interesting. But I don't want to seem too desperate—bad for contract negotiations. "I'd love to talk to you more about that mildly interesting idea. Julian has some time open in his calendar in the next couple of months."

Yeah, like we all do. It's called summer break.

Sara Dimery of CTA inspects my card. "You're a . . . pizza expert?"

My face heats from the inside out. *Dang it, Lyla.* She must have missed correcting that one. I guess you get what you pay for when it comes to employees.

"Just a slight printing error," I say, like that's a normal thing. "*Pizzazz* expert."

She smiles and nods. "All right, then, Mr. Pruitt. I will be in touch."

"I look forward to it, Ms. Dimery," I say, because that seems like the professional response.

She chuckles, waves, and walks away and—*OMG! Wow. Wow. Wow.*

The lobby is beginning to clear out. My parents and Lyla wait for me by the door. Colton was talking to his mom and grandma but now comes running over.

"They said yes," he says with an ear-to-ear grin. He pushes his hair out of his eyes. "They want to go get ice cream with you guys."

And before you know it, Colton Sanford does the weirdest thing ever. He leans in and kisses me on the cheek. And I don't mean an air-kiss. I mean, like, a his-real-live-lips-touched-my-cheek-skin kind of kiss. And he did it right here in the lobby of North Charleston Middle School in front of everyone—my parents, my clients/friends, the other contestants, Mr. Arnold, Mr. Grayson, Miss Troxel, Sara Dimery of CTA. And you know what? It actually *doesn't* feel like the weirdest thing ever. It feels like the coolest thing ever. And nobody even gives us a second look. And most important, I don't feel like I'm going to hurl like I always thought I would the first time I got kissed.

Colton pulls back and shoots me the wicked-cool, stomach-smoothie smile. I'm not sure what the professional thing to do is at a time like this since this is my first boy kiss ever. So I just ram my hands down into my pockets and smile back at Colton.

My phone buzzes/vibrates in my pocket, which kind of makes me jump because I'm not used to getting calls on it. I pull it out and look at the display. I don't recognize the number.

"Hey, um, I need to take this," I say to Colton, sounding way important and professional.

He nods and goes back over to his mom. He gives her a big hug around the waist and she hugs him back. That makes me smile. The phone buzzes/vibrates again in my hand. I flip it open and lift it to my ear.

"Michael Pruitt," I say, because that's how I've heard Dad answer his business calls—with just his name. It sounds very professional.

"Hello, Mr. Pruitt," a female voice says in my ear. "This is Allie Rosen with *Later Tonight with Billy Shannon*."

And—*OMG!*—I think I just peed a little bit.

"Oh, brilliant," I say, slipping into Penelope-the-British-GPS-lady's voice for some reason. "Miss Rosen. It's so lovely to hear from you."

There's a pause on the line.

"Um, yeah. So I got your sizzle reel for Brady Hill," she says.

My throat closes up a little. "You did?"

"Yes, we did," Allie Rosen says. "I loved it. And so did Billy."

"Billy," I say, momentarily losing Penelope's accent. "As in Shannon?"

She chuckles a little. "That's the one."

I don't know what to say. *The* Billy Shannon watched my sizzle reel. I mean, *Brady's* sizzle reel. Directed and produced by me, of course.

"Stupendous, Miss Rosen," I say, recovering my wicked-cool Penelope accent. "That's simply divine, my dear."

"Okay, so." And then Allie Rosen of *Later Tonight with Billy Shannon* says the magic words that every talent agent wants to hear: "I'd like to book your client."

I swallow. Real hard. Because just like that, the Anything Talent and Pizzazz Agency, a division of Anything, Inc., Michael Pruitt—President, Founder, CEO, and Pizzazz Expert, has hit the big time.

RESOURCES

DRAGUTANTE

"Dragutante is a nonprofit that hosts an annual event to provide a platform for young artists (under eighteen) to fully realize their self-expression onstage. This full-day event will create a safe place for young, creative future drag queens to experience the drag lifestyle behind the scenes, as well as onstage! Providing this opportunity to get to know celebrity drag queens will show families who are uneducated about drag culture that it is something to be celebrated."

From the website of dragutante.org.

TRUE COLORS UNITED

"Cofounded by Cyndi Lauper, Lisa Barbaris, and Jonny Podell, True Colors United implements innovative solutions to youth homelessness that focus on the unique experiences of LGBTQ young people. In the United States, 4.2 million youth experience homelessness each year, with lesbian, gay, bisexual, transgender, queer, and questioning (LGBTQ) youth 120 percent more likely to experience homelessness than their non-LGBTQ peers. True Colors United is committed to changing that."

From the website of truecolorsunited.org.

Turn the page
for more from
GREG HOWARD

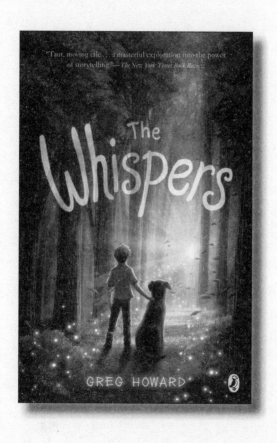

"Taut, moving tale . . . a masterful exploration into the power of storytelling."—*The New York Times Book Review*

The
Whispers

GREG HOWARD

There once was a boy who heard the Whispers.

He heard them late in the day as the lazy sun dipped below the treetops and the woods behind his house came alive with the magic of twilight. The voices came to him so gently he thought it might be the wind, or the first trickle of summer rain. But as time passed, the voices grew louder and the boy was sure they were calling his name. So he followed them.

The Whispers led the boy to a clearing deep in the woods where a rotted old tree stump sat in the center and fallen leaves covered the ground like crunchy brown carpet. The boy stood next to the stump, waited, and listened. He couldn't see the Whispers, but he knew they were there. Their wispy voices surrounded him, tickling the rims of his ears and filling every darkened shadow of the forest.

After waiting patiently for quite some time, the Whispers' garbled words finally began to make sense to the boy, and they told him things. The Whispers knew everything—all the secrets of the universe. They told the boy what color the moon was up close and how many miles of ocean covered the Earth. They even told him how long he would live—26,332 days. The boy was pleased, because that sounded like a good long time to him. But as they continued to whisper knowledge into his ear, they never showed themselves to the boy. He only caught glimpses from the corner of his eye of their faint bluish glow fading in and out around him. He so badly wanted to see them, to know what kind of creatures they were. How big were they? Or how tiny? Were they thin, or fat, or hairy? Were they made of skin and bones like him, or of tree bark, or leaves, or dirt? Or something else entirely?

The Whispers told the boy that if he brought them tributes, they would give him his heart's desires. The boy wasn't sure what a tribute was and he didn't want very much anyway. He could hardly call them heart's desires. Maybe a new pair of sneakers so the kids at school wouldn't tease him about his raggedy old ones. Maybe a better job for his father so he wouldn't worry so much about money. And he would love to see his mother smile again, something she rarely did anymore. But he guessed what he really wanted was to see the Whispers with his very own eyes.

One day, as the boy's mother made a batch of her special blackberry jam, he asked her what a *tribute* was. She thought about it a moment and finally told him that a tribute was like a gift to show respect. The boy eyed his mother's handiwork spread over the kitchen table. Everyone loved her jam. When she took it to the local farmers market, she always sold out. And her blackberry jam was his personal favorite. He was sure it would make an excellent tribute for the Whispers. When his mother left the room, the boy took one of the jars from the table and hid it under his bed.

The following afternoon, as the sun was setting, he went back to the clearing in the woods with the jam tucked under his arm. He left it sitting on the rotted old tree stump for the Whispers. Satisfied with his tribute, the boy spoke his heart's desires aloud and then hurried home as not to scare the Whispers away.

When the boy's father got home from work that evening, his mood was lighter than usual and the lines of worry had completely vanished from his face. He told the family that he'd received a promotion at work and tomorrow the boy's mother should take him shopping to buy him new clothes and shoes for school. This news made his mother smile. The boy was amazed that he'd received three of his heart's desires with only one jar of jam. Surely the Whispers would reveal themselves to him if he took them a tribute even better than a jar of his mother's blackberry jam. And he knew just the thing.

The next day, when the boy returned from shopping with his mother, he snuck out of the house right before sunset and took his new sneakers to the clearing in the woods. He kept them in the box, neatly wrapped in tissue paper so they wouldn't get scuffed or dirty. They were the nicest shoes he'd ever owned, and surely this tribute would persuade the Whispers to show themselves.

When he approached the rotted old tree stump, he saw that the blackberry jam was gone. The boy wasn't surprised. He was sure the Whispers enjoyed his mother's jam just as much as everyone else did. He put the box with his sneakers on top of the rotted old tree stump, stood back, and waited. And waited. And waited. He waited so long, he wasn't sure the Whispers were pleased enough with his tribute.

Finally something tickled the back of his neck with the lightest flutter of breath grazing his skin. It spoke his name and asked him what he wished. The boy froze. The Whispers had never come that close before. They must be pleased with his tribute after all. He was excited, but afraid if he moved it would scare them away, so he closed his eyes and remained perfectly still.

"I wish to see you," the boy said in barely a whisper of his own. "I want to know what you look like. It's my heart's desire."

At first there was no clear answer, only a garble of Whispers conversation that he couldn't understand. Then the words slowly pieced themselves together like a puzzle in his ear.

"If we reveal ourselves, you can never leave us," the Whispers said, their velvety voices caressing his ear through the warm summer breeze. "You must stay here in the woods with us forever, for you will know everything, and that is a burden too great to bear in your world."

The boy swallowed hard. He closed his eyes even tighter and stood very still as sweat trailed down his neck, the Whispers' words chilling him from head to toe.

"Are you sure this is what you wish?" the Whispers asked. "To see us? To stay with us and become a whisper in the wind?"

The boy began to worry. He thought about all the things he would miss if he stayed in the woods with the Whispers forever. He would never get to ride his bike again, or go swimming in the pond with his friends. And he would never see his mother and father again. It seemed like an awfully high price to pay just to see what the Whispers looked like. Besides, he'd already offered them his brand-new sneakers, and they were the nicest things he owned. Wasn't that enough?

"No," the Whispers said, reading his thoughts. "It is not enough. If you see us, you must become one of us. And then you will know everything there is to know. You will hear everything. See everything. But the only tribute we can accept for that is your soul."

The boy stood there with his eyes closed tight, scared he might accidentally see one of the Whispers and then the choice would be made for him. He needed a moment to think. The boy wondered what else there was to know. Because of the Whispers he knew the color of the moon up close, how many miles of ocean covered the Earth, and how long he would live—26,332 days. He knew he had a home to which he could return. He knew his parents loved him and his father worked hard to take care of their family. And the kids at school would tease him a little less now that he had brand-new sneakers.

The boy knew it would be dark soon and if he waited too long he might never find his way out of the woods. Then what would the Whispers do with him? He felt around until he found the box with his sneakers on the tree stump. He grabbed it, turned, and ran as fast as he could. He held the box close to his chest and didn't dare open his eyes. He tripped and fell. Got back up and ran into one tree after another. Branches whacked him across the face and chest, but he kept running blindly through the woods.

Only after he'd gone a good long ways and the tiny voices had faded behind him did the boy dare open his eyes. Even then he was careful not to look around. He stared straight ahead until he got to the tree line and ran the whole way home, never looking back, not even when he reached his house.

After that the boy never heard the Whispers again, but he didn't mind. He already had his heart's desires. He had his mother. And his father. And his friends. And his brand-new sneakers. Plus he knew what color the moon was up close, how many miles of ocean covered the Earth, and how long he would live—26,332 days. He didn't know *all* the secrets of the universe and maybe he never would, but he knew plenty.

This was Mama's favorite story. She told me the story every night until the day she disappeared. Then I started hearing the Whispers. And I followed them.

1

THE WORLD'S WORST POLICE DETECTIVE

Fat Bald Detective thinks I had something to do with it. He doesn't come right out and say it, but the way he repeats the same questions over and over—like if he keeps on asking them, I might crack under the pressure—well, it's pretty clear that I'm suspect number one. I don't know why he thinks I'm guilty, other than the fact that he's not very smart. He's not nearly as good at this as the cops on TV, and they're only actors. He just sits there smiling at me, waiting for me to say something more. But I don't know what he wants from me. I mean, sure I have secrets. Big ones. The kind of secrets you take to your grave. But I would never hurt anyone on purpose. Especially not Mama.

I push my hair out of my eyes and look up at the clock on the wall. It shouldn't be too much longer. Maybe I can just wait him out. I look at the desk in the corner of the cramped office. It's cluttered with books, stacks of file folders, and a darkened computer screen decorated with a rainbow of Post-it notes because Fat Bald Detective can't remember anything. There isn't one inch of clear space anywhere to be seen on his desk. It's very unprofessional.

That was one of our words from the calendar—I think from last January. It's still on my wall.

Unprofessional is when someone or something doesn't look or act right in the workplace.

Good, Button. Now use it in a sentence, Mama would say if she were here.

Then I would say something like, *Fat Bald Detective's office is very unprofessional because there's crap everywhere and it smells like Fritos.*

That would have made Mama laugh. I could always make her laugh when we played the word-of-the-day game. Mama says it's okay if you don't always remember the exact dictionary definition of a word as long as you can describe the meaning in your own words and you can use it in a sentence. Now that I think of it, there should be a picture of Fat Bald Detective's office beside the word *unprofessional* in the dictionary.

His office is nothing like the ones in the police stations on TV. There aren't any bright fluorescent lights in here, or cool floor-to-ceiling walls of glass so he can see the whole department and wave someone in at a moment's notice just to yell at them. There's only one small window with a view of the parking lot, and Fat Bald Detective seems to prefer table lamps to fluorescent lighting. And although you can't smell the offices of the police stations on TV, I always imagined they'd smell like leftover pizza and cigarette smoke—not Fritos. I guess it's better than doing this in one of their interrogation rooms. At least in here there's a couch for me to sit on before they lock me up and throw away the keys. Then it hits me. It's the couch. The couch smells like Fritos.

"And what happened after that, Riley?" Fat Bald Detective says—*again*.

Fat Bald Detective has a name. It's Frank. He said I could call him Frank the first time he brought me in for questioning. Mama doesn't normally approve of us calling adults by their first name, but Frank told me to and he's the law. I figure I should probably cooperate as much as possible so he doesn't get any more suspicious than he already is.

Frank actually has three names. They're all printed on his door and on the triangle nameplate on his desk. Grandma says that people who use three names are *puttin' on airs*, but I don't think Frank has any airs to put on. He's short, and bald, and round, and looks like Mr. Potato Head without the tiny black hat, so I think *Fat Bald Detective* every time I look at him.

"I don't remember," I say.

He keeps asking me what happened that day and I keep telling him I don't remember. We've played this little game for almost four months now. I was ten when we started. I'm a whole different age now. I've had a birthday and a summer break since then. I even moved up a grade in school. Detective Chase Cooper on *Criminal Investigative*

Division: Chicago can solve a case in an hour. Forty-four minutes if you fast-forward through the commercials. But Frank will never be as smart as Detective Chase Cooper. Or as handsome. Frank's really not a bad guy, though. He means well. But I don't think he's ever going to crack this case, at least not before I turn twelve. He's running out of time. So is Mama.

Frank and his officers should be out there trying to find the perp—following up on leads, canvassing the neighborhood. That's the way they do it on TV, and they *always* catch the guy. They don't sit in poorly lit rooms that smell like Fritos questioning the eleven-year-old son of the missing person over and over. But maybe this is just the way cops do things out here in the country. Maybe they don't watch much TV.

"Tell me again what you do remember," Frank says in that smiley-calm voice of his that I hate. Like I'm ten or something and if he talks real soft and slow, I'll spill my guts.

I sigh as loudly as I can, just so my irritation is clear. "Like I already said, Mama was taking a nap on the sofa in the living room."

It *was* strange because we only use the living room for special occasions, like on Christmas morning to open presents, or when the preacher from North Creek Church of God used to visit. Somehow the couch in the living room is called a *sofa* and the one in the den is just a *couch*. The living room furniture is not very comfortable, but Mama

says it's not supposed to be. Like that makes any sense—
furniture that's meant to be uncomfortable. I've told Frank
all that before, so I don't repeat it. I've learned only to repeat
the important stuff. Otherwise Frank finds new questions
to ask. I don't like new questions.

Frank laces his fingers together on top of his basketball
of a belly and smiles again. I don't like his smile. It looks
like a plastic piece of Mr. Potato Head's face that he can
pop on and off anytime he wants.

"And where were you while your mother was lying
down in the living room?"

I roll my eyes at him. Daddy wouldn't like that.

Be respectful of authority, he would say. *Frank is just trying
to help.*

But I've answered this same question so many times. If
he can't remember, then why doesn't he write it down on
one of his five thousand rainbow Post-it notes, or turn on a
tape recorder like they do on TV. I wonder where he went
to detective school. Probably one of those online courses,
but poor Frank got ripped off. If Mama were here, she'd add
a *bless his heart.* It sounds nice, but I don't think it's meant
to be.

"I was outside playing with my friends," I say.

Frank raises a bushy eyebrow at me. "And . . ."

"And when I came back inside, Mama was lying on the
sofa in the living room. Like I just said."

"And then what did you do?" the world's worst police
detective asks.

"I touched her hand to see if she was asleep." I say it like I'm quoting a Bible verse I've been forced to memorize and recite on command.

Frank looks down his snap-on nose at me. "And how did it feel, touching her hand?"

This is a new one. What the heck does he mean, how did it feel? It felt like skin and Jergens hand lotion, that's how. And how is this going to help them find Mama? Why doesn't Frank ask me more about the suspicious car that was parked in front of the house that day? I told him about it the first time they hauled me down here for questioning, but he hasn't asked about it since. Instead he's wasting time asking about me touching Mama's hand. *World's. Worst. Police. Detective. Ever.*

"She felt a little chilled, so I pulled the cover up over her hands. I didn't want to wake her, so I went back outside to play."

Frank scrunches his face like that wasn't the answer he was looking for. He thinks I'm hiding something. Like *I'm* a suspect, which is crazy because I want them to find her. I promise I do.

"And that's the last thing you remember?" he says. "Touching your mother's hand while she was lying down on the sofa? Nothing else?"

He knows it is. Unless he somehow found out about Kenny from Kentucky. Or the ring.

Stick to your story, I tell myself. That's what people on TV who are accused of a crime always say—*stick to your story and everything will be fine.* No one has actually accused me of anything yet. But they might as well, the way they all look at me—like they know I'm hiding something.

"Yes, sir," I say, being respectful of authority. Even Frank's authority. "That's the last thing I remember."

Frank squints his eyes at me. Yep. He thinks I'm lying. Or crazy. Or both. But technically I'm not lying. Kenny from Kentucky is long gone and they've never asked me about the ring, so I've never told them. Besides, Daddy will blister my hide if he finds out I have it. I wonder if the ring is considered evidence. Can they put me in jail for withholding evidence? I think there was an episode of *CID: Chicago* about that. I can't remember what happened, but I'm sure Detective Chase Cooper solved the case in forty-four minutes.

Frank's talking now, but I can't understand what he's saying. His voice sounds like that teacher from *The Peanuts Movie*, which Mama and I watched together.

. . . wah waah wah wah, waah wah waah . . .

I nod my head every now and then to be polite and respectful. Frank has some real wacky theories about what might have happened to Mama that day, so whenever he starts speculating like this, I turn on my internal Charlie Brown teacher translator.

Speculating is like when poorly educated police detectives make dumb guesses about a case without having any evidence.

Use it in a sentence, Button, I imagine Mama saying.

Frank needs to get off his big round behind, stop speculating about what happened that day, and go find Mama before it's too late.

Frank glances over at the clock and lets out one of his *this isn't getting us anywhere* sighs because he knows I'm not listening anymore.

"Your father's probably waiting for you outside," he says. "You know, Riley, it's been nearly four months now. I'd much rather you tell me what happened on your own, but if you can't—or won't—I can help you fill in some of the blanks if you'll let me."

Oh crap. I know what Frank's talking about from the cop shows on TV. It's when they start telling the perp what *they* think happened. They make their accusations over and over, louder and louder, until the perp finally confesses.

"How's the case going?" I ask, changing the subject. "Any new leads? New information? Have you found their car yet?"

Frank inhales slowly, then releases a long stream of sour-smelling air through puckered lips. "There's no new information, Riley. You know that." He stands and waves me toward the door. "If you remember anything before I see you again, have your dad call me, okay? It's very important."

I get up and walk out, shaking my head so Frank knows what a disappointment he is to me. What are we paying these people for with Daddy's hard-earned tax dollars if they can't even find my mama?

2

TWENTY-EIGHT WORDS
IN THREE DAYS

We eat supper early that night—just the three of us at the kitchen table. We haven't eaten in the dining room since Mama disappeared. We used to eat dinner in there every night. Now it sits dark and empty like a tomb or a shrine. I don't think we'll use it again until Mama comes home safe and we can all sit in there as a family again. We can eat, and talk, and laugh like we used to. Daddy will tell lame jokes, Mama will ask us about our day at school, and my brother won't be mean to me anymore. But for now it's just a dark room collecting dust on our memories of her.

We sit in silence, Danny wolfing down his mashed potatoes like it's his last meal ever, and Daddy staring at his plate like he's reading tea leaves. Every couple of minutes, he moves some food around with his fork, but that's about it. He hasn't always been like this, just since Mama was taken. I don't think he knows how to *be*, without her here holding us all together. That was her department, not his.

Before Mama disappeared, Daddy laughed a lot. And he always loved scaring Danny and me, or pinning us down on the floor and tickling us until we almost peed ourselves. He'd do the same thing to Mama sometimes until she would scream and laugh and holler like a crazy person. Now when I look over at Daddy, all I can see is the bald spot on top of his head. I don't think he likes to look at us anymore, least of all me. I know it's because I can't remember what happened that day. And because I look the most like her. And because Mama and I share a name and a birthday. But also because of *my condition*.

Or maybe he blames me and that's why he can't look at me. Maybe he thinks I could have done something to save her. Called out for help. Gotten the license plate number of the fancy car that was sitting in front of the house that day. Locked the front door after I went outside. But Mama was in the house, so why would I lock the door? And how did I know something bad was going to happen to her? She just disappeared without a trace, right out of our front living room. That's another reason we don't go in there anymore. It's like a crime scene that no one wants to disturb in case there's still some undiscovered shred of evidence hidden in there. Fibers in the carpet or something. I'm surprised Frank hasn't put bright yellow police tape across the door. Maybe he should. Who am I to say? Detective Chase Cooper would know what to do.

Since no one is talking or looking up, I glance around the kitchen as I pretend to eat. I see Mama in every nook and cranny. Like the dish towels hanging on the oven door handle with the words *As for me and my house, we will serve the*

Lord embroidered on them in red frilly letters. I was with her when she found those at the Big Lots in Upton. She loved them so much she bought two sets. But that's not a lot of money at the Big Lots. Probably like three dollars or something. And the Precious Moments cookie jar on the counter—she found that at the Salvation Army store. It has a picture on the front of a boy and a girl with really big heads and droopy eyes sitting back to back on a tree stump.

Love one another.

Mama likes things with nice sayings printed on them.

She says, *It can't hurt to be reminded to love each other every time you reach for a cookie, right, Button?*

Mama loves baking cookies. She makes them for me to take to school for my teachers and to sell at Mr. Killen's Market to raise money for the church. She even made a big batch last Christmas for the prisoners at the work camp outside of Upton. She's real good at cookies, but one time she tried making me blackberry jam like in the story of the Whispers and it was terrible. It was so bad that we laughed and laughed while we ate some of it on toast that I burnt. Another time she tried to teach me how to make biscuits and gravy, but I burned my hand on the stove, so that was the end of my cooking lessons.

All I'm allowed to make now are frozen fish sticks and Tater Tots in the oven. Frozen fish sticks are gross but we've eaten them a lot the last four months. I don't mind the Tater Tots. But Grandma supplied tonight's meal even though Daddy tells her she doesn't have to do that anymore.

Grandma hates the idea of us eating fish sticks and Tater Tots so much. I wonder what Mama's eating right now. Or if she's been eating at all. What if whoever took her doesn't give her enough food to stay alive until the police can find her?

"Frank said there aren't any new leads in the case," I say, breaking the unbearable silence. My words hang in the air like lint.

Daddy looks up from his plate and stares like he doesn't even recognize me. Danny stops eating and glares at me from across the table. He never wants to talk about Mama's case. Even Tucker lets out an anxious groan under the table, like he knows I should have kept my big mouth shut. He misses Mama too. He hasn't been the same since she disappeared, but the vet can't figure out what's wrong with him. I think he's just depressed.

"Finish your peas and take Tucker outside," Daddy says, looking back down at his plate.

I think that makes a total of two dozen words Daddy's said to me in three days, so I hit the jackpot this evening. I eat my peas one at a time and with my fingers. I know it annoys him. If Mama were here, she'd give me the Mama side-eye. But she's not. And Daddy doesn't even look up to scold me. He just plows circles in his mashed potatoes with his fork. If Danny or I did that, he would yell at us and tell us to stop playing with our food.

Daddy used to like me. He even took me on my very first roller coaster ride, and he wanted it to be the same one he took his first ride on—the Swamp Fox at Family Kingdom Amusement Park in Myrtle Beach. It's one of those old-timey wooden coasters that make that loud *clack, clack, clack* noise when they go up the first climb. The newer coasters don't make that sound anymore and Daddy says it's not the same without it. I was so scared and screamed my butt off the entire ride, but Daddy didn't mind. He just laughed and laughed like a crazy person with his hands raised high in the air the whole time.

When I was six, we were on vacation in Florida and Daddy took us to an alligator farm. He picked me up so I could get a better look at the big, slimy creatures. Then he thought it would be real funny to pretend like he was going to throw me over the fence like gator bait. A fat one spotted us and slowly came crawling our way while Daddy kept up his act for *way* too long, swinging me back and forth and back and forth.

One, two . . .

On *three,* I almost crapped my pants. But he never got to three, so I'm pretty sure Daddy wasn't trying to feed me to the alligators. I screamed bloody murder anyway. But Daddy didn't mind. He just laughed and laughed like a crazy person. To this day I can't even look at an alligator on TV. But I have to admit, it was fun. Daddy was fun. Not anymore.

Danny's phone vibrates on the table, which gets him a hard look from Daddy. His phone is supposed to be off during dinner. Danny grabs it and tucks it into his lap. It's probably some girl from school calling. Danny likes girls now. *Ugh.*

"Sorry," he says to Daddy without looking him in the eye.

Daddy stares at him a moment, and finally his face softens. Just a tad. He doesn't yell at Danny. He would have yelled at me, but Danny's a daddy's boy just as much as I'm a mama's boy. And I don't have a phone yet. It's okay. I wouldn't want any girls calling me anyway.

Daddy gets up and goes to the window over the sink. He mumbles as he lifts it open, "It's stifling in here."

Wow. Twenty-eight words in three days. But those last four I have to share with Danny.

"What does that mean, Daddy?" I say, although I have a pretty good idea. I just want him to notice me.

"What does what mean?" he kind of grunts back.

"*Stifling.*"

He looks over his shoulder at me and gives me a flat look. "It means it's hot and stuffy."

I push my luck, trying to lighten the mood. "Use it in a sentence, Daddy."

He squints at me like he can't remember my name or why I'm here. "What?"

"Use the word *stifling* in a sentence," I say, feeling hopeful.

"I just did." He looks out the window, dismissing me with a slight shake of his head.

Danny stuffs his mouth and grunts his agreement with Daddy. Danny eats like a pig and always sides with Daddy.

Actually Danny does *everything* Daddy does, so now that Daddy doesn't like me, Danny doesn't either. He used to play with me before Mama disappeared. Now he just acts like I don't exist. He barely even talks to me. Stays in his room with the door closed doing Lord knows what, and hangs out with his new high school friends in Upton. He's only three years older than me, but he treats me like a baby.

Tucker must have sensed the tension in the room, because he lets out a long, flappy fart that sounds like a balloon deflating under the table. Danny looks at me and his lips curl up, exposing teeth caked with mashed potatoes and gravy. Danny never smiles at me anymore, but he thinks farts are hilarious. Especially dog farts. Even I can't help but smirk, just a little. But we both freeze, waiting to see how Daddy will respond. It could go either way. The seconds tick by long and slow like they did during the sermons at North Creek Church of God when we used to be churchgoing people.

I dare to look over at Daddy standing at the sink. His shoulders are shaking a little. Laughing or crying, I can't tell. He turns to face us and I see that it's both. He's laughing softly, but at the same time his eyes are moist. I'm surprised because I don't think I've seen Daddy crack even a polite smile to anyone in the last four months. His laughter sparks life into the room and we know it's okay now. We have permission to join him, and we do. Hard. It's the first time since Mama disappeared that there's been any laughter in this house. It sounds amazing, echoing around the kitchen and then drifting out the window. Tucker scrambles from under the table, barking excitedly and joining in our rare moment of happiness. Daddy's laughter eventually dies down, though. His smile doesn't totally disappear, but it fades a little. His eyes are still misty.

A strong honeysuckle-scented breeze rolls in through the open window and brushes my cheeks. I close my eyes and breathe it in deep. It's almost like she's here, like she heard us laughing and rushed into the kitchen to see what all the fuss was about. Mama loves the smell of honeysuckle. She always yells at Daddy for cutting back the bushes in the yard. It grows like crazy around our house. Mama taught me how to pinch off the bottom of the blooms, slide the stem out, and lick the nectar off. She calls it nature's candy. Now whenever I catch a whiff of honeysuckle, I think of her and I wonder if I'll ever see her again. Right now, it's like she's reaching out to me from wherever she's being held captive—calling to me to come find her. To rescue her. The police are useless, so I may be her only hope.

"Take that gassy mutt outside, Riley," Daddy says, his smile completely fading.

Wow. He said my name. And he wasn't yelling or cross sounding or anything. Just said it like normal. Like he would say Danny's name. I hop out of my chair with a small jolt of satisfaction, or pride, or something pumping in my veins and guide Tucker to the kitchen door.

Looking back over my shoulder, I smile at him. "Okay, Daddy."

But he doesn't see me. He's already turned his back on us again. He stands at the sink, his shoulders shaking. I'm not sure if he's laughing again or if he's gone back to crying. I don't think I really want to know for sure, so I grab Tucker by the collar and hurry out the door.

ACKNOWLEDGMENTS

I loved writing Mikey's story. It took me back to a much simpler time in my life when I turned our family's laundry / storage room off the carport into my business, the Anything Shop. Yes, I gave croquet lessons—fifty cents a lesson, and that included a glass of milk with ice that had to be consumed before the lesson began. The ice was very important for some reason that escapes me now. And the cardboard general store my dad built in our front yard for me was no match for a baby tornado. It was tough sometimes being twelve and running a business empire all by myself, which is why I am so grateful for all the help I had crafting this story about it.

My heartfelt thanks go to . . .

My agent, Bri Johnson—I literally would not be writing this if you hadn't found me in your slush pile and given me a chance. It has been an absolute joy working with you and I look forward to many wonderful years, laughs, and successes to come.

My editor, Stacey Barney—for your patience with me while writing this book as life threw me a few curveballs. You dragged me over the finish line and helped me create something that I am so in love with.

My publicist, Lizzie Goodell—for getting the word out, looking after me, and never laughing when I tell you my pie-in-the-sky publicity dreams.

Publisher Jen Klonsky and the rest of my amazing Putnam/Penguin family from sales, to marketing, to accounting, to school and library, to the art department and everyone in between. You will probably never know just how grateful I am for all of you.

Cecilia de la Campa and the sub rights team at Writers House—for rocking so hard.

Caitlin Tutterow and Allie Levick—for keeping me informed and on task, for getting me things (I feel like) I need, and for the encouraging words.

Lindsey Andrews—for a wicked-cool cover and your keen eye for detail. With you I never worry that the end product will be anything but super-crazy fabulous.

Michael DiMotta (michaeldimotta.com)—for your gorgeous cover illustration and especially for not firing us through the process. It was totally worth it, right?

Melissa—for the daily encouragement and pep talks.

Michelle—for reading the earliest pages of this book and laughing out loud. That gave me the courage to keep writing this story.

Drag kids extraordinaire Desmond is Amazing (Instagram @desmondisamazing), Katastrophe Jest (@katastrophejest), E! The Dragnificent (@ethedragnificent), and Lactatia (@queenlactatia)—for inspiring me to bring Coco Caliente to life in the middle-grade world. You are all so beautiful and perfect in every way. God bless those in your orbit who have supported and nurtured your gifts.

Teachers and librarians everywhere—for fighting the good fight every single day, and for your perseverance and bravery. Never doubt for a minute that you are changing lives.

Travis—for all the things.

© Jamie Wright Images

GREG HOWARD was born and raised in the South Carolina Lowcountry, where his love of words and stories blossomed at a young age. Originally set on becoming a songwriter, Greg followed that dream to the bright lights of Nashville, Tennessee, and spent years producing the music of others before eventually returning to his childhood passion of writing stories. Greg writes young-adult and middle-grade novels focusing on LGBTQ characters and issues. He has an unhealthy obsession with Reese's Peanut Butter Cups and currently resides in Nashville with his three rescued fur babies—Molly, Toby, and Riley.

You can visit Greg Howard at greghowardbooks.com or follow him on Facebook, Twitter, and Instagram at @greghowardbooks